THE LOST HERD

THE CROCKETTS' WESTERN SAGA: TWELVE

ROBERT VAUGHAN

WOLFPACK PUBLISHING
— EST 2013 —

The Lost Herd
The Crocketts' Western Saga: Twelve
Paperback Edition
Copyright © 2022 Robert Vaughan

Wolfpack Publishing
5130 S. Fort Apache Road, 215-380
Las Vegas, NV 89148

wolfpackpublishing.com

Paperback ISBN 978-1-63977-988-8
eBook ISBN 978-1-63977-987-1
LCCN 2022941756

THE LOST HERD

CHAPTER ONE

WILL AND GID CROCKETT WERE IN ROUTE TO CALIFORNIA for no particular reason other than that is where they wanted to go. As a result of a burning trestle, their train was delayed at Ash Fork, Arizona. In order to pass the time, they joined several other passengers in the local saloon. Will saw a seat open at a poker table, so asked to join the game. After about five hands, he determined that none of the other three players was a professional gambler, and it was a convivial game with winning and losing about evenly spaced, except for one player. That player, Kurt Beaumont, lost several hands in a row, until he announced he was out of money.

"Damn, I was going back to New Orleans, but I've gambled away all my traveling money," Beaumont said. "I, uh..." he reached into his inside vest pocket and pulled out an envelope.

"I need to raise some money. I don't plan on playing cards any longer, but, like I said, I need some traveling money, so I've got a proposition for anyone who's interested."

Beaumont's proposition was that he would sell his gold mine, which was near Prescott, Arizona. The other players scoffed at the proposal, but there was something that made Will interested enough to accept Beaumont's offer. After a telegram to Prescott, Will learned that the mine was legitimate. So it was that Will and Gid found themselves in the unusual position of owning and operating The Axis. Although the mine, with hours of physical labor, turned out to be productive endeavor, one night they had a conversation that changed things for both of them.

"Will, I'll do whatever you think we should do, but I don't mind telling you, that I'd just as soon we were somewhere else, doing something else."

"What else would you have us do, Little Brother?" Will asked.

"I don't know, anything else. I just get tired of going down a hole every day, and bringing out a lot of rocks."

"Rocks with gold," Will said.

Gid sighed. "Yeah, rocks with gold."

Will chuckled. "Well, to tell you the truth, I feel the same way. I don't think either one of us was born to be miners."

"All right, then. You're the smart one, what do you think we should do now?"

"I think we should sell The Axis."

Shortly after the two brothers came to that decision, they were offered a rather generous sum of money for their gold mine and they wasted no time in selling it.

It took a couple of days for Will and Gid to clear out their belongings at the mine. Then they went to see Woman, who lived in the little cabin that was just to the side of their mine. Woman was a Yavapai Indian who had refused to go to the Apache Reservation at San Carlos when her tribe had been ordered to leave. Even though Prescott was less than ten miles away, Woman had never gone to the community.

It could be said that Woman worked for Will and Gid, because she did cook their meals, and sometimes provided game for them, but there had never been any formal employer, employee relationship. She was there in the cabin when Will and Gid took control of the Axis mine, and now that they had sold the mine and were about to leave, Woman was still there. She would remain there after the Crockett brothers left.

After explaining to Woman what was going to happen and saying goodbye to the placer miners on Lynx Creek, they headed into Prescott. It took less than a week for the completion of the paperwork to transfer the title of the Axis and for the delivery of the bank draft finalizing the transaction.

It was with both joy and sadness that they headed to The Beatrice Saloon to tell their friends goodbye. There, they learned that Nigel, the British owner, and Penny, one of the girls who worked there, were going to be married.

"Congratulations," Will said.

"We're going to be married in London," Penny said, happily.

"Is that right? Well, it'll be good to visit where Nigel grew up," Gid said.

"It isn't a visit, we're moving there," Nigel said.

"Oh? You don't think there'll be a problem?" Will asked.

Will's question was based upon the fact that the Duke of Clarence was actually quite virile, and had produced ten illegitimate children, six boys and four girls. Had they been legitimate, the oldest boy would have been king.

As it turned out, the oldest boy of those ten, Percival Housewright, was Nigel's father. If of legitimate birth, he would have been king, and now that he was dead, Nigel would be king, instead of Victoria being queen. That unpleasant fact of succession had forced Nigel to leave the country.

"Queen Victoria has given me the title of Baron, and I'm going to be able to resume my musical career," Nigel said. He chuckled. "Apparently, the Secretary to the Sovereign is no longer concerned that I might make an attempt to claim the crown."

"Is there any way we could get you two to stay?" Sheriff Bower asked the Crockett brothers. "The territory needs good men."

"Afraid not," Gid said. "We've been here long enough and it's time to move on."

"Where will you go?" Penny asked.

"We don't really know," Will said. "But for the first time in our lives we have a piece of real money, so it might be good to think about some way to hang on to it."

"Thirty thousand dollars *is* a lot of money," Nigel agreed.

Will looked at Nigel in surprise. "How did you know how much we got for the mine?"

Nigel chuckled. "Everybody in Prescott knows. At least everyone who has read the *Prescott Advocate*, thanks to our crusading editor."

Nigel handed the folded newspaper to Will who opened it, then read the headline.

CROCKETT BROTHERS SELL AXIS GOLD MINE FOR $30,000

Will sighed. "I wish Ben hadn't done that."

"Don't be too hard on him, Will," Sheriff Bower said. "Ben Weaver's a newspaper man, and you have to admit that this is news."

"I guess it is," Will said. "But I wish he would have waited until after we were gone before he ran the story."

———

THE NEXT MORNING Will and Gid left Prescott for what would be a two-day ride to Phoenix. They had five hundred dollars in cash, and a certified bank draft, for twenty-nine thousand, five hundred dollars.

"You know where I'd like to go?" Gid asked, as they rode south.

"Where?"

"Well, before we wound up in Prescott, we'd started out for California. I think I'd like to go there, if for no other reason, than just to say we'd been there."

"All right, that's as good a place as any, I guess."

Before leaving Prescott, the kitchen of the Reed Hotel had prepared a lunch for them to have while on the trail, and at noon, they stopped to enjoy it.

"What do you want to do in California?" Will asked.

"You'll laugh," Gid said.

"Maybe not. Try me."

"Well, sir, what I'd like to do, is stick my foot in the

Pacific Ocean. I've wet my foot in the Mississippi River and the Gulf of Mexico. I've never been to the Atlantic or the Pacific, but if I get to the Pacific, I'll only have one left to do."

Will smiled. "Sounds like a good plan to me."

They had made coffee for their lunch, and Gid was reaching for the pot when a bullet suddenly struck the pot, sending hot coffee spraying. At almost the same moment they heard the sound of the shot that had propelled the bullet.

Will and Gid drew their pistols, then rolled over into a shallow depression. They looked toward the sound of the gunshot.

"They's four of us, 'n only two of you," a voice called out to them. "'N we all got rifles."

"What do you want?" Will called back.

"We want that thirty-thousand dollars you fellers is a' carryin'."

"We don't have thirty thousand dollars," Will called back.

"The hell you don't. You think we can't read? We know what you got for that there mine of yours."

"That's true, but we don't have thirty thousand dollars—all we have is a bank draft made out to the two of us. That means it wouldn't do you any good."

"What? What are you talkin' about?"

"Since it's made out to us, if you take it, it won't be worth any more than a piece of paper. So, you might as well go on about your business, and leave us alone."

"Ha, what if we take that draft away from you, 'n just tell the bank, we're you? They'd give us the money then, wouldn't they?"

"You'll never find out, because you'll never get the draft."

"We'll just see about that."

The last comment was followed by a barrage of rifle shots. The bullets whined harmlessly over their heads, and Will saw the puffs of smoke which displayed the shooters' location.

First Will, and then Gid fired toward the smoke.

"Ha! That ain't goin' to do you no good," the same man called. And again, all four of their assailants fired at them.

Will examined the depression they were in, and saw that it stretched at least two hundred feet in each direction.

"Gid," he said quietly, then he pointed. "You go to that end and I'll go to the other end. Then we'll work our way up to them, and have them surrounded."

"Surrounded?" Gid asked with a chuckle. "How can you surround four people with just two people?"

"Maybe flanked would be a better word. You'll be on one side and I'll be on the other."

"How will we know when we're both in position?"

"I'll find some way to let you know."

"All right."

"Let's reload, then we'll shoot at 'em one more time from here, before we move out."

They punched the empty shell casing out of each pistol and replaced it with a new bullet. Then, at a nod from Will, they both fired again.

As Will expected, their adversaries returned fire, and as the bullets whipped by over where they had been, the two brothers started out in opposite directions to execute Will's plan.

When Will reached the end of the depression, he looked back toward Gid, gave him a signal, then moved out.

Will was able to take advantage of rocks, bushes, and the depression, until he was in position to see the men who were after them. He didn't recognize any of them by name, but he had seen them a few times, and he knew they were miners.

"If you men will throw down your rifles, we'll let you live," he called.

"The hell we will," one of the men shouted back, surprised to hear someone in a new, and unexpected location. He fired toward the sound of Will's voice.

Initially, the rifles had given the four men the advantage, but now, in close proximity, the advantage went to pistols. Will returned fire and one of the men went down. Gid brought another down and the remaining two assailants dropped their rifles and threw up their hands.

"Don't shoot no more, we give up!" one of them shouted.

"Hold your fire, Gid!" Will called.

Will stood up, then started toward the two remaining assailants, and he saw Gid approaching from the other side.

"Don't shoot us, Crockett. Please don't shoot us," one of the two men pleaded.

The two men who had been shot were sitting up now, attending to their wounds, one a shoulder wound, the other shot in the leg.

"All right. Leave your guns here, 'n get these two men back to town to the doc."

Will watched as the two wounded men were loaded

onto their horses, then, as they were riding away, he tossed the rifles into some low-growing vegetation. When they returned, they would have to look for their rifles, and by then, he and Gid would be far down the trail.

CHAPTER TWO

ON THE MORNING OF THE THIRD DAY AFTER LEAVING Prescott, Will and Gid arrived in Phoenix. They stopped at the Bank Exchange which, despite its name, was actually a hotel, restaurant, and saloon.

"You boys new in town?" the bartender asked.

"Just passing through. We'll be taking the train to San Francisco tomorrow."

"San Francisco. Great town, you'll love it," the bartender said. "What'll you have?"

"Beer," Will said.

"Me, too."

When the beer mugs were put in front of them, Will wrapped his hand around the glass, then jerked it back.

"This beer's cold," he said.

"Yeah, most people like 'em better that way."

"But I don't understand. How did you get it cold?"

The bartender smiled. "We may be out in the desert, but we're livin' in modern times. We got us our own ice factory, right here in Phoenix."

A couple of the percentage girls, wearing dresses

that exposed their sexual charms, approached the two brothers.

"You two are new in town," one of them said in a throaty voice.

"How do you know we're new?" Will asked.

"Because as handsome as you two are, if we'd ever seen you before we'd remember it."

"Well now, see, that's where I know you are wrong because there's nothing at all handsome about this big, ugly man standing here beside me," Will teased.

"Oh, no, you're wrong. I like big strong men," the other young woman said. She smiled up at Gid. "My name is Alice, what's your name?"

"Gid."

"And I'm Will. What's your name?"

"Jeanie."

"Well, Alice and Jeanie, how would you two pretty young ladies like to have supper with my brother and me?" Will asked.

"Oh, that would be lovely, but..." Alice started to say, but Will interrupted her with a raised hand.

"We'll pay you for your time, just as if we were going upstairs with you," Will said.

Both girls broke into a broad smile. "Well, then, yes, we'd love to," Jeanie said.

After a good meal and a pleasant visit with Alice and Jeanie, Will and Gid checked in to the Bank Exchange Hotel for the night. The next morning, they sold their horses, then boarded the train for the trip to San Francisco.

———

THEY WERE in their second day of travel, and Will had been quiet for a long time, just staring through the window at the passing country side.

"You're being awfully quiet," Gid said.

"Yeah, I reckon I am. I'm just lost in thought, is all."

"Really? What are you thinking about?"

"I don't know, maybe settling down somewhere, I guess."

"Settling down? Wait, are you telling me you're tired of travelling around? I mean, you'd give up seein' so much of the country?"

"I don't know if I'm ready for that or not. I'm just thinking, is all," Will said.

"Hey, what would you think about settling down in San Francisco?" Gid asked.

"Seeing as neither one of us has ever been to San Francisco, I don't think I can answer that question. But I'm willing to explore the possibilities."

"You know what? With the money we've got, we could buy us a saloon," Gid suggested.

Will shook his head. "No. I don't know what I want to do, but I know what I don't want to do, and one of the things on my 'don't want to do' list would be to get involved in a saloon."

"All right then, let's just say that San Francisco is a place to visit and have some fun."

Will chuckled. "Neither one of us has much experience in just 'having fun,' so how will we know when we're having it?"

"We'll just have to do some things that we haven't done before, then decide whether or not it's fun."

"What if it isn't fun?"

Gid laughed. "If it isn't fun, we'll stop doing it."

Will joined him in laughter. "All right, I'll go along with that."

———

AFTER THREE DAYS OF TRAVEL, they reached San Francisco. Neither Will nor Gid had ever seen a city as large as San Francisco. The streets were illuminated by electric lights, and cable cars moved people through the city.

"You know what Little Brother? We thought we would need to buy a couple of horses, but there's no need to," Will said. "Looks to me like if we want to go anywhere, we can ride on one of those contraptions."

"How do those things move around? I don't see any horses pulling them, and I don't see any steam comin' out of 'em."

"I don't have any idea, but they seem to be working," Will said.

"What do we do first?"

"I think we should find a bank to deposit our money and then find us a hotel," Will said.

"What about finding some place to eat?"

"We can do that," Will agreed.

They chose a restaurant called Maimie LeCler's. It was a more elegant establishment than either of them was used to.

"Damn, maybe should have waited until we were better dressed before we came in here," Will said.

A waiter, wearing a white jacket and tie, came to their table then. "*Menu de table messieurs?*"

"Uh, yeah, I think," Will replied.

The waiter handed them a menu, then withdrew.

"What the hell?" Gid said as he looked at it. "I can't read this. How can I order what I want to eat, if I don't have any idea what it's sayin'?"

"I think it's in French," Will replied.

"Are you going to tell me that you can read it?"

"No. I'm not going to say that."

"Then what are we goin' to do, just point our finger at somethin' 'n tell this fancy-dressed fellow that's what we want?"

"Hold on," Will said, as he raised his hand to signal the waiter.

The waiter with the haughty air returned. "You are ready to order, sir?"

"Not yet. We'd like a menu in English."

"In English, sir?" the waiter asked, the words clipped and patronizing.

"Yes, in English. This is America and the language we speak here is English. Now I assume you do have menus printed in English."

"To be sure, sir," the waiter replied.

"Then, get us one written in English."

"Will, you think I'd get in trouble if I knocked that snooty son of a bitch on his ass?" Gid asked, as the waiter left the table to retrieve the English language menus.

Will laughed. "I think, like as not, you probably would. But it is kind of fun to think about, isn't it?"

"You damn right, it is."

The waiter returned.

"Your...*English*...language menus, sir."

When the waiter returned a few minutes later to take their order, Gid ordered Roast Prime Rib of Beef.

"Sir, you may wish to reconsider your order," the waiter said.

"Why, is there something wrong with the beef?"

"Oh, quite the contrary, sir. You'll find that we have the finest beef in the city. I was only suggesting that this may be a little...out of your budget."

"I'm hungry, I'll have a double order," Gid said.

"One order will be enough for me," Will added.

"Very well, sir. Your meal will be here shortly," the waiter replied, then he turned to leave.

"Look at the way that son of a bitch walks. Tell me, Will, do you think he really walks like that, or does he just have a cob up his ass?"

Will laughed. "Gid, remember, you are the one who wanted to come here."

The prime rib was delicious, and both men ate with gusto. When they were finished, the waiter returned, with the check.

"I do hope you have sufficient funds to pay for the meal," the waiter said.

The cost of the meal was three dollars and fifty cents. Will paid for the meal with a five-dollar bill.

The waiter returned a moment later, with the change, and a receipt, on a small plate. As Will reached for the money, the waiter gave a small cough.

"Sir, it is customary for the diners to leave a gratuity in appreciation for the service."

"What service?" Will asked, as he picked up the change.

"Well, I never," the waiter said.

"Never get a tip? I don't doubt it, the way you are. You might try being a little friendlier, and a little less of a horse's ass," Will said.

By the time they left the restaurant, a fog had rolled in, so thick that they could barely see ten feet in front of them. As a result of the lack of visibility, they would hear hoof beats on the coble-stoned street, then a team of horses and carriage would appear, as if by magic, then after only a moment of being seen, they would be invisible once more. It was in just such a way that two men suddenly appeared right in front of them. Both men were holding guns.

"Well now, Jack, what do we have here?" one of the two men asked. He was a little shorter than average, with a misshapen nose and a drooping eye.

"Oh, I'd say we've found a couple of pigeons with a fat purse, just ready for the plucking, wouldn't you, Sam?" Jack answered. Jack was taller, with long hair and a stringy beard.

"Yeah, that's what I was thinkin', too."

"You two, hand over all your money, 'n maybe we'll let you live," Jack said.

"Which one do you want, Little Brother?" Will asked, calmly.

"I'll take the bigger one," Gid said. "You can have the little one."

"What?" Sam asked, surprised by the reaction of the two men they had just encountered. "What the hell are you two talking about? We're the ones holdin' the guns 'n..."

That was as far as the one called Sam got before Will stepped in to him and dropped him with a sharp uppercut. As Will was taking care of business with Sam, Gid picked up Jack, then threw him. Now, with both men on the ground, Will and Gid took their guns from them.

"Hey, Will, do you think it would be all right if I break their arms and legs?"

"No, don't do that."

"What about if I just break all their fingers?" He started toward the two men.

"Yes, you can do that if you want to."

"No! Keep that big son of a bitch away from us!" Sam called out in fright.

"All right," Will said. "If you two will run away, I'll try and keep my brother away from you."

"What about our guns?"

"I'll tell you what. We'll turn these guns in at the police station, and you can go there to get them."

"Are you crazy? We ain't goin' to go to the police station and ask for guns that we used to try 'n rob somebody."

"I guess you have a point there. All right, Gid, go ahead and break their fingers."

"No!" Sam shouted and he turned to run, with Jack just behind him. They disappeared in the fog bank within a matter of seconds.

"Damn, I wish you would have let me break their arms and legs. That would have been fun," Gid said with a little laugh.

"Maybe next time," Will said.

"I'm goin' to hold you to that promise," Gid said.

CHAPTER THREE

——————————————

THE FOG HAD ROLLED AWAY BY THE NEXT DAY, SO WILL and Gid took that opportunity to view the water. They saw the San Francisco Bay, what was called the Golden Gate, and the Pacific Ocean. They also saw an island that they were told was called Alcatraz.

"Anybody live on the island?" Will asked.

"A few soldiers. Oh, there's also a lighthouse there."

Going down to the water's edge, Gid sat down, took off his boot and sock, then, as he had previously stated, stuck his foot in the water.

"You want to put your foot in the water?" Gid asked, with a broad smile on his face.

"No thank you."

"Someday, forty or fifty years from now, I'll be able to tell my grandkids that I stuck my foot in the Pacific Ocean. What will you be able to tell your grandkids?" Gid asked.

"I don't know, maybe that I had enough sense not to do something like that, do you think?"

After Gid put his boot and sock back on, the two continued their perusal of the city.

The brothers were awed by the size of San Francisco. It was a huge metropolis, with a population of two hundred thousand. The streets were paved, and it had an impressive skyline. Dozens of ocean-going ships were docked at the wharves, which teemed with activity. Five railroads made San Francisco their terminus, and it had become the banking center of the West.

"Hey, Will, you think this town has a saloon?" Gid asked.

"Of course it will have a saloon. Dozens of them, I expect."

"Then let's find one. At least I won't feel as lost there, as I am out here."

"Let's see what we can find in the paper," Will suggested, and stopping at one of the many street-vendors, they picked up a copy of *The Gazette*.

Will looked through the paper for a moment, then he chuckled. "Read this," he said, handing the news-paper to his brother.

"What is it?"

"Just read it, then we'll talk about it."

The Barbary Coast is the haunt of the low and the vile of every kind. The petty thief, the house burglar, the tramp, the whoremonger, lewd women, cutthroats, murderers, all are found here. Dance-halls and concert-saloons, where bleary-eyed men and faded women drink vile liquor, smoke offensive tobacco, engage in vulgar conduct, sing obscene songs and say and do everything to heap upon themselves more degradation, are numerous. Low gambling houses, thronged with riot-loving rowdies, in all stages of intoxica-

tion, are there. Licentiousness, debauchery, pollution, loathsome disease, insanity from dissipation, misery, poverty, wealth, profanity, blasphemy, and death, are there. And Hell, yawning to receive the putrid mass, is there also.

Gid laughed. "Our kind of place. That sounds like something we might want to explore. How do we get there?"

"Maybe we can hire that thing to take us," Will suggested, pointing to a vehicle that was, at the moment, discharging a man and a woman.

"What the hell is that thing?" Gid asked. The driver of the thing Gid asked about, was sitting on a high seat which was above, and behind, an enclosed passenger area.

"I don't know what it's called, but I have a feeling it's something we can hire," Will replied.

Will and Gid approached the vehicle after the passengers had left.

"What do you call this thing?" Will asked the driver, who was wearing a jacket and a high hat.

"Why, it's called a Hansom Cab, sir," the driver replied.

"Is it a private carriage?"

"It is for hire, sir," the driver replied.

Will smiled. "Ah, good, then we would like to hire it."

"Very well, sir. Where to?"

"Do you know where the Barbary Coast is?"

The driver chuckled. "I do indeed. Climb aboard, and I'll take you there."

It was about a ten-minute ride from where they

started to the area known as the Barbary Coast. The first thing they saw were about half-a-dozen ships lying alongside the piers that stuck out like fingers from the docks. A few minutes later they stopped on Pacific Street, a street that was lined with buildings from one story to six stories high.

"Gentlemen," the driver said, pointing. "There, you will find your dens of iniquity."

"Our whats?" Gid asked.

"Bars, brothels, and opium dens," the driver said.

Will and Gid stepped down from the cab, paid the driver, then with a word of thanks, he snapped the reins against the single horse, and drove away.

"These don't look like any saloons I've ever seen," Gid said as he examined the row of buildings which appeared to be all brick and glass. Absent were the false fronts.

"If we can get a beer, what difference does it make what it looks like?" Will said.

"You're right. What do you say we check one of them out?"

The building they chose to enter had PACIFIC BAR painted on the large window. The entrance wasn't guarded by swinging bat wing doors, but just a regular door. But, when they stepped inside, there was some similarity to the saloons they were used to, in that there was a long bar running down the left side of the room, and there were tables out on the floor. The biggest difference though, was in the clientele. Whereas the saloons they were used to were generally filled with ranch hands and men who were employed in jobs of the West, the Pacific Bar's customers were, for the greatest part, sailors.

Will and Gid stood just inside the door and for the moment, doing nothing but looking around. They felt out of place in their denim trousers, chambray shirts, boots, and Stetson hats. The conversations were foreign to them, some actually speaking a foreign language, but even those who were speaking in English were using terms that were unknown to them, with words like 'going by the board, giving a wide berth, or batten down the hatches'.

One thing that was similar to the saloons they were used do, was that there were scantily dressed, attractive women moving among the customers. Two of the women were Chinese, and they were the two who approached Will and Gid.

"I am Lei Jing," one of them said.

"I am Chu Sahn," the other said.

"You buy drink for us?" Lei asked.

"Sure, why not? We've never had a drink with a beautiful Chinese woman before," Will said.

As the two brothers followed the girls to a table, they overheard one of the sailors talking.

"Whooee, look at that big son of a bitch there. Hell, I bet he could give ole' Taylor a run for his money. Too bad he's on his way to Hawaii now."

"Hell, he don't look all that tough to me," another said.

"Can we get something to eat, here?" Gid asked one of the girls, ignoring the discussion about him.

"You bet, very good Chinee food in here," Chu said.

"What do you say, Will? Can we eat something? I'm hungry."

"Think you can eat Chinese food?" Will asked.

"If it's food, that's all that matters."

Will chuckled. "Why did I even ask?"

They invited Chu and Lei to have supper with them. It was the first time either of them had even eaten Chinese food, and the first time either of them had ever tried to use chop sticks. Chu laughed, as she kept trying to instruct Gid, who struggled with them for the entire meal. Will, on the other hand, picked it up rather quickly.

"You know, Gid, if we had to eat all meals like this from now on, I'd be the big one and you'd be the little one."

"Well, the good thing is we won't be eating our meals like this from now own," Gid replied as he dropped one of the sticks trying to convey a piece of pork to his mouth. Chu and Lei laughed again, then she picked up the dropped stick, took the other one from Gid's hand, and easily recovered the piece of pork and transferred it to Gid's mouth.

"Hey, what are you two hayseed lookin' sons of bitches doin' in a sailors' bar?" The man who asked the question was a big man, wearing the garb of a seaman. He was also the one who had made the declaration that Gid didn't look all that tough to him.

"We're trying to figure out how to use these sticks to eat," Will said.

"Yeah, well why don't you go to some place where hayseeds like you belong?" the belligerent sailor asked.

"Oh, we probably will after a while," Will said. "But we're new in town, and we thought it might be fun to do a little exploring."

"Well go explore somewhere else. This here is a sailors' bar, 'n you ain't welcome. 'N them two whores you're with got no business bein' with the likes of you.

They're sailors' whores 'n they should be with sailors. Now I'm tellin' you to get out of here, while the gettin' out is good."

Will sighed, and put down his chopsticks. "Mister, I've been trying to get on your good side, but you don't seem to have a good side. So, I'm going to ask you to go away and leave us alone."

"And if I don't?"

"Then I'll have my little brother throw you out."

"Throw me out? And just how is he supposed to throw me out?"

"Gid, this loud-mouthed bastard is disturbing my meal. Would you take care of it, please?"

"I will, if you'll quit trying to make me eat with these little sticks, and let me eat with a knife and fork."

"All right."

Will and Gid were discussing the issue as calmly as if Will had asked his brother to close a window. And that, the calm discussion of the two brothers, as opposed to the loud challenges of the big sailor, got the attention of everyone else, and all other conversation quieted as the other patrons looked on.

Gid stood up from the table. "Would you go away please? You're bothering my brother."

"I ain't goin' nowhere, Mister, 'n you can't make me."

Without another word, Gid threw a punch He felt the sailor's jaw break under his fist, and the sailor went down.

With the sailor down, Gid picked him up, slung him over his shoulder, walked over to the front door, opened it, then tossed me man out.

"Would you get me a knife and fork, please?" Gid asked Chu.

"Yes, I get you knife and fork," Chu said. She smiled at him. "You very strong man."

When Gid sat back down the other patrons, perhaps fearing that staring at him would be taken as some sort of confrontation, returned to their own drinks, card games, and quiet conversations.

"Ahh," Will said, putting the chopsticks down. "Chu, get me a knife and fork, too, if you would, please."

"You my man," Lei said. "I get you knife and fork."

"Thanks," Will replied with a broad smile.

———

WITHIN A WEEK of taking in all the sights of the city, Will and Gid were beginning to feel closed in, not only by the tall buildings, but by the mass of people. They were in the Old Ship Saloon when Gid made an observation.

"I feel like a milk cow in the middle of a herd of steers," Gid said.

Will laughed. "I agree with you, that's a good way of putting it. So, what do you want to do now?"

"I don't know, but whatever we do, let's do it somewhere else," Gid said. "I've had about as much of California as I want."

"All right," Will answered.

"So, where are we going to go?"

"We'll let one of the girls decide," Will said with a smile, nodding toward a group of three percentage girls who were standing together at the end of the bar.

"Wait a minute, we're going to ask a bar girl to tell us where we're going next?"

"In a manner of speaking." Will motioned toward

the girls, and, with broad smiles, all three of them approached the table.

"There are three of us, and only two of you. It looks like you gentlemen are going to have to choose," one of the girls said.

"What are your names?" Will asked.

"I'm Hattie, this is Angelina, and this is Rosie," Hattie said, pointing to the other two girls.

"Well, ladies, we're going to buy drinks for all three of you. But Hattie, I would like for you to ask the barkeep for a piece of paper and a pencil, if you would, please."

A moment later Hattie returned with the pencil and paper.

"All right, little brother, let's come up with a list of places. I'll start with Arizona." He wrote Arizona on the paper.

"No, I don't want to go back to Arizona, we just left there."

"We'll let Hattie decide."

"Me?" Hattie said. "Decide what?"

"You'll see. New Mexico," he added to the list.

"Wyoming," Gid said.

"Idaho." And again, Will added to the list. They concluded the list with Oregon, Texas, Colorado, and Kansas.

Once Will had all the names written, he began tearing them from the paper, then folding them over. "Give me your hat, Gid."

"My hat? Why not yours?"

"Because if we use your hat, you won't have a bitch about where we wind up going."

Will dropped the names in the hat, then held it out

toward the girls. "All right, I want each of you to pull out one piece of paper, but don't open it to look at it."

By now a few of the others in the saloon, curious as to what was going on, had come over to the table to see.

When the three names were drawn, Will emptied the hat of the names that were left, then directed that the girls put the names they had drawn back into the hat.

"Hattie, you draw one of the names, then hand it to my little brother."

"This is exciting," Rosie said.

Hattie drew a piece of paper from the hat, then handed it to Gid.

Gid opened up the paper, then smiled.

"We're going to Texas," he said.

CHAPTER FOUR

THEY BOUGHT A TICKET TO FORT WORTH, TEXAS, AND because they had the money to do so, they travelled first class. First class travel afforded them a private compartment for sleeping. There were comfortable seats for daytime travel in the sleeping car, and there was also a porter assigned specifically to their car. The porter provided the first-class passengers with drink and food at their bidding.

"Gid, we've got more money than we've ever had in our life," Will said.

"Yeah," Gid replied with a broad smile. "It feels good, doesn't it?"

"So, the question is, what are we going to do with it?"

"Here's an idea. Let's spend it."

"All right, that sounds good to me."

"Wait a minute," Gid replied with a confused look on his face. "I was just teasing. You mean you really do want to spend it?"

"Yes, as long as we spend it on the right thing."

"And what would that be?"

"Well, we're going to Texas, aren't we? I think we should spend it on a ranch."

"A ranch?" Gid questioned. "I guess that's one idea. We'll be cattlemen."

"It'll probably be a lot of hard work," Will said.

"Hard work, huh? Well, maybe you've forgotten how hard Pa made us work on the farm."

Will chuckled. "You've got that right."

"Besides, if things hadn't happened the way they did, we'd be there now," Gid said.

"But things did happen," Will replied.

The two brothers were quiet for the next several minutes, and Will couldn't help but let his mind slip back in time. It was twenty years ago, now, but the memory was as fresh as yesterday.

———

Southwest Missouri, 1863

THE WAR WAS in full swing, and it had been over a year since Will and Gid had seen their parents. But now, with General Price's Division bivouacked outside of Springfield, the two brothers took a leave of absence to go home. Home was the Crockett Farm just north of St. Leger, Missouri.

"Hey, Will, do you think maybe Ma might have cooked up a pot of chicken 'n dumplin's for us?" Gid asked as the two rode along the road that led to the Crockett farm.

"Well, I don't know, do you think the sun will come tomorrow?"

Gid laughed. "Yeah, I think she'll have 'em when we get there. Say, maybe we can have our next-door neighbors over."

"The whole family, or just the daughter?" Will teased.

"Well, if I'm going to marry the girl, I need to show the family that I'm a good person, don't I?"

"That's probably a good idea, but..." Will paused in mid-sentence and pointed ahead. "Gid, look at that smoke."

"My God, it looks like it's comin' from home!"

The brothers broke into a gallop, racing toward the smoke. When they arrived, they saw that the house and the barn were burning, both buildings entirely invested with flames. Black smoke roiled into the sky.

"Where's Ma and Pa?" Gid asked as the two men looked in vain for their parents.

"There's Rhoda," Gid said. "What's she doin' standing out in the field all by herself?" Rhoda was the family's mule.

"My God, Gid, she's not by herself," Will said, pointing to two shapes on the ground.

Again, Will and Gid urged their horses into a gallop. Even before they got to the middle of the field, they recognized the shapes on the ground. Their mother was naked, and leaping down from the saddles the two men hurried to their parents.

There were bullet holes in their father, and their mother had bruises all over her body and a bullet wound in her chest.

"Will! Ma's still alive!"

The two knelt beside their mother.

"Ma!" Will said, fighting the lump in his throat.

Amanda, seeing her son, smiled. "I prayed to stay alive until I could see the two of you one more time. My boys." She put her hand on first Will's cheek, then Gid's.

"I'm going to get the wagon so we can get you to the doctor," Gid said.

"No," Amanda answered. "Not now."

"Just to get the wagon," Gid said.

"No, please, God let me live to see you one more time. I know I'll die before you get the wagon. I want you to spend the rest of my time with me."

"Ma, who did this?" Will asked as he held her hand in his.

Amanda took a couple of gasping breaths. "Hoffman. He said his name was Otto Hoffman."

"Isn't he the leader of that bunch of redlegs?" Gid asked.

"That's him—the dirty rotten bastard," Will said.

"Move me over beside Drury," Amanda said. "I want to be with him when..." again, she had to gasp for breath.

"Don't talk, Ma, we'll move you to him."

Working together, the two men moved their mother as gently as possible to lay her beside their father's bullet-riddled body. Will placed Drury's hand in hers.

"Yes," Amanda said. "Yes, my sweet darling, I know you're waiting. I'll be with you soon."

She took her last breath.

———

On board the train

"I wish things could have been different," Gid said after several moments of silence between them.

Will knew then, that Gid was reliving the same, painful memories. He nodded his head but said nothing.

———

It was mid-morning of the third day, when they arrived at Fort Worth. When they stepped down from the train, they were in an environment more akin to what they were used to, and Gid commented on it.

"Do you get the feeling that we've come home?" he asked.

"Home?"

"Yeah, I mean compared to San Francisco. I read that the population of San Francisco is two hundred thousand, Fort Worth is six thousand."

Will chuckled. "As odd as that sounds, it makes sense. We don't belong in a big city. As a matter of fact, Fort Worth is too big as far as I'm concerned."

They watched as their panniers were taken from the baggage car and put on a wagon that had been drawn aside, then they stepped into the depot and sought out the station manager.

"Yes, sir, what can I do for you gents?" the station manager asked.

"We just arrived," Will said. "Where is the nearest hotel?"

"Well sir, it isn't the nearest one, but you won't go wrong by staying at the Clark House," the station manager replied with a broad smile.

"Are you paid to recommend that hotel to arriving passengers?" Will asked.

"Well, uh, yes sir, I am," the station manager admitted. "But it really is a fine hotel. I wouldn't lie to you about that."

Will chuckled. "Since you were truthful about being paid to recommend it, I'll believe you are also truthful about the hotel. My brother and I will stay there."

"If you would, sir, would you be kind enough to tell the desk clerk that Hodge Deckert told you about the hotel?"

"I'll be glad to."

"Thank you, I appreciate that."

When Will and Gid left the depot, they walked over to one of the hackneys that was waiting for passengers from the arriving train.

"Clark House Hotel please," Will said, as he and Gid put their luggage into the boot of the two-wheeled carriage.

The driver chuckled. "Deckert told you about it, did he?"

"He was nice enough to offer a recommendation, yes. Is anything wrong with the hotel?"

"No, it's fine. And it's in the middle of town, so you'll find everything convenient."

The Clark House was an impressive looking three-story building, made of brick. When they checked in, Will mentioned that Hodge Deckert was the one who had told them about the hotel.

"Mr. Deckert is a good man, and you'll find that he didn't steer you wrong," the desk clerk said as the two signed in, then passed over the keys to their rooms.

"Let's get our bags put away, then come down for dinner," Will suggested.

"Oh, sir, we won't be serving dinner until six o'clock this evening," the clerk said.

"What are you talking about? I see people eating in the dining room right now," Gid said.

"Yes, sir, they're having their lunch."

"Yeah, well, whatever you're calling it, I'm ready to eat," Gid said.

After taking their saddlebags to their rooms, the two went down to the dining room for lunch.

"What do we do next?" Gid asked.

"Next thing we have to do is open a bank account and then start looking for a ranch to buy."

"Hey, maybe someone at the bank will know of a ranch that's for sale," Gid suggested.

"Damn, Little Brother, you aren't just a handsome face, are you? That's a good idea."

When they had arrived in San Francisco, they had deposited the certified check they had brought with them from the bank in Prescott. When they left San Francisco, they got another certified check, this time for twenty-nine thousand dollars.

After depositing their bank draft, Will asked if they could meet with the bank president.

"Yes, sir," the teller replied enthusiastically. "Mr. Montgomery will be glad to meet with you gentlemen. Come with me."

Will and Gid followed the bank teller down a hallway that led to the back of the bank. There, the teller knocked lightly on the door, then stepped inside, closing the door behind him. A moment later the door reopened and a tall, rather dignified looking man stood there with the teller.

"Mr. Montgomery, these are our most recent depositors, Mr. Will and Mr. Gid Crockett."

"Charles Montgomery," the man said extending his hand. "Come in, gentlemen, please."

Montgomery's office was comfortably large, and in addition to his desk, there was a round table and four chairs. Montgomery held his hand out toward the table in invitation.

"Now, what can I do for you?" he asked when they were all seated.

"We want to buy a ranch," Will said. "We don't want a great big spread, but we want it to be big enough to make us a little money. Do you have a suggestion as to where we might start to look?"

A broad smile spread across Montgomery's face. "Why, I'd say you've already started."

"Oh?" Will questioned.

"I happened to know the Brown Spur may be just what you're looking for."

"The Brown Spur?"

"It's a ten-thousand-acre ranch near Saginaw, which is about twelve miles northwest of Fort Worth. It's got good grass, and in this part of the country, it's got the most important thing—water. Just last week General Redling, that would be Ben Redling, came to ask me if I knew of anyone who might be interested in buying his property."

"Is it a working ranch now?" Will asked.

"Oh, yes indeed. For its size, it's one of the most productive ranches in Tarrant County."

"If the property's that good, why does he want to sell it?"

Montgomery got a solemn look on his face. "The General is a recent widower. He was devastated by the loss of his wife, and he's lost all enthusiasm for his ranch. He wants to go to Chicago to live with his daughter and son-in-law. Would you be interested in looking at the ranch?"

"Absolutely," Will replied.

"How soon before we can see it?" Gid asked.

"Why, I can write you a letter of introduction so you can ride out there at your convenience."

"Thank you, we'd appreciate that," Will said.

"All right," Montgomery said as he took a paper with the letterhead of the bank, then wrote the letter and handed it to Will.

"Show this letter to General Redling. It will verify that you are legitimately interested in exploring the possibility of purchasing the ranch."

"All right, thank you," Will said as he took the letter.

Ranchers' Bank of Fort Worth
803 E. Belnap Street
Fort Worth, Texas

General Redling,

This letter will introduce the Crockett brothers, Will and Gid. These gentlemen have expressed an interest in purchasing a ranch in our area, and it is my belief that the Brown Spur will be exactly what they are looking for. I can further attest that they have sufficient funds to enter into this transaction, should you wish to do business with them.

Charles Montgomery
President, Ranchers' Bank

Will glanced at the letter, then put it into the envelope Mr. Montgomery had provided. "Thank you, sir, for your time. My brother and I will be back to see you."

"My pleasure," Montgomery said as he rose from the table. "Let me see you to the door."

———

"WHAT ABOUT HORSES?" Gid asked as they stepped out into the hallway. "We need to buy a couple, don't you think?"

"We could always hire one of those hackneys to take us out to the ranch," Will suggested.

"Come on, Will, tell me you're kidding."

Will laughed. "Yeah, Little Brother, I was just playin' with you. We'll go down to the livery and see where we can pick up a couple of good..."

Before Will could finish his sentence, there was a commotion in the lobby of the bank.

"Hands up, ever'body! We're robbin' this bank!"

CHAPTER FIVE

WHEN WILL AND GID REACHED THE LOBBY, THEY SAW three masked men. All three were waving guns around in an attempt to intimidate both the employees and the customers of the bank.

"You two," one of the men shouted, seeing Will and Gid suddenly appear from the back of the bank. "Get your hands up!"

"Gid, if you can handle the one on the right, I'll take care of the other two," Will said.

"What the hell are you talking about? I told you to get your hands up!"

"Now," Will said, speaking so quietly that only his brother heard him.

Will and Gid made lightning draws of their pistols, doing so, so fast that they caught the bank robbers by surprise. There were three gunshots, coming so rapidly that there was scarcely enough separation between them so that the individual shots could be counted.

Gid's shot hit his man in the center of his chest. Will

hit both of his targets in the head, and all three went down.

With smoking guns still in their hands, Will and Gid checked the would-be bank robbers.

"They're dead," Gid said, and with his pronouncement he and Will holstered their weapons.

"Is everyone all right?" Gid asked the customers and employees of the bank, all of whom were now looking at the brothers in shock.

"Uh," one of the tellers replied. "Uh, yes, we're, uh, we're all fine, nobody was hurt."

Montgomery, who had heard the shooting, now appeared from his office, and with a quick glance, took in what had just happened.

"Gentlemen, you just saved our bank and likely, the lives of several people," he said, awestruck by the scene before him. "We are forever in your debt."

"Well, it seemed like it was the thing to do," Will said.

"Geoffrey?" Montgomery said to one of the tellers who seemed to be in a state of shock.

"Yes, sir?"

"Go get Sheriff Maddox."

There were two customers in the bank, a man and a woman, and they moved away from the dead bodies, but said nothing until the sheriff arrived a few minutes later.

"What happened here?" Sheriff Maddox asked.

Now, everyone who had been standing around in silence, began talking at the same time. Finally, the sheriff picked one man to speak, and that was the teller who had taken the Crocketts' deposit.

"Mr. Grant, you want to tell me what happened here?"

"It beats anything you ever saw, Sheriff," Grant said. "These men already had their guns drawn," he pointed to the three, masked bodies on the floor, "when these two men, Mr. Crockett and Mr. Crockett came back from a meeting they were having with Mr. Montgomery. Their guns were still in their holsters, but they drew them so fast that you could hardly follow it. And they shot all three of the robbers, before the robbers could even get off a single shot."

"Crocketts?" Sheriff Maddox asked. "What are your first names?"

"I'm Will, this is my brother Gid."

"I don't think I know either one of you," Maddox said. "Are you just passing through town?"

"More like just arriving," Will said

"Sheriff, these two men just made a rather significant deposit," Montgomery said. "They've expressed an interest in buying the Brown Spur ranch."

"You don't say," Maddox said. He smiled. "Well, I hope you boys do that. The Brown Spur is a good ranch, and the county could use a couple of good men like you."

By now one of the sheriff's deputies, as well as the undertaker had arrived. The deputy had pulled the mask off one of the dead robbers.

"Sheriff, you know who this here'n is?" the deputy asked.

"I haven't looked close enough to identify any of 'em yet," Sheriff Maddox said.

"Well, I don't know all of 'em, but this here'n is Lon

McMurtry," the deputy said, pointing to one of the bodies.

"McMurtry, huh?" Sheriff Maddox looked over at Will and Gid. "Boys, this is your lucky day. There's a five thousand dollar reward offered for McMurtry. There's probably paper on these other two as well, as soon as we find out who they are."

———

AFTER SUPPER THAT NIGHT, they sat on the upstairs balcony of the hotel, just looking out over the city.

"With the twenty-nine thousand dollars that we deposited, plus this five we're going to get for this McMurtry guy, we're damn near rich," Gid said. He chuckled. "I never thought I would say that I was rich."

"Well, we aren't rich, not really. I mean, not like the railroad tycoons, and people like Rockefeller, or Astor," Will said.

"Yeah, but there've been times when we had less than twenty dollars between us," Gid said. "Compared to that, we're rich."

Will chuckled. "Yes, I'll give you that. We're certainly better off now than we've been before. We've chased down many a man for a bounty, but this McMurtry literally just fell at our feet."

The next morning, Will and Gid walked down to the sheriff's office, where they were greeted by a smiling Sheriff Maddox.

"Here's a bank draft for you, for nine thousand dollars," he said.

"Nine? I thought you said it would be five," Will replied.

"Five thousand for Lon McMurtry, two thousand for LeRoy Page, and two thousand for Sid Collins. That's quite a pay day."

Will and Gid smiled, broadly. "Yes, sir, it is."

———

"How is it that you weren't killed, Draco?" Damon Boswell asked.

"I was waitin' just across the street with the horses. When I heard the shootin' I waited, figurin' that it was McMurtry 'n the others what was doin' the shootin', but when they didn't come out, 'n the sheriff went in, I knew somethin' must've gone wrong, so I stepped into a saloon, figurin' to wait until I found out what happened."

"And what did you find out?"

"Well, pretty soon the news was all over, people was a' talkin' about what happened. They was two men, it seemed, who kilt Lon, LeRoy, 'n Sid all three."

"Who were they? Bank guards? Sheriff's deputies?"

"No, sir, they was just two men the gossips say just come into town. They was in the back talking to Montgomery when the boys went it. They say they was brothers by the name of Crockett."

"Too bad 'bout McMurtry 'n the others," Weasel said. "They was good boys."

"Yes. Well, I told them they might be biting off more than they could chew," Boswell said. "But McMurtry was convinced he could pull it off, and he was determined to put his plan into operation."

"Are we going to get some more men to replace them?" Reed asked.

"No, I don't think that will be necessary. I will just make certain that any operation we undertake will be the result of careful planning. And the fewer of us there are, the greater will be our share of the endeavor."

"What?" Mathis asked.

Draco laughed. "You know how educated the boss talks. What he said was, if there ain't too many of us when we do a job, why it'll just be more money for us'ns."

Boswell and the six men with him were camped on the Trinity River, where they had planned to rendezvous with McMurtry and the others after they robbed the Ranchers' Bank in Fort Worth.

"Gentlemen, having learned of the failure of our erstwhile friends, I think it would behoove us to leave this place and return to our hideout."

"But we didn't get no money while we was here," Cooley said.

"As soon as we get back, I'll plan a new operation for us," Boswell promised.

CHAPTER SIX

Brown Spur Ranch

GENERAL BEN REDLING, OWNER OF THE BROWN SPUR
Ranch, was standing under a big live oak tree which was
growing about one hundred yards from the house. He
was looking down at a gravestone.

Here lies
Edna Redling
Precious Flower, you have left
The bonds of this earth to go to
Where a more fitting place awaits you
And there to be forever kept
In the Hands of the Lord
As long as blood courses through
The veins of the hands that pen these words
Thy memory will be forever kept green
Gone but not forgotten,
With much love forever, your Ben

From a distance, it might just look like a man was standing there with his head bowed. But if anyone came close enough, they would be able to hear that he was actually talking to his late wife.

"Once I sell this place, Edna, it won't be as if I'm actually going to be leavin' you, 'cause the truth is, you'll be here in my heart, for as long as I live." Ben placed his hand over his heart. "And the time will come when we'll be together again.

"It's just that I can't stay here anymore, because everywhere I look, it reminds me too much of you, and Sweetheart, that hurts just more than I can stand. So, I've decided to sell Brown Spur, and go to Chicago to live with Sue Ann. That way I'll have some of you with me in actual flesh and blood."

It had been two months since Edna had died, and the pain was still but a breath away from Ben's very existence.

"General Redling?"

Ben looked up to see his foreman coming toward him.

"Yes, Abe?"

Abe was Abe Barker, a man in his mid-forties, dark hair and eyes, and with the sun-browned, weathered skin of someone who spent much time out of doors. He also had a scar on his face, a dark, puffy streak from his left eye, down to the corner of his mouth. This was the result of a saber slash he had received from a Confederate officer.

"The roan and the gelding need shoe work. Do you want me to take them into town to the blacksmith or do you want me to take care of it myself?"

"There's no need to take them to town," Ben said.

"You know you're as good as any blacksmith for something like that, so you go ahead and do it, if you want to."

"All right, I'll get right on it," Abe said. He started to walk away but then he turned back. "General, are you really planning on leaving the Brown Spur?"

"Yes, Abe, I am. I just can't stay here without Edna. When she died, well, it's like a part of me died, too. I'm thinking that if I go to Chicago and spend time with Sue Ann and my grandkids, I can get over this hurt."

"Yes, sir, Mrs. Redling was a wonderful woman, and I can see why you miss her so much. It's just that the men are going to, well, I'm going to miss . . ." Abe let the sentence hang, incomplete.

"I know, Captain. You've been with me for many years," Ben said.

"Since Shiloh, when I was assigned as your aide de camp," Abe said.

"And a better man I never had," Redling said with a smile.

"You know it's not going to be the same, me not being with you."

"I feel the same way, Abe. But I've got to go." Ben had an expression on his face, that showed what agony he was experiencing.

"I can understand that," Abe replied as he nodded his head. "I'll not be asking you again."

"You're a good man, Abe. I know you'll be a great asset to whoever buys the ranch."

"Yes, sir," Abe said as he looked down, not wanting the General see the emotion that he was feeling. "I'd best get to work on shoeing those horses."

Ben Redling, late brigadier general of the Union

Army, watched his foreman walk away, and remembered the first day he had ever seen him.

———

Pittsburg Landing, Tennessee, April 6ᵗʰ, 1862

THE BATTLE HAD BEGUN when the Confederate Army launched a surprise attack on Union forces near a little church known as Shiloh, at a place called Pittsburg Landing in southwestern Tennessee. Up until that time, the war had been more parades and drills than actual battle. But in this engagement, casualties were running unusually high. There were peach trees near Shiloh Church, and their white flowers fluttered down like snow, from the direct hits and even the shock waves of the bullet and cannon fire.

The height of fighting that day took place on a field where all the units from Illinois, under command of Brigadier General Benjamin Redling had dug themselves in along a worn wagon path, called the "Sunken Road," which was at one edge of the field. A couple of hundred yards away, Confederates lined the other edge of the clearing.

On the whole, the Confederates did well on April 6ᵗʰ. They forced the Union men back toward Pittsburg Landing and the Tennessee River. But General Grant, never panicking as his army was decimated, arranged his troops in a final defensive line that held as night came on.

Lieutenant Abe Barker was with the 29ᵗʰ Illinois, which formed a part of the Illinois Brigade, which was commanded by Brigadier General Benjamin Redling.

After a day of intense fighting and heavy casualties, a sergeant approached Barker where he and the rest of his company, lay resting, and licking their wounds from the day's fighting.

"Lieutenant Barker?"

"Yes, Sergeant?"

"Cap'n Marshal says you're s'posed to report to Gen'rul Redling."

"What for?"

"I don't know, Lieutenant, he didn't tell me. All he said was that you're s'posed to report to the gen'rul.

Abe located the General's headquarters on the bank of the Tennessee River.

"General, Redling, I'm Lieutenant Barker, and I was told to report to you, sir."

"Yes, Captain," General Redling said. "Tragically, my aide-de-camp was killed today, and I would like for you to take his place."

"I'm a lieutenant, sir."

Redling smiled. "Perhaps you are for now, but if you're willing to take this job, you'll be a captain."

Abe's smile was even broader than Redling's smile. He saluted. "Sir, Captain Barker reporting for duty."

The battle continued with each army suffering intense casualties. Then, after initial successes, the Confederates were unable to hold their positions and were forced back, resulting in a Union victory.

General Redling found Barker's duty as an aide de camp to be exemplary, so he kept him in that position for the rest of the war.

When the war ended, Ben came to Texas where he bought the Brown Spur Ranch. He brought Abe with him, making him the foreman of the ranch. It was one of the wisest moves he made, because Abe had done an outstanding job for him.

General Redling had also brought his wife with him. His daughter, having married one of the officers in General Redling's command, had remained in Illinois, and now lived in Chicago.

Abe was unmarried when he arrived, but a year ago he met and married Julia Wallace who was an exceptionally beautiful woman, while Abe, who wasn't particularly handsome in the first place even before the disfiguring battle scar, caused others to wonder how he had come to marry such a beautiful woman.

The memories of Shiloh and his time with General Redling occupied Abe's thoughts as he worked to shoe the horses. It was only when he heard the loud guffaws of Walt Chambers, one of the hands who worked on the ranch that the memories slipped away. He was no longer on the battlefield and Pittsburg Landing, he was, once again, in this time and place in Texas, in the barn on the Brown Spur Ranch.

———

Fort Worth

WILL and Gid were having supper in the hotel dining room, when a waitress approached them and offered to fill their coffee cups. It was very late and the dining room was nearly empty. The waitress looked tired, and Gid asked if she would like to join them.

"I'd love to, but I don't think I can," the woman said, as she gathered up the dirty plates.

"Can you join us in eating a piece of pie?" Gid continued.

The woman looked around the room. "I suppose that would be all right. I've not had my supper yet, and there is a piece of apple pie that has my name on it." She smiled.

"Then bring whatever pie you think is good and join us," Will said pushing a chair aside. "In fact bring two or three pieces for my brother. He has a big appetite."

When the waitress returned, she had apple, lemon, chocolate and three pieces of a custard pie.

"This pretty much empties out the pie safe," she said, "so I think Mr. Snyder will be happy."

Will reached for a piece of the custard pie and Gid slid all the others except for the apple in front of himself.

"What's your name," Gid asked as he began eating.

"My name is Lena. I don't think I've seen you two in here before. Are you just passing through?"

"We hope not," Will said. "We want to buy a ranch, and Mr. Montgomery over at the bank has given us a tip on one that's not too far away."

"I'll bet it's the Brown Spur," Lena said.

"That's right," Gid said. "How did you guess?"

"General Redling comes in here when he gets in to town. He's such a nice man, but since his wife died, you can just see in his eyes how much he misses her." Lena shook her head. "And I suppose he'd want to get away from Julia Barker." She said the name in a disgusted tone.

Will raised his eyebrows. "And who is Miss Barker?"

"Not Miss Barker—it's Mrs. Barker. But everybody knows she doesn't remember that very often."

"Oh, and how does she figure in to the Brown Spur ranch?" Will continued.

"She's married to General Redling's foreman, Abe Barker," Lena said. "Abe is a man who's the salt of the earth." She stopped talking. "I think I've said too much. I'm just saying—if you do buy the Brown Spur, just be wary of that woman. She's a hussy if you know what I mean."

"We'll watch out for her," Gid said as he began eating the last piece of pie.

Just then a gentleman entered the restaurant. He looked familiar, and when he saw Will and Gid, he came to their table.

"I know you don't remember me, but you fellows may have saved my life today." He held out his hand. "Geoffrey Killdeer. I'm a teller over at the Ranchers' Bank."

"You didn't tell me you two are heroes. Everybody who came in today was talking about what you did. Did you really kill three men?"

"It's not something we're particularly proud of," Will said as he drained his coffee cup.

"Well you should be," Killdeer said. "The sheriff says those three men were all part of Boswell's gang."

"Boswell? Who's Boswell?"

"Damon Boswell. He's an outlaw who is causing trouble all over this part of the state," Kate said.

"Well, he won't be our problem," Will said. "It would seem to me that someone like this Boswell person would be the law's problem."

"Yeah, you would think that, wouldn't you? But so far, the law hasn't been able to do anything about him, and now that he knows who you two are, he'll probably come for you. It seems this man is free to rob and murder at will."

"Thanks for the warning," Will said. "If we wind up buying the Brown Spur, or any other ranch around here, we'll keep Mr. Boswell in mind."

———

AFTER LEAVING THE RESTAURANT, Will and Gid decided to go get a beer, but when they passed by the sheriff's office the light was burning. They stepped in to visit Sheriff Walter Maddox.

"Listen, I want to thank you guys again for stopping the bank from being robbed. Hell, the whole town is thanking you."

"Well, the reward you gave us was thanks enough," Gid said.

"Oh, believe me, I didn't give you that reward. The State of Texas did," Sheriff Maddox said with a little chuckle.

"Yes, well, I'm just glad we were there at the right time," Will said.

"So am I. So, what can I do for you gents?"

"We told you yesterday that we were considering buying the Brown Spur Ranch."

"Yes, you did. The Brown Spur is a good ranch, and the man who owns it, is a good man, he'll treat you right."

"What should we know about Boswell?" Gid asked.

"Ah, yes, Damon Boswell," Sheriff Maddox replied. "You've heard of him, have you?"

"No, other than we were told the three men we

killed were part of his gang. There was a suggestion that he might be someone we should look out for."

"Well, he's been causing his share of trouble, not only in Tarrant County, but Dallas, Denton, and Collin counties as well. He leads a gang of cutthroats and they've held up the stage a few times, and we think they robbed a bank in Collin County. In the process, there have been several people killed," the sheriff said. "I have to be honest, when Geoffrey Killdeer came runnin' in here telling me some bank robbers had been shot, I went down there hoping it might have been Boswell. But it wasn't and now what's curious to me is why he wasn't with them."

"Has this Boswell done any cattle rustling?" Will asked.

"Nothing major that we know of, but we think his gang probably stole a few cows, here and there. Most likely for their own use, but if you buy a ranch, you might want to keep an eye out for him."

"Thanks, we'll do that," Will replied.

CHAPTER SEVEN

——————

EVEN AS WILL AND GID WERE DISCUSSING BOSWELL, THE subject of their conversation, along with the six men who made up what was left of his gang, were standing by their horses on a road leading into Denton.

"How much money do you reckon this coach is a' gonna be carryin'?" Draco asked.

"There's no way of knowing, of course. However, it is a money shipment from a bank in Dallas, so I have every expectation that it will be quite a significant sum," Boswell replied.

"Yeah, well, I just want to be sure it's worth our time waitin' out here, is all."

"Tell me, Draco, how much money you got 'n your pocket right now?" Mathis asked.

"Hell, I ain't got two nickels to rub together," Draco answered.

"Well, if it's just enough to give us all two nickels apiece, then you'll be ahead of where you are now, won't you?"

The others laughed.

"Mr. Sloan, if you would, please, climb up there and take a look. The coach should be in sight by now," Boswell directed.

"All right," Sloan answered.

Arnie Sloan climbed to the top of the little hill, then looked south toward Dallas.

"Here it comes!" he called. Then, quieter and to himself, he said, "Son of a bitch! Boswell," he called down.

"Yes, I heard you, the coach is on the way."

"No, that ain't what I'm talkin' about," Sloan said. "They's four men ridin' with the coach."

"That don't matter none, does it?" Reed asked. "They's seven of us, 'n only four of them."

"Five of them," Boswell said. "Don't forget the shotgun guard."

"Yeah, but we open up on 'em a' fore they even got 'ny idea we're here," Reed said.

"No," Boswell said. "Our success has been predicated upon always having a position so superior that any resistance would be futile. We will not engage unless our advantage is unchallengeable."

"I ain't sure what you said, but it sounded kind a' like you was sayin' that we won't be a' hittin' that coach," Draco said.

"That's exactly what I'm saying. Gentlemen, we will proceed no further into this operation. I suggest we retire from the scene before any of them are made aware of our presence."

Draco laughed. "You're the damndest talking feller I've ever know'd."

"I don't know why you should say that, Mr. Draco, I

am speaking English after all, not some indecipherable patois."

"Now you're a' doin' that of a pure purpose, ain't you?" Draco said. "Talkin' in them fancy words that there don't nobody know just what the hell it is that you're a' sayin'."

"I don't know, I do seem to be able to make myself understood," Boswell replied.

"Yeah, I reckon you do. But, look here, iffen we ain't goin' to hold up this here stagecoach, when 'n where at are we goin' to get some more money, 'cause it's liken I said, I ain't hardly got no money left a' tall."

"I will study the possibilities before us, and ascertain which would be the most productive with the least amount of risk," Boswell said.

"What's that?" Draco asked.

"He said he'll find us some other way to get us some money," Weasel said.

"Oh, well, good, 'cause I can sure use some," Draco replied.

Although the six men who composed the Boswell gang were very vocal for the ride back to the small abandoned line shack that was acting as their outlaw headquarters, Boswell remained quiet.

———

BECAUSE THEY HAD SOLD their horses before they left for San Francisco, the first thing the Crockett brothers did the next morning, was buy new horses from the livery. They chose quarter horses—both were clay-red, but Will's horse had a white mane, while Gid's horse had a black tail and mane. Will named his horse, Dancer, Gid called his horse, Pug.

The town of Saginaw, which was the nearest town to the Brown Spur was, as Charles Montgomery had pointed out, twelve miles north, and slightly west of Fort Worth.

"Who would have ever thought that we would want to be ranchers" Gid said as they started their ride toward Saginaw.

"Why not?" Will asked. "Like you said earlier, at one time we were going to be farmers."

"Ranching isn't the same thing," Gid said.

Will chuckled. "No, it isn't. When you are a rancher, you ride a horse, but as I recall when we were farmers, we walked behind a plow pulled by a mule. Perhaps you've forgotten that."

Gid chuckled as well. "Come to think of it, that's right, isn't it?"

Within an hour after they left Ft Worth, Will and Gid rode into the town of Saginaw.

"Damn, these sure are wide streets for such a small town," Gid said.

"That they are," Will agreed.

"How are we going to find out where the ranch is?" Gid asked.

Will pointed to the Blacksmith shop. "I'd say the smithy would know."

When the two men dismounted in front of the shop, they could smell the smoke from the forge and hear the loud clang of the smithy's hammer as he was working on a piece of gleaming, red-hot metal.

The smithy was a powerfully built man, wearing a full-length apron and a visor. When he saw Will and

Gid, he stopped hammering and looked up, lifting his visor as he did so.

"What can I do for you boys?" he asked.

"We're looking for the Brown Spur Ranch," Will said.

The Smithy pointed toward a road. "Follow this road west for about two miles, you can't miss it."

"Thanks."

"I don't believe Barker is a' hirin' though."

"Barker? We heard that he was the foreman. We need to see Ben Redling, the owner," Will said.

"Redling is the owner all right, but Abe Barker, bein' the foreman 'n all, well, he's that does all the hirin' and firin' that gets done."

"We're not looking for work, we're looking to buy the place," Gid said.

The smithy smiled. "Are you now? Yes, I knew that the General was wantin' to sell. Well, in that case I expect we'll be doin' business from time to time. My name is Leo Watson."

"It's good to meet you, Mr. Watson. My name is Gid Crockett, this is my brother, Will."

"Crockett? Are you boys any a' kin to Davy Crockett?"

"We've been told Davy was a cousin," Will explained.

"Well, I'll be damn." Watson smiled, and reached out his hand. "I'd like to shake hands with you two boys. Davy Crockett is a genuine hero of Texas."

They shook hands, then Watson said, "If there's anything I can do for a kin o' Davy Crockett, you just ask, 'n I'll do it."

"You've already done it, Mr. Watson," Will said. "You've given us directions to the Brown Spur."

"I hope you boys buy the ranch. It'd sure be good to have some of ole' Davy's kin livin' among us."

"Well, we can't actually take advantage of Davy, seeing as he was a distant cousin, and he died before we were even born," Will said.

"But we're proud of being his relative," Gid added.

"Yeah, well I would sure as hell think so," Watson said.

———

A LITTLE LESS THAN half-an-hour's ride after they left town, they saw a sign that arched over a little road that connected the ranch to the main road. The sign read, "BROWN SPUR RANCH" then beneath that were the words "Ben Redling, Proprietor".

"It looks like we've found it," Gid said.

They passed under the sign, then rode about a quarter of a mile farther until they reached a cluster of buildings: a red barn, a bunk house, a kitchen and dining hall for the hands, a small house, and a larger, two-story white house with a porch that spread all the way across the front.

When Will and Gid reined up in front of the house, they were met by a man who appeared to be in his mid-forties. He had dark hair, sun-browned skin, light blue eyes, and a long scar that started just below his eye, and cut through the corner of his lip.

"Can I help you gentlemen?" the man asked by way of greeting.

"Mr. Redling?"

"No, I'm Abe Barker."

"Ah, yes, we were told about you, you're the foreman, I believe," Will said.

"I am."

"Is Mr. Redling in?"

"Yes, he's in the house."

"Would you tell him we'd like to meet with him?"

"That depends. What are you here for?"

"The banker told us, this ranch might be for sale and we're interested in buying."

"All right," Abe replied, as he stepped back inside.

No more than a moment later, Abe reappeared at the front door. "Come on in," he invited. "General Redling is in the drawing room."

Ben Redling stood to greet them when they entered the room. Redling was a big man, in his seventies, with white hair and beard, and a ruddy complexion.

"Mr. Redling, or should I say General Redling, my name is Will Crockett, this is my brother, Gid. Mr. Montgomery told us the Brown Spur Ranch might be for sale. If that's so, we're interested."

Redling laughed. "As I'm long past being a general, I go by Ben, and yes, Brown Spur is, indeed, for sale. I don't mind telling you it's the finest ranch in Tarrant County. It has ten thousand acres of grass, it's well watered, and if you're interested, I'll make you a good price on the cattle as well."

"How many head do you have?" Will asked.

"Abe, what are we running now?" Redling asked his foreman who was standing just inside the room.

"I'd say close to twenty-five hundred head," Abe replied.

"How late is that count?"

"That was about a month ago."

"Then it should be fairly accurate."

"Uh, General Redling, if you don't mind, I need to go. I've got the boys movin' some of the beeves onto the north range," Abe said.

"Sure, go right ahead."

"Mr. Crockett, Mr. Crockett," Abe nodded at each of the brothers by way of saying goodbye before he left.

"Good bye, Mr. Barker, I'm sure we'll meet again," Will said.

"Twenty-five hundred head," Redling said, continuing their conversation. The market will probably be somewhere around forty dollars a head, I'll let you have them for some less than that, say, thirty–five dollars. That would give you an immediate profit of twelve–thousand, five hundred dollars if you brought them all to market."

"Sir, that's a very generous offer, but I'm afraid we won't be able to afford the ranch and the cattle," Will said.

"Ah, there's no need for you to worry about that. You won't have to pay me for the cattle until after you sell them."

"What are you asking for the ranch?" Gid asked.

"Two dollars an acre for the land, twelve hundred dollars for the house and outbuildings. That would come to twenty–one thousand and two–hundred dollars. That's a very good price, gentlemen, and..."

Will interrupted Redling in mid–sentence. "We'll take it."

"It's not negotiable, I have to have at least that much to..." Redling continued, then he stopped. "I beg your pardon; did you just say you'll take it?"

"Yes."

"That's great! We can ride into the bank at Saginaw and make all the arrangements. You'll have no problem in getting a loan on the property."

"If it's all right with you, we'd prefer to do business at the Ranchers Bank in Fort Worth," Will said, and he showed Redling the letter Montgomery had written.

Redling read the letter, then smiled and nodded.

"That's a most informative letter. Fort Worth, yes, that will be good. If you can wait a couple of days, I can sign the ranch over to you and then I can catch the train to Chicago." He smiled. "That's where I'm going. My daughter lives there."

"That would be fine," Will said. "We're staying at the Clark House."

"But you do want to look over the ranch don't you? And you need to meet the hands—that is if you intend to keep them on, and I hope you do. They're all good men." Redling said. "And of course you'll want to meet Julia."

"Julia?" Gid asked.

Redling smiled. "Julia is Abe's wife." He shook his head. "She's a beautiful young lady and she's got a great business head on her shoulders. After my wife passed, I sort of depended on Mrs. Barker for a lot of things."

"Mrs. Barker sounds like an interesting lady," Will said. Neither he nor Gid commented that they had heard her name earlier.

"Very much so. I have an idea. If you can stay, I'll invite Abe and Julia to have supper with us tonight."

———

WHEN ABE BARKER brought his wife to supper that evening, Will couldn't help but notice the unlikely pairing of the two. Abe had the rustic look of a man who spent most of his time outdoors. He also had a badly scarred face. By contrast, Julia was an exceptionally good-looking woman, with long black hair, brown eyes shaded by long, dark lashes, high cheekbones and pouting lips. There was a sensuality to her movements that reminded Will of a cat.

The only other person present was Maria Sanchez, Redling's cook. She was an overweight, Mexican woman, with a face and eyes that Will would describe as kind. She had prepared Swiss steak with mashed potatoes, string beans cooked with bacon, and biscuits for supper. She was a very good cook, and Gid was eating with great relish.

"Oh, I like a big man who likes to eat," Julia said with a seductive smile.

"Well, my little brother does like to eat," Will said.

"*Little* brother?" Julia asked, surprised by Will's comment.

"He's younger than I am, and I can remember when he was smaller."

Julia laughed, her laugh low and throaty. "Well, he's not smaller than you now. Why do you still call him your *little* brother?"

"Old habits die hard, I guess," Will replied.

"Is it true that you handsome men will be buying Brown Spur Ranch?" Julia asked.

Julia's overt sexuality made Will a little uneasy and he glanced over at Abe, who was eating his dinner with little notice of his wife's coquetry.

"We're certainly considering it," Will said. "But we'd

like to get a really good look at the ranch before we make our final decision."

"Oh, well, I would be delighted to show you around," Julia said.

"I appreciate your offer, Julia, but I think it would be better if I showed them the ranch, and they've agreed to take a couple of days to get a really good look at it," Redling said. "After all, I'm the one who will be selling it."

"Yes, of course, General," Julia said. "I was just offering my help."

"I know, and I appreciate it," Redling replied as he reached over to pat her hand.

After dinner everyone retired to the parlor where the conversations continued.

"Six months ago, my wife died," Redling said. "I thought I could go on, but without Edna, it's just too painful, and I have nothing to keep me here. My daughter and son-in-law have invited me to come to Chicago to live with them, and that's what I intend to do."

"Are you from Texas, Abe?" Will asked.

"No, like General Redling, I'm from Illinois."

"Abe was one of my officers, my aide de camp in fact," Ben said. He smiled at Abe. "And in my opinion, there was no finer aide de camp in the entire Union army."

"And what about you, Mrs. Barker? Are you from Illinois as well?"

"Oh, heavens no, and call me Julia. I'm from right here in Texas. Abe and I have only been married for a little over a year."

"Will you be spending the night with us?" Redling asked.

"No, we have rooms at the Clark House in Fort Worth, but we'll be back out here tomorrow morning for the tour."

"Good, we'll be looking for you."

CHAPTER EIGHT

THAT EVENING, FOUND THE BROTHERS WILL AND GID IN Casey's Saloon on McLeroy Street in Saginaw. They were sitting at a table, nursing a beer and discussing their plans when a rather rotund man approached their table.

"Casey's the name, John Casey. I own this here saloon," he said extending his hand.

"It's good to meet you, Mr. Casey. I'm Will Crockett, this is my brother Gid."

"I don't believe I've seen you fellers before. You boys just passing through our fair town?"

"Well, we hope it turns out to be a little more than that. We're looking to buy the Brown Spur Ranch."

"Oh, that's a fine one, it is," Casey said. "And Ben Redling is as good a man as you're likely to find, despite the fact that he was a Yankee General. Too bad about his wife. Her dyin' sure left him some tore up."

"You been in the area long, Mr. Casey?" Gid asked.

"Please, call me John. I've owned this place for some fifteen years now, ever since I come back from the war.

And if you boys do stay around, why, I hope you become good customers."

"This seems like a pleasant enough place, and the beer is good, so I expect we'll be in here from time to time," Gid said.

"Oh, and if you boys do decide to stay here, that fella that just came in, is someone you ought to meet. That's Percy Coats—he's the town marshal."

Coats was tall and well proportioned. He had dark hair and a moustache that curled down around each side of his mouth, but no beard.

"Percy," Casey called. "Percy, come over here, I've got a couple of fellers I'd like for you to meet."

Coats approached their table with an amiable smile on his face.

"Percy this here is Will and Gid Crockett."

"Crockett you say. You're the two who took down those three galoots in that attempted bank robbery in Fort Worth, aren't you?"

"You know about that?"

"Well, the news of something like that travels fast," Coats said. "What brings you to our fair, little community?"

"They may be about to buy General Redling's place," Casey said.

"Well, you won't find a finer piece of property in the entire county than the Brown Spur." Coats said. "I hope you stay around. We could use a couple of good men, especially with someone like Boswell running around causing trouble. Have you heard of him?"

"Oh yes, we have heard of Boswell. What can you tell us about him?" Will asked.

"Not much, but to be honest, I mean, he ain't caused

me no actual trouble yet, but if 'n when he does, it would be nice to have a couple of boys like you two around to help out."

"Anytime my brother and I can be of any assistance, feel free to call on us," Will said.

"Thanks, I'll keep that in mind," Coats said. "I need to be on my way, but I hope everything goes well for you and for the general, too."

"Yeah, me too," Will replied.

A moment after Coats left the table, a very attractive young woman approached. "John says you two gentlemen plan on buying the Brown Spur."

"That is our intention, Miss..."

The young woman laughed. "Oh, heavens, call me Suzie, everyone else does."

"Very well, Suzie it is. Would you consider having a drink with us?"

Suzie laughed. "That's funny. You know that's my job."

For the next several minutes Will, Gid, and Suzie conversed over their drinks. Suzie had been a 'working girl' in New Orleans, then married one of her 'friends.' But when her husband died, her in-laws didn't want to have anything to do with her, so she left New Orleans, winding up in Saginaw.

"It's worked out better 'n I thought," Suzie said. "John treats all the girls just real nice, and nobody's run into anyone who's been mean, or brutal to us." She smiled. "I don't think either of you two would be mean, or brutal, would you?"

"There have been more than a few men we've been mean and brutal to," Will answered, easily. "But they were mean and brutal first."

"And we aren't likely to be mean and brutal to any of folks—either men or women, who don't get on our bad side first," Gid added with a grin.

"Oh heavens," Suzie replied, her smile matching Gid's. "I'll just have to tell all the girls to stay on your good side."

A few minutes later, one of the other girls, who identified herself as Millie, came over to join them."

"Oh, and you should meet Abby too," Millie said.

"She's our newest girl, and as sweet a girl as you'll ever meet. Do you mind if I call her over?"

"The more the merrier," Will said with a wide grin.

Abby came over when summoned and Will's first impression of her was that she was quite young.

"Abby, this is Will and Gid Crockett," Millie said. "These gentlemen are thinking about buying Ben Redling's place, so I expect we'll be seeing a lot more of 'em."

"How do you do," Abby said. There was a quiet, shyness to her tone, and an innocence about her which was in contrast to her profession. Will couldn't help but wonder how someone like this wound up as a percentage girl.

They visited for almost half an hour before the three women excused themselves, saying that they had to get to work. Will and Gid watched them as they went from table to table, like bees going from flower to flower, greeting the customers as they came in.

"You know, Abby . . ." Gid started, but Will interrupted.

"Yes, I was wondering the same thing. What's a girl like her doing in here?"

———

LATER THAT SAME EVENING, as they rode back to Fort Worth, the two brothers began discussing what was ahead of them.

"Are we doing the right thing, by buying a ranch?" Gid asked.

"Gid, we discussed this at some length on the train coming down, I thought we'd made our decision."

"Yeah, I guess so."

"Are you having second thoughts now?"

"Sort of. I mean, we've never done anything like this, we've always just sort of..." Gid let the sentence hang.

"Sort of what?"

"Sort of moved around, going from one place to another."

"That's something to consider," Will said. "But we didn't think we were miners either, and look what we got out of it? A lot of money that we need to do something with besides just spend it all."

"I agree." Gid smiled. "Besides, it might be somethin', being a big cattleman and all."

Will chuckled. "Little Brother, no matter what we do, you're always going to be big."

Gid joined him in laughing. "You're right about that."

"I'm looking forward to the next couple of days. I want to take a really good look at this ranch."

"Yeah, me too."

———

OUT AT THE Brown Spur Ranch, the cowboys in the bunk house were talking about the upcoming sale of the ranch.

"You think they'll keep us on? Or do you think they'll hire all new hands," Doodle Hawkins asked.

"Why wouldn't they keep us on?" Jim Clay asked.

"It's just that I know that sometimes, when folks buy a ranch, well they get to thinkin' that maybe they want all their own men, so the first thing they do, is they fire ever' one that's already workin' there."

"I don't think the Crocketts would do nothin' like that. Not the Crocketts that I know," Mike Latham said.

"Whoa, wait a minute. Are you sayin' you actual know the Crocketts?" Stan Mitchell asked.

"No, I don't actual know 'em. But I know about 'em, on account of I've read about 'em. They's been books wrote about 'em. You might say that they's famous."

"Uh, uh. If they was famous, why, they'd more 'n likely be livin' in some big city somewhere, like Kansas City, or St. Louis or Chicago, or some such place. They wouldn't be out here in the middle of Texas, fixin' to buy a ranch," Walt Chambers said.

"No, but that's what's made 'em famous you see, is bein' out West runnin' down outlaws 'n such. I read about 'em in one o' them dime novels," Latham said. "*Texas Shootout*, I think it was that the book was called.

Walt Chambers laughed. "Well, hell, they ain't none o' them books true. Them's all just made up stories."

"Yeah? Well, I don't think they'd write books about 'em, if they warn't true. And in the dime novel that I read, the Crocketts was both, good men."

"Well, I hope they are," Latham said. "On account of

pretty soon they're goin' to be the bosses of all of us. That is, if they actual keep us on."

———

WILL and Gid passed under the Brown Spur Ranch sign at a little after eight o'clock the next morning.

"I hope we're not too early," Gid said.

"Gid, this is a ranch. There's absolutely no way that everyone isn't up, yet."

Will's declaration was validated when, half-way up the road they were met by a man who was dressed like a working cow-hand.

"You two must be the Crocketts," the man said with a wide, welcoming smile.

"We are. I'm Will, and this my brother, Gid. Who might you be?"

"Stan Mitchell."

"You're one of the hands, are you, Stan?"

"Yes, sir. General Redling, he sent me out here to look for you. I'm supposed to take you up to the Big House when you get here."

"That's all right, we were here yesterday. We know the way," Will said.

"Yeah, but the thing is, I think I'm s'posed to shoot you if you change your mind and try and ride away," Mitchell teased.

Will and Gid both laughed. They didn't actually need a guide, because as Will said, they had already been to the Big House. But they knew that General Redling had obviously provided the young man to lead them, as a courtesy. The three horses moved up the long road at a trot. When they reached the Big House, they were met by Julia Barker.

"The general is waiting for you," Julia said. "Come, I'll take you to him."

"I'll take care of your horses," Mitchell offered as Will and Gid dismounted.

"Thanks, Stan," Gid said.

Mitchell smiled at being addressed by his first name from someone who would probably soon be his boss.

Will opened the door for Julia, who preceded them into the house.

"General, the guests you were expecting have arrived," Julia called out.

"Gentlemen, welcome. It's good to see that you arrived early this morning. Julia, would you be a dear and ask Maria to bring coffee?"

"Yes, of course. Will, Gid, I hope everything goes well and that I will see much more of you," she said with a flirtatious smile.

"I'm sure you will," Gid said, politely.

"You gentlemen indicated yesterday that you were predisposed to buy the ranch," Redling said. "I hope that your being here means that's still your intention."

"We haven't changed our minds," Will said.

"Good, good, it really is a fine ranch." Redling paused in mid-sentence, then took a deep breath and continued, "As I told you yesterday, my wife died, or I would never even think about selling this place. It's just that everything I see around here reminds me of her, and it's hard." He stopped again. "I need to be with my daughter and her children, not only to escape the melancholy of this place, but just to be with someone who'll cheer me up. You know, I have a grandbaby I haven't even seen and that's just wrong."

At that moment, Maria came into the room, carrying a tray. There were three cups, a coffee pot, a pitcher of cream, and a container of sugar. There was also a plate of doughnuts.

"*Gracias,* Maria," Redling said.

"I tell you what, this is certainly a good start," Gid said with a broad smile as he took two of the doughnuts.

"Ha! Maria makes doughnuts two or three days a week," Redling said.

"I'm so sorry for your loss, General," Will said.

Redling forced a smile, then shook his head. "I had no right to bring such a pall over the proceedings. This is supposed to be a happy day for all three of us. Drink up, boys. After you finish your coffee, we'll start out."

———

THEY STARTED their tour at the barn where two of the hands were saddling their horses. Stan Mitchell was standing by his, already-saddled, horse.

"You've met Mitchell," Redling said. "The one there with the beard and moustache is Walt Chambers, and the other one is Mike Latham. Gents, this is Will and Gid Crockett, if everything goes as it's supposed to, they'll be your new bosses, so you'd better treat them well."

The four men exchanged handshakes.

"Where are you headed?" Redling asked.

"Jim 'n Doodle have most of the cows moved to a new pasture," Chambers said. "They's some of 'em that didn't want to leave the crick so me 'n Mike's goin' out to go get 'em."

"You'll have all the cows gathered then?"

"Yes, sir."

"Good, I want you to get a good count," Redling said.

"Yes, sir, we can do that."

"Are our horses still saddled, Stan?" Gid asked.

Mitchell nodded and smiled. "Yeah, I figured you two would want to ride out again. Yours is saddled too, Gen'rul, iffen you want to come along."

"Yes, thank you, I believe I will."

A short time later, the men left the barn, riding south. Will and Gid took everything in as they rode, noticing that the fences were in a good state of repair, the fields were abundant with graze, and the waterways clean and accessible. It was obvious that the ranch was well tended.

While on their inspection tour, they encountered Jim Clay and Doodle Hawkins, then while Will and Gid visited with Clay and Hawkins, Chambers and Latham rode off to bring a few of the errant cattle back in to the gather.

"Boys, what I want to do now, is count the herd to see how many head I actually have," Redling said.

"How are we goin' to do that boss, without losin' count?" Doodle asked.

"I have a suggestion," Will said. "Suppose we move them all into that adjacent field, moving them ten at a time. That way we can't lose count."

"What about the cows Mike 'n Walt's goin' after?" Doodle asked.

"That's no problem," Mitchell said. "We'll just count them last."

The men began the count then, moving ten head with each transfer into the new field. Gid used his knife to cut a small notch into the fence post for each one hundred transferred. They worked until mid-afternoon, then Walt and Mike returned with twenty-three more beeves.

By the end of the day, every cow was transferred, and Gid examined the scratches on the fence post, then announced the total.

"Two thousand, six hundred and fifteen head," Gid announced.

As they rode back toward the housing compound, Mitchell invited Will and Gid to have supper with them in the cowboy's kitchen and dining hall. "Uh, is that okay with you, Gen'rul, if Mr. Crockett 'n Mr. Crockett eat with us?"

Redling chuckled. "I'm not the one to ask. I would think that decision would be up to Will and Gid."

"Well, if it'll help you make up your mind, I'd say that Moses is just about the best cook of any ranch I've ever worked on," Mitchell said.

"You've convinced me," Gid said.

"Yeah, it sounds good," Will added.

CHAPTER NINE

BACK AT THE FOREMAN'S HOUSE, ABE WAS READING THE paper when Julia came into the room.

"I got another letter from my brother," she said.

"Oh? What does Harry have to say?"

"He's breaking in a new fireman. The one he had before has left the railroad, he said he didn't like all the travelling."

Abe chuckled. "If he didn't like travelling, why did he become a fireman on a locomotive?"

"Who knows, here's the letter if you'd like to read it." Julia handed the letter to Abe.

"Harry's a real interesting fella, being a railroad engineer and all. When are you gonna invite him out, so I can meet him?"

"I don't know, he's always so busy. I'll ask him, sometime. But for now, I want you to invite the Crocketts to have dinner with us tonight." she said.

"Oh, I don't think we can. Stan told me he was gonna invite them to have supper with the men tonight."

"You're the foreman, you can just tell Stan Mitchell that Will and Gid will be dining with us."

"No, I wouldn't want to do that, because I don't think that would be right. If these two buy the ranch, and I'm pretty sure they're goin' to, then they need to get to know all the men who'll be working for 'em. And I get the feelin' they don't know much about ranchin'.'"

"Don't you think they need to know the foreman then?"

"Oh, I think they know us, all right. And don't forget, we've already had one meal with them."

"Yes, but that doesn't count. Mr. Redling was there."

"Of course, it counts. And like I say, the men need to get to know who they are going to be working for."

"Abe, why do you let those men push you around like that? You're their boss and you have absolute authority over every hand on this place," Julia said. "The most important relationship on any ranch is the one between the owner and his foreman."

"I think they realize that, and once they actually take over the ranch they'll come to know that even more."

"If you say so," Julia said. "I'm going to go lie down for a while, I've got a headache."

"Well, there you go, if you have a headache, it's a good thing the Crocketts aren't eating with us."

"Ohh, you. You just don't understand, do you?" Julia said in a challenging voice.

Julia strode pointedly into the bedroom, then lay on the bed. She had been counting on having the Crocketts as their guests tonight. They were both so handsome and it would have been enjoyable to share a meal with someone other than her husband. He was always so business oriented that he rarely ever paid any attention to her. And, with that terrible scar on his face it was growing more and more difficult to look at him anyway.

She had known about the scar when she married him, but she thought his position as foreman would provide her with a comfortable life. At least, it would keep her off the line. That was a part of her history that she never shared, so Abe had no idea she had ever been engaged in the world's oldest profession.

————

THE COWBOY KITCHEN and dining hall was a separate building from the bunkhouse. It had one long table with six chairs on each side, providing seating enough for every hand, and then some. Moses had fried chicken for tonight's supper and a huge bowl of mashed potatoes, another bowl of gravy and a platter of biscuits were set at the head of the table.

As the men ate, they bantered back and forth about ranch conditions, and they teased Scooter Simpson, who at twenty-two, was the youngest of all the cowboys.

"You should 'a seen Scooter when he tried to collect the rattles offen a snake what just had its head cut off. Well sir, you know how a dead snake will twitch 'till sundown, 'n what this dead snake done was, whip around as iffin he was about to bite 'im. He screamed so's you could hear 'im a mile away."

The others laughed again, as Scooter stared down at his plate in embarrassment.

Scooter wasn't the only one to come under attack as nearly every cowboy present was the butt of some tale.

Doodle Hawkins was the victim of a story told with much glee by the others. It seemed that one night he became inebriated with drink at the Casey's Saloon, then mounted his horse for the ride back home. And when he got back, he unsaddled the horse, then lay down in the stall with him, and went to sleep right there.

"But here's the thing," Jim Clay added, with a chuckle. "That horse had just been bought from over to Chris Dumey's place, so when it come home, it went right back to where it come from. 'N when Doodle woke up the next mornin', why, he warn't here at all, he was lyin' in Chris Doomey's barn."

"When are you going to buy the place?" Mitchell asked, after the joking was over.

"We want to spend tomorrow here as well, then I suppose we'll be about ready," Will answered. "The general wants to take the train out of Fort Worth as soon as possible."

"Well, I'll be lookin' forward to it. You two look like you're a couple of good men, 'n I won't mind workin' for you. Don't get me wrong, Gen'rul Redling is a man anyone would be willin' to ride the river with, 'n I was happy workin' for 'im, but seein' as he's goin' to be leavin' the ranch, well I'm just glad it'll be someone like you two that'll be takin' his place."

———

As SCOOTER LAY in his bunk that night, he thought about the teasing he had received at supper. He didn't mind it, and he realized that it was all in good fun. He knew, also, that teasing meant that he had been accepted by everyone.

His being a cowboy in the middle of Texas, would

come as a huge surprise to anyone who had served with him on board the *Sea Serpent*, a clipper ship, of 2594 tons, built for James Baines Shipping Company out of Norfolk, Virginia.

Scooter thought of his last cruise, and the reason he had left the sea.

———

One year earlier, at sea

A QUICK-BUILDING STORM had hit them, and the *Sea Serpent* was plowing through heavy seas. As her bowsprit dipped and poked through a large swell, the wave broke over the bow and threw its spray the entire length of the deck.

"Mr. Hanlon, we're into heavy seas, send some men aloft to take in the sail," Captain Greenly ordered.

"Aye, aye, sir," Hanlon, the first mate replied.

A handful of sailors, led by Ed Bivens, scrambled up the foremast, as it was the only mast that was square-rigged, and thus required hands aloft to furl sail. Scooter Simpson was among the sailors that had gone aloft.

"See that there is a proper furl, Bivens," Hanlon shouted into the wind.

"Aye, aye, sir," Bivens shouted back, his voice sounding thin in the wind that now buffeted them.

The wind was blowing with gale force now, and the ship was crashing violently through the waves. Scooter and the others furled the topsail with enough authority to satisfy Hanlon, and returned to the deck. But the wind continued to build until suddenly a sail on the foremast ripped open from top to bottom.

"McKinley! Grab some men and lay up to furl that gallant sheet before it blows to tatters," Hanlon ordered.

"Aye, aye," McKinley replied. "Wilson, Jenkens, with me!" he shouted.

McKinley and the men he had summoned climbed the mast and began working on the torn sail, but no sooner had they finished with it and returned to the deck, than the mizzen topsail tore loose and began flapping in the breeze, threatening to pull away and take with it the top part of the mizzenmast, which was now vibrating like a wand.

"Damn!" Hanlon swore. "Simpson get up there."

"Mr. Hanlon, Simpson's a little young for that," Bivens said. He started for the mizzenmast. "I'll go up."

"No, I'll go," Scooter shouted, but Bivens, his best friend, was in the rigging as soon as he shouted and within seconds was nearly to the errant sail. But now the howling wind was of near-hurricane velocity, and the mountainous waves were battering against the hull of the ship with the impact of a cannon ball. The *Sea Serpent* would be lifted by one swell, hang quivering over the trough between the waves, then slam back down into the sea, only to be caught up by another, even larger wave. That would have the effect of knocking the ship to the side, slapping at it as if it were a helpless victim in the claws of a tiger enjoying a macabre sport.

Bivens made the mistake of trying to step from the braces to the weather spreader, but just as he did so, a violent roll of the ship jerked the spreader away and his foot came down on empty air. He had already committed the transfer of body weight from one foot to the other, so he lost his footing. He made a desperate grasp for the gaff, missed it and fell, pitching headfirst toward the deck more than seventy feet below.

Scooter was watching, and he gasped and felt his stomach rise to his throat as he saw Bivens pitch forward. Bivens didn't make a sound ... or if he did, it was drowned out by the fury of the storm. He made a final, futile grab for the mainsail as he fell, but, as with the gaff, he missed, and a split second later he crashed onto the deck with a sickening thump, then lay very still.

Seaman Pounders was less than six feet from where Bivens hit when he fell, and, in fact, was lucky that Bivens didn't fall on him. He leaned down to examine the young sailor for a moment, then stood up and looked back at the captain, his eyes reflecting the shock of what he had seen.

"How...is...he?" came the faint yell from quarter-deck. Captain Greenly was standing at the taffrail, holding his hand cupped around his mouth.

"He...is...dead!" Pounders yelled back.

Now, one year later, Scooter could recall the agony of that moment. As soon as the ship made port, Scooter left the sea.

———

WHEN WILL and Gid came back out to the ranch the next morning, they asked Redling if they could use his parlor to meet with everyone who was riding for the brand, one at a time. "We'd like the opportunity to get to know them better."

"Of course, you can, and that's a good idea. While

you two are doing that, I'll ride into town to tell some folks goodbye. Besides, it's probably good that you meet them on your own, because I think they would open up to you better with me not being around."

"You're the foreman, Abe, do you have any problem with that?" Will asked.

"No, sir, not at all."

"Good, we're going to depend on you to send them in to us, and you can choose whichever ones you want in any order you decide."

"All right," Abe agreed. "I guess I'll start with me. Before the war I was a county board member in Bond County, Illinois. During the war I was a captain, and General Redling's Aide de Camp. After the war, the general bought this ranch, and he hired me on as his foreman. Then, about a year ago, I met, and married my wife who you've already met."

"And you come highly recommended by the General," Will said. "Now, if you would, please arrange for the others to come meet with us."

"All right," Abe said.

———

"WHY ARE they wanting to see us one at a time?" Mitchell asked. "Are they lookin' to see which ones of us they're goin' to keep on?"

"No, I don't think it's anything like that at all," Abe said. "As far as I know, I think they intend to keep all of us. They just want to meet everyone on a person-to-person basis, is all, and I think it's a good idea."

"Yeah," Mitchell agreed. "Now that I think about it, it all right."

When Mitchell went into The Big House, it was obvious that he was uneasy, not only because he was going to be interviewed by his new bosses, but also because he was so rarely a visitor to The Big House.

"Have a seat, Stan," Will offered. Will and Gid were sitting on the sofa, and they had pulled one of the overstuffed chairs over, facing the sofa. Mitchell sat down, still just a little anxious.

"How long have you ridden for the Brown Spur?" Will asked.

"About five years," Mitchell said.

During their interview with Stan Mitchell, they learned that he had worked at another ranch before he came to the Brown Spur, and before that he had been a teamster for a freighting outfit in Dallas.

Walt Chambers, their next interviewee, was from Memphis, and had come west for the adventure, ten years ago. The Brown Spur was the only place he had ever worked.

Mike Lathum had been born and raised in Southeast Missouri, in the town of Winchester. His background was somewhat similar to that of Will and Gid, in that he had been a farmer, then a soldier under General Jeff Thompson in the Confederate Army. He came west after the war, because he said there was nothing left for him at home.

Jim Clay had lived in Texas for his entire life. His father had been with Sam Houston, when Texas won its independence from Mexico. He had been on a couple of cattle drives, and couldn't think of any other kind of work but with cattle. He had been with the Brown Spur Ranch for twelve years.

Doodle Hawkins, whose real name was Cephus, had

been with Custer on his last campaign. Specifically, he had been with Reno during the fight, and so was spared the fate of so many of the men of the 7th Cavalry. He left the army shortly afterward, and had worked at quite a few jobs before winding up as a drover on the Brown Spur.

Moses Dixon was a cook, and he had been in the Confederate army with Abe and General Redling. When the war was over, and Redling bought the ranch, Moses had come to the ranch with them. He had been a cook for the ranch from its very beginning.

The last drover Will and Gid interviewed was Scooter Simpson. Scooter was the youngest of all the ranch hands, and the Brown Spur was his first experience as a ranch hand. Scooter had been raised by a single mom in Newport News, Virginia. She died when he was twelve years old, and he had gone to sea. In his six years at sea, he had been all over the world, crossing both the Atlantic and the Pacific. He had been cowboying for the last four years.

Their interview of Maria Sanchez, the cook and housekeeper of the Big House consisted only in asking if she would be willing to stay on in the job, and she happily agreed to do so.

"And make doughnuts from time to time," Gid added.

"Si, señor," Maria answered with a little laugh.

———

"So, what did you think of the crew?" Redling asked that evening, after the long day of personnel reviews.

"General, I think you've put together as fine a group of men as you'd ever want to meet," Will said.

"I agree, but to be honest, I have to give Abe credit for that. He's the one that checked them out, and he's the one who hired them."

"I'm glad he's staying," Gid said.

"Yes, me, too," Will said.

"So, I take it that there are no further questions," Redling said. "Are you ready to make the purchase?"

"We are," Will said. "And, if it's all right with you, we'll ride into town tomorrow to take care of business."

"Would that be Saginaw?" Redling asked.

"No, our money is deposited in the Ranchers' Bank of Fort Worth, so that's where we'll go, if it's all right with you."

Redling smiled, broadly. "That's great," he said. "We can take care of business, and afterward, I'll be able to catch the evening train heading north."

"Does your daughter know you're coming?"

"Are you kidding? I would never spring anything like that on her, without telling her first. Besides, she's the one who invited me to come live with her. When I get into town tomorrow, I'll send her a telegram first thing."

"That's probably a pretty good idea," Will agreed.

"Then we'll find the best restaurant in Fort Worth, where we'll have a goodbye dinner, my treat."

Gid laughed. "That's an even better idea!"

CHAPTER TEN

THE NEXT MORNING, IT TOOK THEM JUST A LITTLE OVER AN hour to ride in to Fort Worth, where they would conduct their business at The Ranchers' Bank.

"Well, it looks like you two gentlemen took my advice reference the Brown Spur Ranch," Charles Montgomery said as he extended his hand to Ben Redling. "Are we ready to do some business?"

"Yes, but before we do, we've decided that we want a lawyer to make certain the transfer deed is properly drawn," Redling said.

"To be sure," Montgomery replied. "Do you have a lawyer in mind?"

"I've used Daniel Norton in the past. I think I'd like to use him," Redling said.

"Excellent suggestion, Mr. Norton's a good man. I'll send Geoffrey for him."

Dan Norton, a rather short man with thick glasses arrived a few minutes later. He read the agreement Will had drawn up that specified how the transaction would proceed.

He smiled. "Tell me, Mr. Crockett, have you ever read for the bar?"

"No, sir," Will said. "If there's anything that doesn't look right, please change it."

"Oh, no, I'm not criticizing this document—I'm merely saying it seems that you have thought of everything. Are you satisfied, Ben?"

"I am," Redling said. "They've even agreed to take care of Barney until he dies."

"Your horse," Norton said. "He must be close to twenty years old."

"Eighteen." Redling cleared his throat and looked down. "Let's get these papers signed so I can get out of here."

Mr. Montgomery took over. He prepared a certified bank draft payable to Ben for $21,000 for his ranch, plus $200 in cash. Then he presented Will and Gid a promissory note for $88,600, the sum representing thirty-five dollars a head for two thousand, five hundred and sixteen head of cattle. That was $25,000 less than what the cattle would bring on the current market. It was a plan in that would benefit both the buyer and the seller.

Gid let out a long sigh as he picked up the pen. "I never in my life thought that I'd sign a note for this much money."

"Think of it as a business arrangement rather than an actual note," Norton explained. "It won't come due until the cattle are sold and until that day, the cattle will still belong to Mr. Redling. You, of course, are attesting to the fact that you will in good faith, do everything you can to keep the cattle healthy."

"We understand," Will said as he signed the piece of paper and then slid it over to Redling.

"It has been a pleasure doing business with you," Daniel Norton said. "If you have a need for a lawyer, I hope you will keep me in mind."

"We will," Gid said as they all stood to go.

Charles Montgomery opened his drawer and pulled out two cigars. "To the two newest residents of Tarrant County. Welcome."

———

FROM THE BANK, Will and Gid walked General Redling to the railroad depot, where he bought a ticket to Chicago. The Western Union office was right next door, so he stepped in to compose a telegram to be sent to his daughter.

HAVE TODAY SOLD BROWN SPUR RANCH TO TWO GOOD
MEN STOP WILL TAKE TRAIN TO CHICAGO TOMORROW
STOP WILL ARRIVE IN CHICAGO NINE AM THURSDAY

   LOVE, DAD

"That will be seven dollars and fifty cents, sir," the clerk said.

Redling paid the telegraph fee, then turned to Will and Gid. "Gentlemen, what do you say we find a nice place to have a bite to celebrate?"

"How about the Clark House restaurant?" Gid suggested.

Redling smiled. "Edna and I ate there many times over the years. She would approve that the Clark House would be where I eat my last meal in Fort Worth."

When the three men entered the restaurant, Lena, seeing Will and Gid, hurried over to meet them.

"Did you buy the ranch?" Lena asked.

"They know about the ranch?" Redling asked.

Will chuckled. "I can answer both of your questions with one word. Yes."

"Oh," Lena said, "that means you won't be coming in here as much, doesn't it?"

"Oh, I expect we'll be coming to Fort Worth rather frequently," Will said. "It's not that far, and there'll be some things that we just can't get in a town as small as Saginaw."

"Well, you'll always be welcome here," the waitress said. "What will you have?"

After they had each ordered fried pork chops and baked beans that Lena had said were good, they sat back to wait for their food.

"How do you feel about all this, General?" Will asked.

"I'm not sure how I feel. On the one hand, I'll be glad to be with my daughter again, on the other hand, I'm sad about selling the ranch and leaving Edna's grave." Redling smiled. "But, what's done is done, and I have enough money that I won't be a burden to Sue Ann and her family."

"We will do our best to keep the Brown Spur in as good a condition as we are getting it," Gid said.

"I'm sure you will," Redling said.

———

SOME FIFTY MILES west of Brown Spur Ranch, seven men were encamped behind a ridge which was high enough to keep them out of sight of anyone who might be traveling on the Millsaps Road.

"Ha, lookie here, I pissed that grasshopper right offen that blade o' grass there," Draco said.

"I bet that really pissed him off," Mathis replied, to the laughter of the others.

Boswell was sitting on a log watching the antics of the men who comprised his gang, though he preferred to use the word organization, rather than gang.

Damon Boswell was an unlikely subject to be leading a gang of cutthroats and desperados. Boswell held a master of *juris prudence* degree from Washington University in St. Louis. He had passed the bar in Missouri and, at one time had been a practicing lawyer. But that was all in his past. Now Boswell had put his intelligence and his considerable skills into a criminal career.

Boswell had learned that the next morning a coach, carrying a money transfer to the bank in Fort Worth, would be passing through the small town of Millsap. Millsap was so small that it had no law. Boswell planned to rob the coach when it stopped in the town.

They were waiting just outside Millsap, and while the others were horsing around with each other, Boswell was holding himself aloof from the activity. He had everything planned out to a "T", and it all began on perfect timing.

Boswell took out his watch and examined it for at least the tenth time in the last hour. This was exactly the right time.

"All right, gentlemen, let's put this operation into motion, shall we?"

Approximately fifteen minutes later, the seven men that made up the Boswell gang rode into town. Seeing so many coming into town at the same time was a little unusual for Millsap, because it had a population of less than a hundred people. However, since people who lived in remote areas often came into town, the arrival of the seven men aroused no undo suspicion. All seven riders stopped in front of the depot of the Sunset Stage Line.

While the others waited outside, Boswell and Draco went into the small depot building.

"You fellers needin' tickets?" the station manager asked.

"No thank you. We're meeting someone on the coach," Boswell answered. "Is it on time?"

"As far as I know it is. We ain't got no word otherwise."

"We'll wait outside," Boswell said.

Draco snickered, once they stepped outside. "Yeah, we're meetin' someone. We're meetin' the man with the money." He laughed. "Meetin' the man with the money. That sounds funny."

"It's called alliteration," Boswell said.

"A little what?" Draco asked, confused by Boswell's comment.

"Never mind."

Boswell and his men waited for the coach to arrive, not directly in front of the stagecoach depot, but across the street.

"Here it comes," Mathis said.

They watched as the coach came into town. Usually, stagecoach drivers liked to make a big entrance into town, and the driver of this stage was no exception, as he had the horses at a gallop.

"Whoa!" he shouted. "Whoa there, horses, whoa!"

As he was shouting, he hauled back on the reins, and pulled on the brake handle, bringing the coach to a sliding stop right in front of the coach depot.

When the coach stopped, Boswell and his men, now mounted, approached it.

"Draco, get up there," Boswell ordered.

Using the spokes of the front wheel as steps, Draco stepped out of the saddle and climbed up to the driver's seat. The driver and the shotgun guard were both looking toward the depot, and didn't notice him until he startled them by speaking.

"Hello, boys," Draco said.

Startled, the driver turned toward him. "Here now, what the hell are you doing up here? Mister, you ain't authorized to be up here," the driver said, angrily and authoritatively.

Draco smiled, and pulled his pistol. "You might say I've got me a ticket to be here."

"What do you mean you got a ticket? What do you want?" the driver asked.

"We want the money pouch," Boswell said.

When the driver looked out in front of the coach, he saw several mounted men forming a half-circle around the coach. And like the man who had climbed up on the front wheel, all were holding pistols pointed at the driver and shotgun guard.

A couple of passengers started to leave the train, but Weasel pointed his gun at them.

"How 'bout you folks just stay in the coach 'till our business is done?" he asked.

The passengers, consisting of two men and a woman were at first confused, then frightened.

"Get on back in there a' fore I start in to shootin'," Weasel added, waving his pistol.

Hastily, the frightened passengers scrambled back into the coach.

"I believe we asked for the money pouch," Boswell said. "Throw it down, please, so we can conclude our business."

The driver reached down into the well for the pouch.

"Don't give it to 'em, Billy," the shotgun guard said.

Draco shot him, and the guard, with a surprised expression on his face, slapped his hand over his chest, and with blood spilling between his fingers, tumbled off the coach.

"This is the last time I'm going to ask you to throw down the money pouch," Boswell said, and with shaking hands, the driver removed the canvas bag and held it out toward Boswell.

"I reckon this is what you're a' wantin'."

"Yes, thank you. You have been quite cooperative," Boswell said.

Within seconds, Boswell and his men were galloping away carrying a canvas money pouch. Behind them lay the dead shotgun guard, and a small group of people who were cautiously moving toward the body.

CHAPTER ELEVEN

"What do you think? Should we change the name of the ranch?" Will asked as he and Gid rode back from Fort Worth.

"No, that's bad luck," Gid said.

"That's for ships. It's bad luck to change the name of a ship, not a ranch."

"Yell, well, I think we ought to leave it the same name anyway. What's wrong with Brown Spur?" Gid asked. "Besides, if we changed the name of the ranch, we'd most likely have to change the brand too, seeing as it's a spur."

"You're right," Will said. "Brown Spur is good enough."

Will and Gid left the main road and turned onto the quarter-mile long drive leading up to the house they had just bought. When they did so, they saw a horse coming toward them at a gallop.

"I wonder what that's about?" Will asked.

"Who is it?" Gid asked.

Gid's question, if not Will's was answered a moment

later, when they saw that the rider of the galloping horse was none other than Julia Barker, her long black hair flying in the wind behind her. She reined up as she approached them.

"So," she said with a broad smile. "Am I talking to my new bosses?"

"We bought the ranch," Will said. "I don't know as that makes us *your* boss."

"That makes you Abe's boss, doesn't it?'"

"Well, yes, ma'am, I suppose it does."

"Then that makes you the boss of everyone on this ranch, and in case you haven't noticed me before, I am on this ranch." Julia laughed, a musical, wind-chime kind of laugh.

"Well, if you put it that way, I suppose that does make us your boss."

"I've never had such a handsome boss before, and now I have two of them," Julia said, flirtatiously.

"Where's Abe?" Will asked.

"He's working on something in the machine shed. I swear, he spends more time in that machine shed than he does anywhere else."

"Were you going somewhere, Mrs. Barker?" Gid asked.

"Please, it's Julia, and no, I wasn't going anywhere. I saw you, back when you were on the main road, so I thought I would just come to meet you."

"Well, then you can ride back with us."

"That was my plan," Julia said, again smiling.

The three rode up the long drive with Julia talking for the entire length of the drive.

"I suppose you'll be wanting to see Abe," she said when they reached the compound.

"Yes."

"He's in there." Julia pointed to a small, unpainted and windowless building.

"I'll get him," Gid offered.

Because the building was windowless, it had a rather dim interior, illuminated only by what sun splashed through the open door. Abe had a piece of metal secured in the bench vise, and he was filing on it.

"Abe?"

Abe looked up. "Did the sale go through?"

"It did."

"Excellent. I'm glad for the General, I know he wanted to go be with his daughter, but I'm gonna miss him."

"Abe, I wonder if you could gather all the men so we could talk to them?" Gid asked.

"One at a time?"

"No, we already did that, and there's no need for any more interviews. We just want to talk to everybody."

"Sure, I'd be glad to. At least I can get those that are close to the home place."

When Gid returned to Will and Julia, Will was looking quite uncomfortable. It didn't take much for Gid to determine what the problem was. Julia was engaged in some outlandish flirting with him.

"Uh, I told Abe to gather all the men so we could speak with them," Gid said, his words interrupting the scene.

"Good idea," Will said. "Now, we'll be meeting them as owners."

———

It took no more than half an hour to get everyone rounded up, and when they were all gathered under the windmill, Will began talking to them.

"Gentlemen," he began.

"Haw, that's 'bout the first time any of us has ever been called a gentleman," Doodle Hawkins said.

"And you'll never be called that again, if you don't stop interrupting people," Abe chastened.

"Sorry," Doodle said.

Will had stopped when he was interrupted, but he resumed his address to the gathered cowboys.

"Gentlemen, I just wanted you to hear it from the horse's mouth so to speak. It is official now, my brother and I are now the proud owners of the Brown Spur Ranch."

Will's announcement was met with applause from the men.

"You plannin' on makin' any changes?" Walt Chambers asked.

"No, the ranch seems to be running quite well now, and I've always believed that if it isn't broke, don't fix it." Will said.

"Sounds good enough to me," Moses said.

"What about you two?" Chambers asked. "You learned all there was to learn about us. Tell us some about you. Is it true that you two rode for Quantrill during the war?"

"We were irregulars, yes, but the war is over now, and I really don't care to discuss it. My brother and I are more interested in what lies ahead of us. But you do deserve to know a little about us. And, although this will be our first experience as ranch owners, we do have a varied background, and I feel certain that some of our experiences will help us."

"You shot them men that was tryin' to rob the bank in Fort Worth, didn't you?" Chambers asked.

"Uh, yes," Will replied.

"'N you've done that lots of times, ain't you? I been readin' about you two in some o' them books I read."

"He's talking about dime novels," Mitchell said.

Will sighed. "Yes, I'm familiar with those. All I can say is, don't believe everything you read."

"But you make a lot of money offen them books, don't ya?" Chambers asked.

"Not one damn dime," Gid said.

"You don't? Damn, that don't seem right, none at all," Chambers said. "You should be gettin' money for bein' in them books."

"Enough about the books. Neither my brother nor I have anything to do with them, and as I said, don't believe everything you read. Remember, those books are novels, and that implies made-up stuff. Now, gentlemen, if you will, I'd like all of you to go back to whatever it was you were doing."

With a loud "hoorah" the meeting broke up then, and the cowboys all returned to the tasks they had been engaged in, before they were called away.

"What about me?" Julia asked, after everyone was gone. "Are you interested in what I was doing before I married Abe?"

"If you want to tell it," Will replied.

"I was a show girl, I performed in theaters from San Francisco to Fort Worth." She smiled at Abe. "By the time I reached Fort Worth I was tired of it, so I married Abe, and here I am." She finished her presentation by bending her right knee, sticking her left leg out behind her, spreading her arms, and thrusting her chest and head forward.

"Ta, da!" she said, musically. "Now, you must let me show you the house." Julia reached out to lay her hand on Will's arm.

"I don't think that will be necessary," Will said.

"Oh, but please, I insist. It's a beautiful house, and I want you to see all its charms."

"All right," Will agreed, reluctantly.

With a happy smile, Julia led the two brothers across the lawn to what the cowboys called "the Big House." Will and Gid had been here before, but they had seen nothing but the dining room and parlor, so Julia took them through those two rooms with nothing but a cursory notice.

"You should see the kitchen," she said. "Of course, you'll never have to spend any time here, but I want you to understand what a wonderful kitchen it is."

When Julia pushed through the door she was met by Maria Sanchez.

"You already met Maria of course. I imagine you will be keeping her on."

"Yes, of course we will," Gid said. "Anybody who can cook as well as this lady is certainly welcome to cook for us as long as she likes."

"*Gracias, Señors*," Maria replied. "After the señora shows you around, I have coffee and pie if you would like."

"Pie? Maria, you are a woman after my own heart," Gid said with a broad smile.

"Come, I'll show you the rest of the house," Julia said. "You've already seen the parlor, dining room, and kitchen. Maria has a bedroom downstairs, just off the kitchen, and there are four more bedrooms upstairs."

"You go look at it, big brother. I'm going to get a head start on this pie," Gid said.

"All right, but if I'm going up by myself, I get my choice of the bedrooms," Will said with a teasing smile.

"As long as the rooms that are left have beds, you can choose any one you want. Oh, Maria, that looks good," Gid added with a smile as he saw Maria remove the pie from the pie saver.

Julia led Will upstairs, then into one of the bedrooms. "This was General Redling's bedroom and since you have your choice, I'm sure this is the one you'll choose. It has its own private bathing room, as you can see. And it, like the bedroom, is very private. As a matter of fact, it is private enough for you to entertain company without anyone . . . *knowing*." She smiled seductively.

"I uh, do appreciate the bathing room to be sure, but I have no plans, to entertain anyone privately."

"That's too bad," Julia said in a low, sultry voice. "If you entertained the right person, it could be quite . . ." she paused in mid-sentence, then added the word, "pleasurable."

"Do any of the other bedrooms up here have a private bathing room?" Will asked in a planned and specific business point of view.

"Uh, yes," Julia said, realizing that the spell she had tried to establish was broken. "There is one more bedroom with its own bathing room, it's just not as large as this one. I'll show you the other rooms."

When Will had seen the other bedrooms, he came

back down to the kitchen where Gid was half-way through his second piece of pie.

"Couldn't wait, huh?"

"Let me finish this piece, then I'll get another and we can eat together."

"*Oh mi,* Señor Gid, *tienes tanto apetito!*" Maria said. Then, realizing she had spoken in Spanish, she translated. "Oh my, you have such an appetite."

"You don't know the half of it, Maria. You'd better be prepared to cook for at least three men, since my little brother can eat for two."

"Did you check out the bedrooms?" Gid asked.

"Yes."

"Let me guess, you're putting me in a closet."

"Well, if I do, it's your own fault. You could have come up with me to have a look around," Will teased.

"Your bedroom is quite nice, Gid," Julia said. "I think you will be most comfortable there."

"I'm sure it will beat a lot of places I've stayed."

"I had better get back and prepare dinner for Abe," Julia said, excusing herself.

"Thank you," Will said.

"My pleasure," Julia replied, giving Will a very sultry look as she left.

"I'll tell you one thing," Gid said. "That Julia is about the prettiest woman I believe I've ever seen."

"She's trouble," Will said.

"Hmmph," Maria said as she turned to her dish pan.

"What do you mean?" Gid asked.

"I mean watch yourself around her. She could be trouble."

"She said something when she was showing you the bedrooms, didn't she?" Gid asked.

"Just be careful when you are around her. Remember, she is Abe's wife," Will replied, without being more specific.

"That's not a problem for me," Gid said. "You're the one all the women go for. I'm always just a bystander."

"In this case, consider yourself lucky."

"Yeah, well, I've already finished this piece of pie, so that means I can start over and we can have a piece together." He lifted the third piece of pie and put it on his plate.

Will chuckled. "I like your logic."

When Julia returned to the small house that she and Abe occupied, she thought of Will and Gid, and fantasized as to how it would have been if she had met them in her former profession. She had told them that she was a showgirl, and that was true, but that was only a part of her background.

Julia's real name was Wanda Beck. She was born to a prostitute in St. Louis, and had been brought up in a brothel, learning, not only from her mother, but from all the others who worked there. She was always pretty, and had developed into full womanhood at an early age. She was fifteen years old when she had lost her virginity after the owner of the brothel had auctioned her off to the highest bidder. After that, she worked as a very high-dollar prostitute and, unlike some of the girls who did it only for the money, Julia had enjoyed her work.

Wanda married one of her customers who came from a very wealthy family. Unable to function in a monogamous relationship, she found other lovers. When her husband learned of her indiscretions, he sued for divorce. She paid her lawyer with sexual favors, and he arranged for her to leave the divorce with a one-time alimony payment of ten thousand dollars.

After her divorce, she worked on a riverboat, eventually settling in New Orleans. For the next few years, she moved around, alternating between being a show girl, and a prostitute. It was during this time that she changed her name to Julia Coleman.

She had come to Fort Worth with a traveling show, and it was there that she met Art Barker. By then she had grown weary of travel and prostitution, so she set about winning him over and, less than a month after they had met, Julia and Art were married. She sometimes wondered if the marriage was actually valid, since the name she had used was Julia Coleman, instead of Wanda Beck. It gave her some comfort to think that the marriage wasn't valid, that she was just using the marriage as a matter of convenience. Sometimes when she thought of it, she chuckled. If she ever wanted to leave Art, she wouldn't even have to divorce him. Wanda Beck had never married him.

CHAPTER TWELVE

At a small, deserted cabin on the Trinity River some distance from the Brown Spur Ranch, Boswell's men were discussing the job they had just pulled.

"Seven hunnert 'n eighty dollars? That's all there was? I thought this was supposed to be a money shipment from one bank to another," Draco said.

"It was a bank transfer," Cooley said. "It just wasn't as big as we'd been led to believe."

"Well, hell, this warn't hardly no money a' tall," Draco said.

"We're all disappointed in the paucity of the funds," Boswell said. "I'll tell you what I'll do. I won't employ the usual division scheme which is, by our agreement, designed to give me a somewhat larger share than the rest of you. We'll divide it evenly."

"Well, it's good of you to be a' doin' that, but it still ain't much money," Jenkins said.

"Jenkins, you every rode for a ranch?" Weasel asked.

"You know I have."

"How much was you paid?"

"Twenty dollars a month," Jenkins replied.

"Uh huh, we've near 'bout all of us done some ranch ridin' so we know what it's like to bust your ass from sunup to sundown, 'n all for twenty dollars a month, and found. We'll be gettin' over a hunnert dollars apiece from this here job. It'd take you near five months to earn that much money, ridin' for a brand."

"Yeah," Jenkins said. "Yeah, I guess when you look at it like that, you're right. A hunnert dollars ain't all that bad."

"Gentlemen, take your money and go into town so that you might use the money for whatever might bring you enjoyment. In the meantime, I shall endeavor to find us a more lucrative adventure."

"Damn if you ain't 'bout the purtiest talkin' man I've ever heard," Weasel said.

Boswell smiled. "I do try."

————

AFTER THE OTHERS LEFT, Damon Boswell remained behind, alone in the cabin he had appropriated to be used as a hideout. Every other member of his gang had gone into the small town of Peaster, there to spend their money in debauchery.

Boswell had taken a chair outside and was leaning back against the wall of the cabin as he drank a cup of coffee, and looked out toward a nearby thicket of trees.

What was he doing here? He had been a prosecuting attorney back in St. Louis, and a very good one. One case in particular, had been his prosecution of Jabo Bono.

Jabo Bono was a cross country serial killer believed

to have killed no fewer than six people. He had been tried for the murder of Max Owen, and sentenced to death by hanging. But before the sentence could be carried out, a slick lawyer managed to have the conviction set aside so that it became necessary for him to be tried again. This time, Boswell was selected to prosecute the case.

Bono was to be tried not for the murder of Max Owen, but for Theodore Miller another one of his victims. Unlike the first trial, which had been for a murder recently committed, the trial for Miller was truly a "cold case." There was difficulty in establishing the integrity of old evidence, and in finding witnesses who were still alive and could give cogent testimony. Everything seemed to conspire to make this an impossible case to try, but Boswell tried it in less than two weeks and following his brilliant summation, the jury found Miller guilty.

The Missouri Governor, Charles Hardin, had sent Boswell a note of personal congratulations on his prosecutorial brilliance. One week after the trail, Boswell was a witness to Bono's execution by hanging. He still carried with him the article the *St. Louis Globe* had published about the case.

Justice Has Been Served

Jabo Bono is a serial killer who is believed to have murdered no less than six people, two of them in the state of Missouri. He was recently tried for the murder of Max Owen, the store keep of a store Bono had robbed. Bono was able to hire a slick lawyer who, even when the case had been adjudicated and a guilty verdict found, managed to

THE LOST HERD   109

get the finding set aside by the Missouri State Supreme Court.

Damon Boswell, acting as prosecuting attorney for the city of St. Louis, then tried Bono, not for the murder of Owen, which was believed to be the stronger case, but for the murder of Theodore Miller, a much earlier victim. By doing so, he was able to avoid any possibility of violating the double indemnity clause.

Although the evidence was cold, and witnesses were few, Boswell's case was so brilliantly presented that Bono was found guilty of murder a second time, and this time, the prosecution was so well handled, that not even the Supreme Court could overturn the decision of the twelve jurors. Bono paid for his crime by being hanged.

It is believed by this newspaper, that Damon Boswell should present himself for the position of Attorney General for the State of Missouri. Should he do so, this newspaper will offer its full support.

As Boswell thought of that case now, he chuckled. It was too bad Bono was hanged. He could use a man like Bono in his current endeavors.

Boswell's time as a lawyer had been profitable, and held promise of bigger things, such as the St. Louis Globe's suggestion that he would become the Attorney General for the state of Missouri.

But then came an opportunity that he thought was too good to pass. Mrs. Claypool, a very wealthy client, entrusted him to set up a trust fund for her of over half a million dollars. Boswell set it up, but shaved off a hundred thousand for himself.

What Boswell didn't realize, was that Claypool's grandson was also a lawyer, and he caught the attempted theft before it could take place. He brought charges against Boswell which resulted in him being disbarred, and indicted for fraud.

Boswell, who had been released on bail, jumped bail and fled the state of Missouri. No longer able to earn an income as a lawyer, Boswell dedicated his considerable intellect to criminal activities, which brought him to this time and place, as leader of a gang of cutthroats and murderers.

———

Brown Spur Ranch

OVER THE FIRST few weeks after having bought the ranch, Will and Gid worked at getting better acquainted with all the ranch hands, and they actively participated in the various tasks needed to run a ranch. They quickly became liked and admired by the cowboys because, as Jim Clay said of them, "them boys ain't a' feard o' gettin' their hands dirty."

Will and Gid accompanied Doodle Hawkins and Jim Clay on an 'outriding' which was an inspection trip of the range to discover the location and physical state of the scattered groups of stock. They also checked the creek to make certain the water was flowing freely.

"Oh, oh," Doodle said, pointing. "There's a patch of loco weed over there, we need to keep the cows away."

"How do you handle something like that?" Will asked.

"We normally burn it out," Doodle said.

"Yes, but it takes near-bout all of us to keep the fire from gettin' out of hand," Clay added.

"All right, let's burn it," Will said.

Half an hour later, the fire was set, and nearly all the hands, including Art Barker were gathered around the patch of loco weed. All of them were carrying canvas sacks that had been soaked in the creek so that they could extinguish any errant flames. They managed to keep the fire under control and when it finally burned out, all the loco weed was gone.

"Good job, men, good job," Will said congratulation them when the task was completed.

This being the last chore of the day, the men were all in a good mood as they rode back for supper.

———

"You stink," Julia said to Abe when he came into their cottage. "You smell like smoke."

Abe laughed. "We all do, we had to burn off some loco-weed."

"Go eat with the men, so you don't stink up the whole house."

"All right," Abe replied without argument.

After Abe left, Julia made certain that all the windows and doors were open to get rid of the smell of smoke. The house had no window screens, so that meant flies would come in, but she decided that she would rather deal with flies, than with the smell of smoke.

Ranch life was a lonely existence for her, and her only diversion was in her flirtations. Since marrying Abe, she had never followed through with any of her teasing, nor did she intend to. They were diversions only. But, with the arrival of the Crockett brothers, her flirtations took on a more enjoyable turn. She thought both of them were very good looking and fanaticized about how she would react if either of them actually did respond to her.

———

Outlaw Cabin on the Trinity

"GENTLEMEN, I hope you haven't spent every penny you have, because I need to make a deposit in the bank in Graham," Boswell said.

"Hah!" Weasel said. "I thought we was supposed to take money out of bank, not be a' puttin' it in."

"An astute observation, Weasel," Boswell said, "but we can consider this to be seed money. Your participation money will be returned to you, then we will divide any additional funds the bank may have."

Boswell was able to collect three hundred dollars from the others, and adding seven hundred of his own dollars, would create a deposit that was large enough to give the appearance that Boswell was a solid businessman.

And that was exactly what Boswell, who had identified himself as Morris Anderson when he made the deposit, wanted.

"Mr. Steadman, I wonder sir, if I might buy lunch for you, so we could discuss some business propositions," Boswell said to the manager of the Commercial Savings Bank of Graham.

"Why, I would be delighted to, Mr. Anderson. I think you will find that Graham is a very good place to start a new business."

Boswell took Steadman to the Rustic Rock, which was the most expensive restaurant in Graham. He did so, because it helped add to the image he was presenting.

"Tell me, Mr. Anderson, just what business are you in?" Steadman asked, once their meal had been delivered.

"I'm in the real estate business."

"Oh," Steadman said. "Well, to be truthful with you, sir, I'm not sure how much business you'll be able to conduct in and around Graham."

"Oh, you don't understand, Mr. Steadman. I intend to use the entire state of Texas for my real estate transactions. I plan to use Graham as my headquarters, and if your bank is capable of handling the business, then I will be using your bank as my repository."

"Oh, in that case, I think you'll find our bank is perfectly capable of handling any account you wish to establish," Steadman said.

"I'm quite sure there will be a substantial amount of funds coming through your bank. If you don't mind my asking, how much do you have on deposit?"

Steadman smiled. "We have over fifty thousand dollars in reserves."

"Good, good, I'll see you again when we're ready for our first business transaction."

———

ONE WEEK LATER, Sloan and Jenkins rode into Graham together, but stopped at the north end of town. A few minutes after they arrived, Cooley and Weasel came into town, riding all the way through town until they reached the south end of Elm Street. It was half-an-hour later before Boswell, Draco and Mathis appeared. That was the cue for Sloan, Jenkins, Cooley and Weasel to start toward the middle of town so that they reached the bank at the same time as Boswell, Draco, and Mathis. When Boswell and the two men with him dismounted, Sloan, Jenkins, Cooley, and Weasel held the reins to the horses.

With a nod to the other two, Boswell went into the bank.

"Mr. Anderson, it's nice to see you again," Steadman said with a broad smile. "And the gentlemen with you?"

"They are business associates," Boswell said. Boswell pulled his pistol, as did the other two.

"Here, what is this?" Steadman asked, shocked to see the sudden, and unexpected appearance of guns in their hands.

"Isn't it obvious? We are robbing this bank."

"Bank robbery? But you are a businessman!"

Boswell chuckled. "Yes, I am. It just so happens that the business I'm in is robbing banks. Boys, present your containers."

Draco and Mathis produced cloth bags. There were two tellers, and each of them got a bag, along with orders to empty their counter drawers.

"This one is for you, Mr. Steadman," Boswell said. "If you would, sir, please empty the safe."

"Here, you can't do this? The people of this town have their life's savings deposited in this bank."

"And now they are going to be deposited in these bags," Boswell said with a little chuckle.

"Things were going quite smoothly until one of the tellers grabbed a gun and raised it to shoot, but Draco killed him before he even got a shot off. After that, Mathis shot the other bank teller.

"Oh, my God, what have you done?" Steadman shouted as he moved toward the teller who was closest to him.

Boswell shot Steadman.

"What'd you do that for?" Draco asked. "He's the only who could open the safe."

"I'm afraid we have no time for that. The rest of the town certainly heard the shooting, that's for sure. Let's get out of here, now!" Boswell called, and the three men, each clutching a bag of money, ran from the bank. Leaping onto their horses, they galloped out of town, keeping the curious at bay with wild shooting as they left.

———

"Twenty-seven hundred dollars," Jenkins said with disgust after they counted their haul. "Twenty-seven hundred dollars total. Hell, that's only seventeen hundred dollars more than we deposited there in the first place."

"Well, at least we have seventeen hundred dollars more and we can live off that until the boss comes up with our next job," Draco suggested.

CATTLEMEN'S SAVINGS BANK OF GRAHAM ROBBED

In a daring daylight robbery, seven men held up the Cattlemen's Savings Bank of Graham. Three innocent men were killed in the robbery, they being Martin Steadman, who was the bank manager, as well as Timothy O'Riley, and Morrison Cooper, the two tellers. It is uncertain how much money was taken.

There were seven men involved in the holdup, and they fired random shots as they galloped out of town. Fortunately, none of the town's citizens were hit during the robbers' daring escape. Although there is no verification of the charge, at least two of the citizens of Graham have stated that they identified one of the escaping outlaws as Damon Boswell.

Saginaw, Texas

WILL and Gid had come into Saginaw to buy some supplies, and they were standing at the counter of Bailey's Clothing when Marshal Coats came in.

"Hello, Percy," Will greeted.

"I thought I saw you two ride in," Percy replied. "How are things going for you out at the ranch?"

"We're beginning to get into the swing of things, I think," Will said.

"I didn't know it would be so much work, though," Gid added.

"Ha! Gid thought we would just be gentlemen ranchers with hands to do all the work," Will said.

"Well, now, Gid's right. We have some ranch owners who never set foot on their holdings," Percy said.

"Then that's the kind of ranch owner I want to be," Gid said with a chuckle. He rubbed the calluses on the palm of one hand.

"Did you happen to see the article about the bank robbery in Graham?" Marshal Coats asked.

"No, we didn't," Will answered. "We've sort of been hunkered down out at the ranch, so we've been out of touch with what's going on in the world."

"They're saying they think it was Damon Boswell and his gang who did it. I tell you what, I wish you two boys weren't so tied up with your ranch. We could sure use a couple of good men to take care of Boswell and his outlaws."

"That would be the job of Sheriff Maddox, wouldn't it?" Gid asked. "You're the city Marshal of Saginaw aren't you."

"I am, but I'm also a deputy sheriff, which gives me authority all over the county. I'm sure Sheriff Maddox would deputize the two of you if you'd consider going after that bunch."

"I wish we could help you," Will said, "but it's like we said, we're pretty much tied up with the ranch."

"I understand. Don't pay me any mind, I'm just an old man havin' to deal with a problem."

"I hope you get him," Will said.

After leaving Bailey's Clothing store, Will and Gid stopped by Casey's Saloon, because as Gid explained, "To come to town and not get cool beer would be a foolish waste of opportunity."

"Little Brother, you are quite right," Will said.

"Damn, you agree with me? I thought I was going to have to get down on my knees and beg you."

Will laughed. "Now, that would be quite a sight, wouldn't it? A six-foot-four inch, two-hundred-forty-pound man, down on his knees, begging for a beer. I should have held out."

"How were you going to hold out, when you want one as much as I do?"

"I guess you've got me there, I would like a beer before we go back out to the ranch."

"And Julia's little games," Gid added.

"You've noticed."

"Ha! Who the hell couldn't notice? She acts like a saloon girl every time she comes near us," Gid said. "I know Abe sees it, but he never says anything."

They had carried on their conversation while walking from the livery to the saloon. They were greeted as they pushed through the swinging bat-wing doors.

"Well, if it ain't the Crocketts," Casey called out to them. "It's good to see you boys again, I was afraid the ranch would be keeping you holed up out there."

"Believe me, John, it is keeping us busy," Will said.

"Hello, boys," Suzie said, coming over to greet them with a welcoming smile.

"If it's not the prettiest girl in the whole county," Gid said.

"Well, considering that you are out at the ranch with Julia Barker, I consider that quite a compliment."

"She's pretty all right," Gid said. "But she's..." he didn't complete the sentence.

"You don't have to say any more," Suzie said. "I know exactly what you're talking about."

Will and Gid finished their beer, then, exchanging goodbyes with everyone, started back out to the ranch.

CHAPTER THIRTEEN

SIX MEN WERE MOUNTED, WHILE A SEVENTH WAS HOLDING the reins of his horse as he relieved himself against the piling of the trestle. It was dark, but the moon was full and bright, and the twin ribbons of iron gleamed softly as they stretched east and west.

"Damn, Weasel, how long you plannin' on peein'?" Mathis asked. "You been standin' there ever since we got here, 'n that was damn near an hour ago."

The others laughed.

"Well, when you gotta go, you gotta go," Weasel answered. Finished, he buttoned his pants and remounted his horse.

"Hey, Cooley, you ever see any o' them, what they call hydraulic mining operations?" Draco asked. "You know, the way they use steam power to build up the water pressure, then squirt these big pipes of water against the mountain to wash away the dirt 'n such."

"Yeah, I've seen 'em," Cooley answered. "What about 'em?"

"You think we could get any money by rentin' out

Weasel to one o' them mines so's he could piss away some o' the mountain?"

Again there was laughter.

"Well, boys, I'm glad my pecker's providin' you with all this entertainment," Weasel said. "But damn if you don't make me worry a mite about what kind of fellers I've done hooked myself up with."

From the distance came the high, keening sound of a train whistle.

"Train's a' comin'," Sloan said.

"Yeah? How'd you figure that out?" Jenkins asked.

"Gentlemen, please, we would all be better served if there was some comity between us," Boswell said.

"Well, hell, ain't that what we're a' doin? Jokin' is comedy ain't it?" Draco asked.

"Never mind," Boswell said, having no wish to explain the difference between the two words.

They heard the whistle again, and this time, as they looked off in the distance, they could see the faint glow of the gas headlamp. And now, they could hear the puffing sound of escaping steam from the engine.

"Get the fire going," Boswell ordered, and Weasel dropped a match onto the kerosene-soaked pile of wood they had stacked up on the tracks.

"You're sure that'll stop 'em?" Sloan asked.

"There's a bridge here," Boswell said. "If you were the engineer and you saw the bridge burning, wouldn't you stop?"

"Yeah, only the bridge ain't really goin' to be a' burnin'," Sloan said.

"Use your noggin, Sloan," Draco said. "All the engineer is goin' to see is the fire. He ain't goin' to know that it ain't the bridge that's a' burnin'."

———

THOUSANDS OF TINY, glowing, red sparks lifted from the stack and drifted up to join the stars. Smoke, blacker than the night, streamed back along the top of the train.

A great, gleaming and mirrored gas lantern threw a beam of light ahead of the train, while a flickering orange glow bathed the interior of the engine cab.

Austin Prouty was the fireman, and having just thrown in several loads of coal, he closed the door to the firebox and sat down to catch some of the breeze generated by the forward progress of the train.

"What's the pressure like, Clyde?" he asked.

The engineer checked the gauge. "One hundred sixty PSI," he said. "You've got a good head of steam up." Clyde Barnes held a tin cup under the water keg and drew a cup of water, then handed it to his sweating and panting fireman. "Here, have a beer. You earned it," he said.

"Thanks," Austin said, taking the proffered cup. He drank the tepid water, then smiled. "Best beer I ever had."

———

BEHIND THE ENGINE and tender came the dark baggage car, then the express car. There were only two windows in the express car, but they were shining brightly because inside the moving post-office, one of the two messengers was busy sorting mail and putting it into the pouch for drop off at the next town. In a safe in the corner of the mail car, there was an oversized white bag. Dawkins had signed for the white bag when it came aboard, so he knew it contained exactly $3,817.00. That was a lot of money, and he had commented to Morris, that he was responsible for it. Being responsible for so much money made him nervous, and he would be glad when he could be rid of the responsibility.

There were four passenger cars behind the express car. Although this was a night train, there were no parlor cars on this run, because essentially, it was a local, stopping at just about every town along the route. Emil Barret, the conductor, was in the last seat of the last car. There was light in this car, as there was in the other passenger cars, but it was soft and unobtrusive. The illumination came from low-burning kerosene lanterns which were mounted on gimbals on the walls of the car. Some of the passengers were awake and talking quietly among themselves, but most seemed to be trying to grab some sleep, though as the seats did not recline as they did in some of the plusher parlor cars, sleep was rather difficult to come by.

Barret took out his pocket watch and examined it in the light of the lantern that was just over his seat. It was just after midnight, and they were due to arrive in Fort Worth at one.

———

BACK IN THE ENGINE, Clyde saw something on the track that caused a start. "What the hell?" the engineer shouted.

"What is it, Clyde?" Austin asked.

"The damn bridge is on fire!"

Clyde pulled the brake lever and the great driver wheels, as well as all the wheels on every car behind the engine, activated by the Westinghouse air brake system, locked down and began sliding along the steel tracks.

"Here it comes," Mathis said.

The men watched the big locomotive as it approached, gushing smoke and spewing steam from the drive cylinders. The big wheels, driven by the thrusting piston rods, rumbled by, spilling burning cinders from the firebox, and leaving a long, glowing path between the tracks. Then they heard the squeal of locking brakes.

"He has observed the fire, boys, and he is stopping," Boswell said.

Finally, the train came to a jerking, hissing stop. Though still, it wasn't quiet, as water burbled in the boiler, and the overheated journals and bearings popped and snapped.

"Weasel, climb up into the cab," Boswell ordered.

"What's going on?" the engineer asked. "Is the bridge on fire?"

Weasel smiled. "Nah, we just thought it'd be nice iffen you stopped the train."

"What do you want?" the engineer asked.

"I don't want nothin', except for you to stay here 'til we're finished."

"Finished doin' what?"

"Why, robbin' the train, if course," Weasel said, his smile growing larger.

After Weasel made certain the train wouldn't be pulling away, Boswell and the others climbed into the first car behind the express car. The passengers looked up, first in surprise, then in alarm as they saw six armed men coming into the car.

"What? Who are you men? What do you want?" a white-haired, dignified looking man asked.

"What we expect is for you gentlemen to remain seated, and give us no trouble," Boswell said. "You two come with me," he said, speaking to Mathis and Draco but not saying their names. "The rest of you spread out among the cars and keep the passengers quiet."

The two men stepped across the vestibule into the express car.

"You men get out of here," one of the messengers ordered.

"We will leave as soon as you accommodate us," Boswell said. He pulled his pistol and waved it at the two men. "Open the safe."

"Don't open it for 'em, Dawkins," one of the two said.

"Open the safe, if you would, Mr. Dawkins," Boswell repeated.

"Don't do it," the same man said again.

Boswell nodded, and Mathis brought his gun down on the head of the man who had protested. He fell to the floor.

"Morris!" Dawkins shouted in alarm.

"This is the last time I'm going to ask you to open the safe," Boswell said, and Dawkins, with trembling hands, opened the safe, then removed a canvas bag and held it out toward Boswell.

"I reckon this is what you're a' wantin'."

"Yes, thank you," Boswell said. "You've been most helpful."

Less than a full minute later, Boswell and his men were galloping away with the money pouch while the train was still stopped.

———

From the Saginaw Standard

Boswell Gang Holds up Train

In a brazen act, Damon Boswell and his gang of cutthroats held up the Fort Worth local on Friday last. The means by which the robbers stopped the train was to set a fire on the tracks, giving the illusion of a burning bridge. The amount gained by the robbery was not disclosed.

Residents of this part of Texas are well aware of the perfidious operations of Boswell, for he has robbed banks, coaches, and even some remote stores. A reward of fifteen thousand dollars, dead or alive, has been placed upon the head of this outlaw.

CHAPTER FOURTEEN

WITHIN A WEEK AFTER TAKING POSSESSION OF THE RANCH, Will and Gid felt comfortable enough with their new situation to invite Abe and Julia for dinner so they could "discuss some plans."

Abe and Julia lived in a small house that was within easy walking distance of The Big House. They arrived promptly as six, and Julia was dressed as if going to a fancy ball.

"Thank you so much for inviting us," she gushed. "I've been looking for a reason to dress up and look nice, for a change."

Will knew that she was fishing for a compliment, so he gave her what she wanted. "Why, Mrs. Barker, I think you always look nice." He had purposely called her Mrs. Barker in order to make his compliment less personal.

"Oh, please, won't you just call me Julia? That was the way General Redling always addressed me."

"I suppose I could," Will replied.

"So, Will, did you read about Boswell in the paper?" Abe asked.

"Yes, a bank robbery here a while back and now a train robbery. He seems to be quite a busy fellow."

"The general and I were concerned about him. As far as I know, he hasn't done any cattle rustling yet, but it's probably a good idea to watch out for him," Abe said.

"Nonsense, you worry too much," Julia said. "How would he steal any cattle? You don't expect him to just show up and help himself to the entire herd, do you?"

"She may be right," Will said. "I've dealt with Boswell's kind before. He wouldn't want to mess with a few cows here and there and stealing an entire herd is hard work. I expect people like Boswell don't like to work."

"I doubt that you've ever dealt with anyone quite like Damon Boswell before," Julia said. "People say he's a well-educated man, and at one time, he was a very successful lawyer before he ran afoul of the law."

"I didn't know that," Will replied, "but if you don't mind my asking, how do you know that?"

"There was an article about him in the *Star Telegram* a few months back. You have to wonder why a man like that with a good education and respected in his field, would turn his back on such a thing to become an outlaw."

"There had to be something," Will said. "All of us have skeletons in our closets that we'd just as soon not talk about."

Julia didn't respond.

"When are we going to eat?" Gid asked.

Will chuckled. "You'll have to excuse my brother. Maria cooked chicken and dumplin's because that's Gid's favorite meal."

Abe smiled. "Well, chicken and dumplin's certainly sounds good to me."

They went into the dining room where the table, big enough to seat eight, was set for four. As soon as they were seated, Maria brought the food out to the table.

"Oh, my, you do enjoy eating, don't you?" Julia said as Gid filled his plate for the second time.

"Some people like to paint, some like to fish, my hobby is eating," Gid said.

Julia's laughter was melodic. "Well, I do like to see a man enjoy himself." She looked over at Abe, and pouted. "Abraham, on the other hand, eats like a bird."

"I eat enough to stay alive," Abe said. "What else do you need food for?"

After their meal, they retired to the parlor.

"Oh, have you ever played anything on the music box?" Julia asked.

"No, we haven't," Gid replied. "We've been so busy, we don't come into this room very often."

"You must let me show you how it works," Julia said. "Mrs. Redling really enjoyed her music."

Will nodded, and Julia picked up a large brass plate that was perforated with many holes. Putting it on the turntable, she cranked the machine, then set it playing. "This is called *Music Box Dancer*."

The resulting sound was rich and melodic, filling the entire room with a beautiful melody.

"I've seen little music boxes before, but never one this large, and never one to produce such a full sound. Why, in my opinion, this is as good as an organ," Will said.

"It is beautiful, isn't it?" Julia said.

"You said you wanted to talk about what we should do next," Abe said, after the music ended.

"Yes, as you know, ranching is new to my brother and me. What would you say is the most important thing for us to do now?"

"That's easy. Get the cattle ready for market. And for that, we'll be needing to move the cattle from one range to another, so they don't graze one of the ranges out. Then, we'll cull out the calves and brand them."

"Is tomorrow too early to start?" Gid asked.

Abe smiled. "I knew you two would be good to have around. Tomorrow is as good a day as any."

———

WILL and Gid had bought not only the land and cattle, but the twenty horses as well. That was because none of the cowboys, with the exception of Abe, owned his own horse. Abe actually owned two of the horses, a saddle horse and the horse that Julia used to pull the buggy when she went into town.

With Abe leading the way the next morning, Will and Gid participated in the business of moving the cattle to a new range. In the process they separated out several of the new calves for branding.

The brand for the Brown Spur Ranch was a spur, which looked like an elongated letter "C" with a little line protruding from the back of the "C" to form the spur itself.

"Pretty ingenious," Will said.

"The general came up with that design himself," Abe said.

Walt Chambers and Mike Latham worked as a team

in branding the calves. When the cowboys would bring a calf to them, Chambers would hold it down, while Latham applied the brand. It was a quick and smooth operation.

———

Casey's Saloon

WHEN JOHN CASEY looked up from what he was doing, he saw an attractive young girl standing at the bar.

"What can I do for you, young lady?"

"I, uh, want a job."

Casey got a concerned look on his face. "How old are you?"

"I'm uh, twenty-one."

"I have to tell you, you don't look no twenty-one to me."

"Why? You think I look older than twenty-one?"

Casey laughed. "All right, what's your name?"

The girl paused for a moment.

"You haven't forgotten your name, have you?" Casey joked.

"No, uh, my name is Abby."

"Abby, what made you choose this place to work?"

"Sally, at the Cozy Home Saloon in Fort Worth told me about it."

"You worked at the Cozy Home, did you?"

"Yes, for a little while."

"Why did you leave? You didn't get in any trouble, did you?"

'No, I, uh, well Sally just told me that you were a nice man to work for."

Casey nodded. "Well, Sally's a good woman, and if she recommends you, that's good enough for me. Just a minute."

Casey walked down to the other end of the bar and talked to a woman who was standing there. The woman nodded, then, with a smile, came down to meet the young woman.

"My name's Suzie," she said with a warm smile. "John says you want to work here."

"Yes, ma'am."

"Oh, heavens, I'm Suzie, not ma'am."

Abby smiled. "Thank, you, Suzie."

"Well, John's a good man to work for, and the other girls are friendly. I think you'll like it here."

Abby smiled. "Yes, I think I will."

"May I give you a suggestion?" Suzie offered.

"Yes, of course."

"I don't know what got you to this place, and I don't ever want to know. All of us have some shadow in our background that caused us to do what we do, but whatever it is, it isn't anybody's business. Sometimes a man you will be with will get curious and want to know more about you. My suggestion is that you keep all that to yourself."

Abby smiled, and nodded her head. "Thanks," she said. "I'll remember that."

———

BY THE END of their first month as ranch owners, Will and Gid had gotten a full taste of what ranch life was like. They worked in the blistering sun and in the pouring rain. They pulled cows from the mud, led them to water, and moved them from pasture to pasture.

One night, after a full and exhausting day, Will and Gid were sitting out on the back porch, engaged in deep conversation.

"I haven't worked this hard since we were back on pa's farm," Gid said.

Will chuckled. "Well, Gid, if I remember correctly, you did agree to buy this ranch."

"Yeah, I guess I did, didn't I? Why didn't you just hit me upside the head and ask me what was I thinking?"

"Why don't we take a break? Let's go into town tomorrow," Will suggested.

"Yeah," Gid said, "that is if the boss will let us have a day off."

Will laughed. "I think that can be arranged."

"Maybe we can go into Casey's and one of the girls there can buy me drink."

"I don't think that's the way it works. I think we buy *them* a drink.

"Oh, yeah, now that you mention it, I believe that is how it works. Either way, tomorrow I plan to have a drink with a pretty girl."

————

THE NEXT MORNING Will and Gid left things in Abe's capable hands and rode into town. They took care of some ranch business first, stopping by Sikes' Hardware store to buy some barbed wire, then to McGill's feed and seed store to buy some salt blocks. After making a few more general purchases, they went to the livery stable and arranged for a wagon to deliver the items to the ranch.

Then, with all their business taken care of, they tied their horses in front of Casey's Saloon.

"Well, if it isn't the two best looking ranchers in all of Texas," Suzie said, greeting them with a smile.

"Ah, you're only saying that 'cause it true," Gid replied.

Suzie laughed, and hit Gid, playfully, on the shoulder.

"Go find a table, I'll bring each of you a beer, then join you," Suzie said.

"Sounds good to me," Gid agreed.

"Oh, and we have a new girl working here now. Her name is Abby. She's only twenty-one, and she's a little shy. I'll bring her with me, if you promise to be nice to her."

"We're always nice," Will said.

A moment later Suzie approached the table with another young lady. Abby was small and delicate looking. She was attractive, with her long, auburn hair, but the expression on her face, despite her practiced smile, was one of anxiety. Suzie was carrying the two beers, and Abby was carrying a couple of small shot glasses containing the percentage drinks for her and Suzie.

"Abby just joined us this week," Suzie said.

"Well, welcome to the big city of Saginaw," Gid teased.

The four visited over the next several minutes, and Will and Gid's tales of their adventures as new ranchers had both of the girls laughing.

"There you are, you bitch!" a man shouted, pointing

at Abby. He walked over to the table. "Give me my money back."

"I don't know what you're talking about," Abby replied in a frightened voice.

"The hell you don't! You got me so drunk yesterday that I passed out. And when I came to, all my money was gone."

"Angus, you managed to get yourself drunk without any help," Suzie said.

"You come upstairs with me now, I'm goin' to take it out in trade," Angus said.

"No, I'm busy."

"I said you're coming upstairs with me, bitch!" He reached down to grab Abby by the shoulder.

The moment Angus's hand touched Abby, Gid stood, then he jerked Angus away from Abby, and threw him on the floor.

"Why you big son of a bitch!" Angus yelled. He made an awkward grab for his gun, but dropped on the floor. By now the ruckus had caught the attention of everyone in the saloon, and they watched as John Casey came over wielding a double-barrel shotgun.

"Angus, if you try and use that gun, I'm goin' to blow your head off," John said. "You came in here yesterday and got drunk, so drunk that Miss Abby left you at your table. Then, you joined a poker game and lost all your money within half-an-hour. I'm going to ask you to leave now, and don't you come back in here again until you've learned a few manners."

"I, uh..." Angus started, then looking around the saloon, he saw no friendly faces. "I'll be going now," he said in a much more contrite voice. "Maybe I...maybe I was wrong." He picked his pistol up from the floor and put it back in his holster, then pushed through the bat wing doors as he exited the saloon.

"Thank you," Abby said to Gid, grateful for his intervention.

"You let me know if he gives you any more trouble," Gid said. "And thank you, John."

Gid didn't really need John's intervention. There was no way Angus would have managed to shoot him, but by intervening, John knew who was right and who was wrong in the argument.

For nearly an hour after that, the four continued their visit, not like bargirls and customers, but like four old friends.

As soon as Will and Gid stepped out of the saloon, Angus was standing in the middle of the street. He was already holding his pistol, and he fired at Gid, the bullet carrying away Gid's hat.

In a lightning move, Will drew and returned fire. Angus went down.

Will stood there, holding the smoking gun in his hand as he looked around to see if anyone else posed a danger to them. When he saw that there was no further threat, he holstered his gun.

"Damn," Gid said, "I sure wasn't looking for anything like that to happen."

"Me neither," Will said. He and Gid walked over to look down at Angus's prostrate form.

"Did you kill him?" Gid asked.

"I didn't have time not to."

By now several people had gathered around Will, Gid, and Angus's body. After less than a minute, Percy Coats came working his way through the group of gawkers.

"What happened here?" Coats asked.

"We came out of the saloon, and this man started shooting at us," Will said. "I had no choice but to return fire."

There were more than a dozen witnesses to the event and all were eager to tell the marshal what happened.

"He's tellin' the truth, Marshal," one of the witnesses said. "Them two no more 'n come outta the saloon when ole' Angus here commenced a' shootin' at 'em."

"Angus has given me trouble before, but it isn't like him to just start shooting at someone. Did you know him?"

"Not before a few minutes ago," Will said. "Gid and I were visiting with a couple of the girls when this man came in and put his hand on one of the girls, yelling about her stealing his money."

"Only John and Suzie both said that the man was lying, so I asked him to stop bothering the girl," Gid added.

"You asked him to stop?" Coats asked.

"Yeah, well, it may have been a bit more than my just asking."

"Gid threw him to the floor," Will said.

"I see."

"And, I reckon that's what caused him to get mad," Will said. "I guess he took it out by trying to shoot us, but all he did was poke a hole in Gid's hat."

Gid showed his hat to the marshal, then stuck his finger through the bullet hole and wiggled it.

"Under the circumstances, there won't be no charges," Coats said. "You boys don't even have to come down to the jail."

———

"Oh," Abby said after Will and Gid had left. "That man was killed because of me."

"No, he wasn't," Suzie said. "He was killed because he was a jackass who tried to kill Will and Gid Crockett. You had nothing to do with it."

"I . . . I should have gone upstairs with him."

"Honey, I know Angus Berry, or perhaps I should say that I knew Angus Berry. In the mood he was in today, if you had gone upstairs with him, you know he would have beaten you. I'd think that you'd understand things like that since you're twenty-one years old," Suzie said.

"Eighteen," Abby said in a whisper.

"What? I thought you said you were twenty-one."

"I did say that, because I wanted everyone to believe that. But I just turned eighteen a couple of months ago. Please, don't tell anyone."

Suzie stared at Abby for a long moment. "And I suppose Abby isn't your real name either, is it?"

"No it's..." Abby started.

Suzie held up her hand. "Honey, you don't need to tell me anything. None of us use our real names and Abby's as good a name as any. And don't worry, I won't tell anyone how old you really are."

"You promise?"

"I tell you what. My real name is Lydia Foster, and I'm from Jackson, Mississippi. I don't want anyone to know that, either, so now we each have a secret on the other to keep."

"I didn't know what kind of people I would run into when I...uh, when I started in this business. But you have been very nice. Thank you for being my friend."

"I'm glad to be your friend," Suzie said. "Now, you put Angus out of your mind, and let's hustle a few drinks."

Abby smiled. "Thank you, I will."

CHAPTER FIFTEEN

"You know, Will, we've got quite a commitment with this herd. I'd feel better if we sold them off, then with our share, start another herd where we weren't indebted to the general," Gid said one morning over coffee.

"I've been thinking about that, too," Will said. "Let's see what Abe has to say."

A little later that morning, Will found Abe in the machine shed, filing on a horseshoe he had locked in a vise.

"Abe, if it's all right, how about you and your wife coming up to the Big House for supper tonight? Gid and I have a few things we need to talk to you about."

Abe smiled. "I never pass up an opportunity to eat Maria's cooking. We'll be there."

Will was aware that Abe hadn't asked him what he wanted to talk about, and he appreciated that. He thought it was a subject that could better be discussed if they gave some time to the question.

"I wish there was some way we could just have Abe over for supper," Will said.

"You know there's no way we can do that," Gid said. "Julia would come over, whether she was invited or not."

Will chuckled. "You're probably right."

———

JIM CLAY and Doodle Hawkins were repairing the corral fence when they saw Will and Gid go into the machine shed to talk to the ranch foreman.

"Hey, Doodle, did you hear about what happened in town the other day?"

"What this time?"

"Will Crockett shot Angus Cates."

"Of course I heard about that. Ever'body in town's talkin' about the shootin'. They say Cates already had his gun drawed when Will shot 'im."

"He did," Doodle said. "That's why Will didn't get in trouble with the law."

"Well I, for one, ain't a' goin' to be missin' Angus none. As far as I'm concerned, he was a no count son of a bitch."

"I agree with you there," Clay said.

"What do you think about the Crocketts?" Doodle asked.

"What do you mean?"

"I mean as owners of the ranch. What do you think about workin' for 'em?"

"I think they're a couple of good men," Clay said. "I didn't know what they was goin' to be like in the begin- nin', and I was ready to quit iffen I didn't like 'em. I mean, don't get me wrong, I miss the General and I thought he was a damn good boss, but truth to tell, I like the Crocketts damn near as much."

"Me, too," Doodle said. "'N you know what I like most about 'em?" He laughed. "Them two piles into work just like they's hired hands, instead of the bosses. I mean, they ain't a'feard of gettin' their hands dirty."

"You got that right."

Doodle may have used the term, 'getting their hands dirty' as an allegory, but that very afternoon, Will and Gid actually did get their hands dirty when they worked with the others to free a cow that was belly deep in a mud pit.

As everyone was cleaning up afterward, Scooter asked Will about the shooting incident in town.

"Hey, Mr. Crockett, if you don't mind tellin' me, how is it that you got to be so good with a gun?"

"Well, practice, I guess," Will answered.

"Have you shot a lot of people?"

"Scooter, if you don't mind, I'm really not all that comfortable talking about things like that."

"Uh, huh, but you've shot lots of people, ain't you? Leastwise, that's what I've heard."

"Sometimes it's necessary. But I've never shot anyone who wasn't shooting at me."

"I'd sure like to be able to shoot like that," Scooter said.

"No, Scooter, you wouldn't," Will said easily. "If you shoot too well, you are just putting a target on your back. Trust me, you don't want to live like that."

"No, but I still wish I could draw 'n shoot like you can," Scooter insisted.

———

WILL and Gid stayed busy with chores for the rest of the day then late that afternoon, they returned to the house to get cleaned up for supper.

"What are we having tonight, Maria?" Gid asked.

"Why bother to ask, Little Brother, you'll gobble it up like you haven't eaten in a week, no matter what it is."

"Well, yeah, but I kind of like to know what I'm eating."

"Señor and Señora Barker are coming, *si*?"

"Yes."

Maria smiled. "Then I am cooking something I know the señor will like. Pork chili verde."

"Sounds good to me," Gid said with a wide smile.

Will chuckled. "Little brother, do you even know what that is?"

"No, but if Maria makes it, I know it'll be good, 'cause Maria is as fine a cook as I've ever known."

"Gracias, Señor Gid," Maria replied with a self-conscious smile.

———

ABE AND JULIA arrived just before six, and as before, Julia looked more like a percentage girl in a saloon, than a housewife. Her style of dress and her overt flirtations with both Will and Gid made the two uncomfortable, especially as it was taking place right in front of Abe. He either wasn't aware of it, or he was aware and just didn't care.

They did not discuss their business while they were

eating. Abe, after commenting that this was one of his favorite dishes, ate with as much gusto as Gid.

Will chuckled. "Are you two going to leave any food for Julia and me?"

"It's every man for himself," Gid said as he refilled his plate.

Then, after a well-enjoyed supper, they all went into the parlor, where Will started the conversation.

"Abe, Gid and I have decided that we want to sell the herd so we can give Redling the rest of what is due him, then start a new herd of our own."

Abe nodded. "I think that's a pretty good idea."

"But here's the thing. Since we really don't know what we're doing, we'd like your opinion on what we should do next."

"Well, I can tell you what the general always did. He'd go to Kansas City and book the herd in advance so that he'd have a guarantee of what each animal would bring. If you do that in advance, you should be able to get four or five dollars more per head, than you would if you just showed up with a herd."

"I can see that," Will said. "I suppose if you just show up with a herd, you're pretty much committed to accept anything they want to give you."

"That's sort of the way it works. The buyers figure they have you over a barrel, because you for sure don't want to take the herd back with you."

"I have a question," Gid said. "When we take them, how do we do it? Will we need to make a cattle drive?"

"Well, we could, and that would save the cost of shipping, but it's so much easier to put 'em on a train, that it's worth what it will cost. And by booking your herd in advance, you'll come out enough ahead that the train will be paid for, and then some."

"Abe, you always give good advice," Will said. "Little brother, how would you like to make a train trip to Kansas City?"

"I think I'd like that. It's been a long time since we were there," Gid said. "Say, do you think we'd have time to drop down to St. Leger?"

"We'll make the time," Will said.

"St. Leger?" Abe asked.

"It's a small town in Southwest Missouri," Will said.

"What's so significant about it?"

"It's where we were born and raised," Gid said.

Abe smiled, and nodded. "Yes, I understand. I got back to Bond County last year." He looked over at Julia. "Julia didn't care all that much for Illinois, but I enjoyed going back home."

"What was there to like?" Julia asked, dismissively. "None of your family liked me."

"You just didn't give them a chance."

"I gave them as much a chance as I wanted to, and if we never go back, it'll be fine with me."

"Yes, well, under the circumstances, I doubt very much if we will ever go back, at least, not together. I may go back a time or two, they're my family and I won't just turn my back on them."

"Why do we need family, when we've got each other?" Julia asked.

"Family is important. You've told me very little about your family. I know that you said your parents are dead, and I know you do have a brother because you write to him all the time. I wish he'd come visit because I'd like to meet him sometime."

"Harry lives a life of excitement, rushing down the rails at fifty miles per hour. You would bore him to tears."

"Well, I see no reason why we shouldn't get started tomorrow then," Will said, uncomfortable at being a witness to the discussion going on between Abe and Julia.

"You'll want to turn in early tonight, so we'd better get on back home. Thank Maria for the supper," Abe said. "I know she made it just for me."

"And for me, too," Gid said.

After Abe and Julia had gone, Gid turned to Will.

"If all other wives are anything like that woman, I'd just as soon never get married," Gid said. "The way she acts—the way she talks—why does Abe put up with it? I just don't understand it."

"Yeah, me neither," Will said.

———

Cabin on the Trinity River

"WE AIN'T MAKIN' hardly no money a' tall," Draco said.

"What do you mean we aren't making any money?" Boswell replied.

"I mean we've robbed a stage coach, a bank, and we've held up a train, 'n we only got a little over four thousand dollars total. 'N then we got to divide that all up between the seven of us. Well, ten if you're gonna be actual about it, seein' as you take three shares of everthin'."

"You know, Draco's right," Sloan said. "We joined up with you so's we could make a lot o' money. Onliest thing is, we could more 'n likely make as much as we've been makin', iffen we was to go out on our own."

Draco and Sloan's comments were met with affirmation by the four others.

Boswell nodded, then held out his hand. "You're right," he said. "But, do not despair. I've been planning an operation that will make us enough money that we will be able to withdraw from any additional activity for at least a year or as long as you might like."

"What you got in mind, Boss?" Mathis asked.

"I'm going to keep my plans to myself until it's time to actually implement them. That way, there is less opportunity for our job to be compromised."

"What?" Weasel asked.

"He means he'll tell us when we need to know," Jenkins said.

"Excellent, Jenkins, my good man," Boswell said. "That is exactly when I will tell you."

"Yeah, well I hope it ain't gonna be too much longer off, on account of we ain't hardly got enough money now to get drunk 'n get us a woman," Cooley said.

Draco laughed. "Hell, you got that wrong. Ain't no need for you to get drunk. What you got to do is get the woman drunk a'fore she'll be with you."

"Yeah, even if she is a whore 'n you're 'a payin' her," Weasel added, to the laughter of all the others.

"Just be patient, my friends," Boswell said. "I promise you, you will be rewarded."

———

As BOSWELL LAY in bed that night, he began thinking about the operation he had in mind. He was actually already laying the groundwork for it. It would be the most complex of any jobs they had done, but the reward would be significant, perhaps even enough for him to give up the outlaw life, and return to the position that he once occupied in society. Though of course any such re-entry into society would have to be under an assumed name.

The plan Boswell had in mind was not of his own conception. It had been recommended to him by someone who would, themselves, be entitled to a share of the proceeds. But it would be well worth it. And there might even be a collateral bonus from the partnership.

CHAPTER SIXTEEN

"WILL, WOULD YOU AND GID BE GOOD ENOUGH TO MAIL this letter for me? It's to my brother."

"Absolutely, we'd be glad to," Will said. "Listen, it's none of my business, and I know you said your brother would be bored by coming here for a visit, but I do wish you'd invite him. I'd like to meet him, and I know Abe would."

Julia smiled. "You read my mind," she said. She held up the envelope before she handed it to him. "It just so happens, that this is an invitation for Harry to come visit."

The next day Will and Gid rode into Fort Worth where they posted Julia's letter. After that they bought tickets to Kansas City, making arrangements for their horses to go with them. The train wasn't due to leave until ten o'clock the following morning, so they checked in to the Clark House, then walked down the street to the Cozy Home Saloon.

When they walked in to the saloon, they were greeted by Sally and Millie.

"Where have you been? We haven't seen you in a long time."

"It's been a while, all right," Will agreed. "We've been staying pretty close to a place called Saginaw."

"Oh, yeah, we heard you bought a ranch out there," Millie said.

"We did indeed. Now, why don't you two ladies get yourself a couple of drinks and join us," Will invited.

The drinks were purchased, and the four found a table in the back corner of the room.

"Do you like the ranchin' business?" Sally asked.

"I think we do," Will said, "but it's all because of the people who work for us. Our foreman is the best, and all the hands work well together. I'd say they're doing a good job of breaking us in."

"I'd say they're doing a bit too good a job of breaking us in," Gid added.

"What do you mean?" Sally asked.

Will chuckled. "What he means is, we aren't gentlemen ranchers who watch everything from the front porch. We're out working, side by side with the hands."

"I bet they appreciate that, though," Millie said.

"They seem to," Will agreed.

"What about Julia?" Sally asked.

"Well, I'll say this," Will answered. "She's a pretty woman."

"And has she asked you to take her to bed yet?" Millie asked.

"Uh...no nothing like that," Gid stammered.

"Just you wait," Sally said, "if she hasn't already, it's just a matter of time. Once you are a part of the profession, it's hard to step aside."

"Profession?" Will asked.

"When she got Abe to marry her, she told him she was a show girl, but I knew her back in St. Louis when her name was Wanda Beck," Sally said. "She married one of her wealthy John's, but she couldn't stop her old ways. When her rich husband found out about her entertaining other men, he divorced her."

"Did she work here?" Gid asked.

"Oh no," Sally said. "She came in here one time, but when she saw me and knew that I recognized who she really was, she never stepped a foot in here again. It wasn't long after that, that she married Abe. Nobody knows if she knew him from someplace else or not, but now she passes herself off as some uppity woman—the wife of a foreman who doesn't have the time of day for those of us who are still workin'. She tricked him. That's for sure."

"Sally, that's not fair," Millie said. "You know that girls like us are always looking for an opportunity to turn over a new leaf."

"Yeah, but Julia isn't like us," Sally replied. "There's no way she'd turn over a new leaf unless there's money under it."

"Why are we talking about her, anyway?" Millie asked. "There are two men and two women at this table. We certainly don't need a third woman."

Sally laughed. "Yeah, you're right." She reached out to touch Will. "And I don't plan to share this handsome man with anyone."

At that moment a young woman came over to the table. She smiled, shyly at Gid. "I want to thank you again for coming to my defense a couple of weeks ago."

"Abby?"

"Yes, it's me."

"Hmm, Millie, looks to me like you have some competition," Sally said.

"No, no, I don't mean to intrude," Abby said.

"Nonsense," Millie said. "Pull up a chair and join us."

Abby smiled. "Thanks."

"Abby, what are you doing here in Fort Worth?" Will asked. "Did you quit working for John?"

"No, I'm still working there, but I came into town on an errand. I'll be going back tomorrow, and Sally said I could stay here tonight, instead of having to pay for a hotel room."

"Well, you're good company, and you're welcome to join us," Millie said.

"Yes, we're glad to have you," Will said as he pulled up an extra chair.

The five were visiting for about half an hour when Sheriff Maddox came into the saloon. Seeing Will and Gid, he stepped over to the table to speak with them.

"So, how's the ranching business going?" he asked.

"All right," Will answered.

"Except, that I haven't worked this hard since I was boy working on the farm," Gid added, turning his hands over. "Look at these calluses."

Sheriff Maddox chuckled. "Ranching is hard work," he said. "That is if you do it right. I know, because I've tried it, not as a rancher, but as a hand."

———

WILL and Gid boarded the train at ten o'clock the next morning. The train was scheduled to arrive in Kansas

City at one o'clock the following day, so since it was such a short trip, they eschewed the sleeping car, which would have provided a private roomette, and decided on the Pullman which allowed the seats to provide a pull-down upper and lower bunk for night travel.

"If you could add it all up, how many days do you think we've spent on a train?" Gid asked over lunch in the dining car.

Will chuckled. "It would be easier to figure out how many weeks we've spent on a train."

"What do you think we should do about Julia and Abe?" Gid asked.

"What do you mean, what should we do?"

"Well, do you think we should tell Abe about her? About her being a prostitute, I mean."

Will shook his head. "That's none of our business, Gid."

"It's just that Abe is such a nice guy, I hate to see him being taken in like he is."

"How do we know Abe doesn't already know about Julia's past? Like I said, it's none of our business."

"All right, I won't bring it up again," Gil agreed.

During their twenty-four-hour long trip to Kansas City, the two brothers discussed a lot of things, including whether or not they wanted to keep the ranch.

"I think it can make us a lot of money," Gid said. "Our cut on the cattle we have right now will be several thousand dollars. And that'll be enough to get our own herd started."

"That's true," Will agreed. "And we do have a bunch of good men working for us."

"But that's thanks to Redling. If we have to hire any

new men ourselves, I'm not sure we'd be able to get anyone as good as the men we already have."

Will smiled. "As long as we have Abe to guide us, that's not anything we'll ever have to worry about."

Gid smiled. "That's right, isn't it? We're damned lucky to have him as our foreman."

———

THE TRAIN TRIP to Kansas City was without incident, and when they arrived at the Kansas City depot, it was hauntingly familiar. After retrieving their horses, the two brothers rode out to the Bottom Stockyard.

"Yes, sir, what can I do for you gentlemen?" a young man with blond hair, and a protruding Adams apple asked.

"We're here to sell some cattle," Will said.

"The cattle are here?"

"No, they're still in Texas."

"Oh, then you don't want to sell them," the young man said.

"What? Yes, of course we do. That's why we're here," Will said.

The young man smiled. "No, since the cattle aren't here, you can't sell them. However, you can book them."

"That's right," Gid said. "That's what we intend to do."

"You'll meet with Mr. Peabody and arrange a contingency sale, based upon the delivery of the cattle."

"Will he tell us how much he'll pay?" Will asked.

"Yes, sir, that's the main reason you want to book your cattle."

A few minutes later the two brothers met with

Maurice Peabody, the buyer for the Bottom Stockyard. Peabody was a rather plump man with a double chin and thin strands of hair on a nearly bald head.

"How many do you have?" he asked.

"Twenty-five hundred head," Will said. During the train ride up, they had decided to round off the number of cows they would sell.

"If you will book the cattle with me, exclusively, we can lock in a price of forty-seven dollars a head, once they are delivered," Peabody said.

"Mr. Peabody, you have a deal," Will said, extending his hand.

Peabody smiled. "A handshake will verify the deal, but we'll need your signatures on a contract. And of course, that protects you, as well as it does us, because it will guarantee that you are paid the amount that was agreed upon."

"Yes, sir, we'll be glad to sign the contract."

———

"Wow," that leaves us with twelve dollars a head," Will said after they left Peabody's office.

"What will that be, total?" Gid asked.

Will got a paper and pencil, then did some figuring. "A little over thirty thousand dollars."

"Damn, that's more than we paid for the ranch. It's beginning to look like this cattle ranching is going to pay off pretty well."

"Now that the business part of our trip is over, let's head on down to St. Leger."

"I don't know if we should do that."

"What do you mean, you don't know? You're the one who suggested we go."

"Do you think there'll be anybody there who still remembers us?"

"I'm sure there'll be somebody, and if not, we'll just go by the home place and visit Ma and Pa's graves."

"All right, then, let's do it."

CHAPTER SEVENTEEN

Dido, Texas

WHEN BOSWELL RETURNED TO THE LITTLE CABIN ON THE Trinity, near the very small town of Dido, he saw that four of his men were playing poker, while the other two were watching.

"Damn," Weasel said. "Where the hell did that ace come from?"

"From the deck you dealt," Draco said, laughing as he pulled in the pot. "I'm in the money now."

"Yeah, there's all of six dollars there," Sloan said.

"Well, no more money than we've been able to raise in the last six months, six dollars is a lot of money," Mathis said.

"Gentlemen, our fortunes are about to change," Boswell said as he hung his hat on the peg.

"What do you mean?"

"I have been made aware of an opportunity. If we pull this operation off, and I have learned that all the conditions are right for a favorable outcome, we shall enrich ourselves by several thousand dollars, each."

"Whoa, wait a minute," Draco said. "Are you saying that each one of us stands to make a thousand dollars?"

"No, I'm not saying that," Boswell replied.

"Oh."

Boswell smiled. "I'm saying that each one of you will make several thousand dollars."

"How much?" Weasel asked.

"That depends," Boswell said. "But I would say no less than five thousand dollars apiece."

"Dayum! When do we start?"

"We start right now," Boswell said.

———

Brown Spur Ranch

"ALL RIGHT MEN, let's bunch 'em up 'n move 'em into the west pasture," Abe said, and he and the six ranch hands began bringing in the cows that had strayed away from the main body of cattle.

"What are we doing this for?" Doodle asked.

"I expect the Crocketts will sell the herd while they're in Kansas City, and it'll be easier to get the cows down to the rail head if we have them gathered."

"That makes since."

"What was that?" Scooter asked.

"What was what?" Walt replied.

"I heard something that sounded like a gunshot."

"Where did it come from?"

"I don't know I just heard it. There, I just heard another one."

"I heard it, too," Walt said.

The two men halted their horses and listened for a moment, but they heard nothing else.

"Ah, it prob'ly wasn't nothin'," Walt said, and the two men got back to herding the cattle.

———

BOSWELL and his gang were riding from the Big House, out into the field where the Brown Spur hands were busy rounding up the cattle. The only remaining hand, Moses the cook, was behind them, lying dead on the cook house floor.

"How many do you think there'll be?" Draco asked.

"There will be seven, and that includes the foreman," Boswell said.

"They's seven of us," Weasel said.

Boswell chuckled. "Yes, but the difference will be in the superior firepower. You see, gentlemen, we are armed and they are not."

"Ha, this is goin' to be easy as takin' candy from a baby," Sloan said.

"Not that easy," Boswell said. "The cattle will be spooked by the gunfire, and we will need to gather them up, then drive them away, just like the cattle drives of old. Except this time all twenty-five hundred head will belong to us."

Before undertaking this venture, Boswell had discussed the positives of taking an entire herd. "Think about it, gentlemen. If we only got ten dollars a head for them, and that would be twenty-five thousand dollars."

"Cattle's more 'n ten dollars a head," Draco said.

"Indeed it is. But in order to get the market value, we would have to take the herd to Kansas City either by train or by driving them up there. That would greatly increase our exposure, and thus present us with a higher opportunity to be apprehended. I think it would be best if we lowered that opportunity by selling the cattle somewhere here, in Texas," he explained. "Or perhaps we would need to drive them all the way to Mexico."

"For ten dollars a head?"

"No, I was just using that figure to illustrate how profitable this operation will be for us. But in fact, I have a plan in mind that will garner considerably more than that."

"There they are," Cooley said.

"Draw your guns," Boswell ordered.

———

"Hey, Abe, lookie there. Who do you think those men are that's a' comin' this way?" Doodle asked.

"I don't know," Abe said, "but I don't like the looks of it."

Abe rode out to the forward edge of the herd to meet them. "Who are you men, and what do you want?" he called.

"Interesting that you would inquire, my good man. I am Damon Boswell, and we want your cattle."

"What?"

———

SCOOTER WAS close enough to overhear the exchange. "Damn, Walt, it's Boswell and they're here to rustle the cattle!"

"We ain't got no way to fight back," Walt said. "Don't none of us have guns."

The gunfire started then, and Abe was the first to go down. Scooter was next with a bullet wound to his stomach then, as he lay on the ground he heard more shooting, as well as calls of alarm and pain.

Finally, the shooting stopped.

"Let's go men!" Scooter heard Boswell shout. "You're no longer rustlers, you are now cattle owners!"

"Yahoo!" someone yelled.

Scooter lay very still as the cattle were rounded up, then driven away.

He didn't realize he had lost consciousness until he heard someone calling to him.

"I know you're still alive, Scooter, I saw you move," a voice said.

Scooter opened his eyes and saw Mark Worley squatting down beside him. Mark worked for Chris Dumey, who owned a small ranch adjacent to the Brown Spur.

"Mark," he said, "what are you doing here?"

"We heard gunfire, and Mr. Dumey sent Angus and me over here to check."

"The cattle," Scooter said.

"There're all gone, I saw 'em takin' the herd and I knew what was happenin', so I waited 'til they were out of sight before I came over here."

"Abe," Scooter said, trying to sit up. "Where's Abe?"

"He's dead," Mark said. "I checked on him 'n everbody else 'n theyre ever' one of 'em dead. All of 'em but you."

"Damn."

"You stay here, I'm goin' to get a buckboard 'n take you into the doctor," Angus said. "Mark, you stay here with Scooter."

"Don't worry, I'll still be here."

————

SCOOTER MUST HAVE PASSED out again, because the next thing he was aware of, was when he was being carried into the doctor's office. Marshal Coats was going in with them, and he heard Mark talking.

"They're dead, Marshal, ever' damn one of 'em," Mark was saying. "Scooter here is the only one we found alive. That is, iffen he's still alive."

"I'm still here," Scooter said in a weak voice.

"Scooter, do you have any idea who did this?" Marshal Coats asked.

"Boswell," Scooter gasped. "They shot ever' one of us, then rode off with the herd."

"You sure it was Damon Boswell? He's not known to be a cattle rustler."

"I heard the man tell Abe he was Boswell."

"And the Crocketts? Were they killed too?" Coats asked.

"No, they went to Kansas City. Bookin' the cattle."

"Marshal, I hope you have everything you need now. I've got to see what I can do to save this man," the doctor said.

The marshal nodded his head. "Yes, sir, Doc. I

expect I need to send a telegram to the Crocketts. They need to get back here as soon as they can."

———

With the Crocketts

AFTER BOOKING their herd with the Bottom Stockyard in Kansas City, the brothers took a train trip to Springfield, Missouri, leaving at four A.M. and arriving in Springfield a little after ten in the morning. Then, after their horses were off-loaded from the stock car, they rode the final twenty miles to the place of their birth and childhood, reaching St. Leger just after noon.

"Look, there's Nippy Jones Saloon," Gid said, pointing to the false-fronted building. "I wonder if Nippy is still running the place."

"I expect he is, but the only way we're going to know, is if we go in and find out."

The two tied off their horses in front of the saloon, then stepped inside. There were no more than half-a-dozen customers, and all were sitting at tables. There was no one standing at the bar, but at the far end, behind the bar, a gray-haired, rather heavy-set man was wiping out glasses.

"That's him," Gid said.

They stepped up to the bar, then Gid called out. "Nippy, how about a couple of beers down here?"

"Coming right up," Nippy Jones replied, and taking two of the clean mugs, he held them under the beer barrel spigot. Then, with foamy white heads on the two mugs of beer, he brought them down and sat them in front of the two brothers.

"Here you are, gents, that'll be a dime."

"And a dime well-spent," Will said, placing the coin on the counter. It wasn't until then that Nippy Jones looked more closely at the two men.

"Well, I'll be damn," he said, as a wide smile spread across his face. "If it ain't the Crocketts. Most folks around here thought you two was dead. Sure has been a while since I seen you two."

"Yes, well as you recall, for a while there, we had paper out on us."

"That's true. Ever'body thought you was running with Jesse James."

"That's one thing we never did do," Gid said as he took a drink from his beer.

"We've not been hearing as much about Jesse, lately," Will said. "Does he come this way very often?"

"You did hear about the Northfield bank robbery, didn't you?" Nippy asked.

"Yes, we read about it in the paper. It didn't go over that well for him, did it?"

"The gang got only twenty-seven dollars, and for that, Clell Miller and Chadwell were killed at the scene, Charley Pitts was killed two weeks later, and the Younger boys was all captured. Jesse and Frank got away, but they ain't been all that active since then. Anyway, the law got to wantin' them boys so bad they just plumb forgot about you two. You ain't even wanted in Missouri no more."

"It's nice not to be wanted anymore," Will said. He chuckled. "Although that sounds funny when you think about it, to say you're glad nobody wants you."

"Are you two back to stay?" Nippy asked.

"No, we're just here on a visit." Will said nothing of the business they had conducted in Kansas City.

"We're goin' out to the farm to visit our folks grave, 'n take a look at our old home place," Gid added.

"You'll find some changes there," Nippy said.

"Yes, well, we're expecting that, but we want to visit it anyway."

"I can see that you'd want to do that. I'm glad you came in," Nippy said. "It's good to see you boys and I hope you come by again."

"Oh, I expect we'll stop by from time to time," Will said. "It's like Pa always used to say, you can take the man out of Missouri, but you can't take Missouri out of the man."

Nippy laughed. "That's what all the old timers say, and I think it's true."

————

THE CROCKETTS' Mother and Dad had been killed by the Hoffman Redlegs, a Kansas outlaw guerilla bunch, crossing the state line to make war against Missourians. Hoffman and his followers rode under the Union Flag during the war, but they were not sanctioned by the Union. Indeed, they were regarded as outlaws by both the Union and the Confederacy.

Their parents had been buried on the farm that they once had owned, so visiting their folks' grave, also meant visiting the farm.

They approached Possum Walk Creek, then paused for a moment to look at the creek that had supplied water to their farm.

"You know, I once caught..." Gid started, but Will interrupted him.

"No, you did not catch the biggest catfish that's ever been caught in the whole world," Will said, laughing.

"I never said I did."

"Oh yes you did. You were eight years old, and when you pulled the fish out of that ditch, right about here as I recall, you started yelling that you'd just caught the biggest catfish ever caught."

"Well, it was a big fish for an eight-year-old," Gid insisted.

"I'll grant you that," Will conceded with a little laugh.

After crossing Possum Walk Creek, the two brothers proceeded up what had once been known as Crockett Road. The last time Will had visited the farm it was exactly as it had been after the Hoffman Redlegs had left it, with only blackened timbers to mark the location of the house and barn. They were expecting to see that this time, but were quite surprised to see that there was a new white, two-story house, and a rebuilt red barn.

"Wow, look at that," Gid said. "It looks like someone has built the farm back the way it used to be."

"I wonder who lives here now," Will mused.

"I don't know, but it's kind of nice to see a house here again, instead nothing but burned-out timbers," Will said.

The question was answered a moment later when a tall, sunken cheek, rather cadaverous looking man with a white beard, white hair, and dark brown eyes stepped out onto the porch.

"Somethin' I can do for you fellas?" he asked.

"Uncle Gordon, is that you?" Will asked.

"Well, blow me down if it isn't Will and Gid," Gordon said with a wide grin. "I wasn't sure I'd ever see you boys again."

"What are you doing here?"

"I'm farming the place," Gordon said. "When it went on the auction block for taxes, I paid the taxes off, then took title to the land. I just couldn't bear to think of this land being anywhere but in the Crockett family. I hope you boys are all right with that."

"What do you mean you hope we're all right with it? Why, I think it's great that you've bought the place," Will said.

"I'm glad you feel that way. Truth to tell, I've been somewhat worried 'bout what you boys might think if you knew I had done this."

"Are Ma and Pa still buried here?" Gid asked.

Gordon smiled. "Come with me, I'll show you."

They walked around behind the house, and out to the tree where their folks were buried. The tree was still there, but everything else was different. There was a white picket fence around the two graves, and the simple, unmarked wooden crosses had been replaced by engraved tombstones.

"Nippy Jones said there had been some changes made, but Uncle Gordon, what you've done here is far better than anything we could have expected," Will said. "I can't tell you how good it is to see the farm restored as we remember it."

"How long are you boys going to be here?" Gordon asked.

"Not too long," Gid said. He smiled. "We're land owners too. We bought a cattle ranch down in Texas."

"Ranchers, are you? Well now, that's mighty fine," Gordon said.

"We came up to Kansas City to check the cattle market, then decided to come down here and have a look around," Will said. "I'm glad we did, seeing the farm rebuilt, takes away some of the more unpleasant memories we have of it."

"Can you at least spend the night with us? You're Aunt Mildred is making chicken pot pie for supper."

"That settles it," Gid said with a broad smile. "I don't care what Will does, I'm staying the night."

Will laughed. "I see you remember Gid's weakness."

Gordon laughed as well. "Everyone who has ever met Gid, knows that the boy loves to eat."

———

The Bottom Stockyard – Kansas City, Kansas

"MR. PEABODY?"

"Yes, Michael what is it?"

"There's a boy out here with a telegram for the Crocketts."

"Send him in," Peabody said.

A young boy, no older than fourteen came into Peabody's office then, holding a yellow envelope.

"That's for the Crocketts?"

"Yes, sir."

Peabody reached for it. "I'll take it."

The boy pulled the envelope back. "I can't give it to you, Mister. It's for the Crocketts."

Peabody gave the boy a quarter. "They aren't here right now, give it to me, and I'll see that they get it."

Seeing the quarter, the boy smiled, then handed over the envelope. "You'll give it 'em?"

"As soon as I see them," Peabody said.

———

AFTER THE BOY LEFT, Peabody opened the telegram, even though it wasn't meant for him.

BOSWELL STOLE YOUR HERD KILLED ALL YOUR HANDS BUT SIMPSON STOP COME BACK SOONEST

MARSHAL COATS

CHAPTER EIGHTEEN

WILL AND GID HAD A GOOD VISIT THEIR UNCLE GORDON and Aunt Mildred. They also caught up with some of the other members of the family. Their cousin, Ellen Genoa, was teaching school in Arkansas. Their cousin, Leonard, was a fireman with the Missouri Pacific Railroad.

Before they left the next morning, they took a tour of the farm, which was both gratifying, and a little melancholy. It was good to see the farm restored to the way they remembered it, but they also couldn't forget that awful day when they found both parents killed by Kansas Jayhawkers, and all the buildings burned. The one positive thing of that memory was that they had found, and settled accounts, with the men who had done such a thing.

They boarded the train in Springfield the next morning. Twenty-four hours later they left the train in Fort Worth, got their horses, then took a leisurely ride to the little town of Saginaw.

"What do you say we stop at Casey's for beer before we ride out to the ranch?" Will proposed.

"You do come up with good ideas, don't you?" Gid teased.

Tying their horses off in front of the saloon they stepped inside. It had been a good trip. They learned that the cattle would bring more than they had expected, and they had the pleasure of seeing the family farm restored by a member of the family.

"Hi, John" Will greeted as the two brothers stepped up to the barn. "We'll have a couple of beers."

John looked at them with a surprised expression on his face. The expression was more than surprised, it was one of concern.

"Where have you two been?" John asked.

"We went to Kansas City to sell our herd. Don't you remember? We stopped here, before we left."

John nodded. "So, you are just now getting back?" John asked.

"We got off the train just an hour or so ago," Will said.

"It was a real good visit, not only because the market is up, but we also got to visit some of our family," Gid added, with a broad smile.

"Why are you..." John started. "Didn't you get the telegram?"

"What telegram?" Will asked.

"Percy Coats sent it to you, care of the Bottom Stock-yard in Kansas City."

"Oh, well that explains why we didn't get it. We were only in Kansas City for a very short time."

"Oh, good Lord, then that means you don't know anything, do you?"

"Now you're worrying me. What is it we don't know?" Will asked.

"I think you'd better go down and talk to Percy," John said.

"Why do we need to talk to the marshal?"

"Please, it isn't my place to tell you. Just go talk to the marshal."

"All right, hold the beers. We may, or may not be back for them."

———

"WHAT DO you suppose that was all about?" Gid asked as they walked down McLeroy Street to the marshal's office.

"I don't know but I'm sure we're about to find out. And, I'm equally sure..." Will paused in mid-sentence.

"That it's going to be something we're not going to like," Gid said, completing the sentence for his brother."

"Yeah," Will agreed.

Percy Coats was sitting behind his desk when they stepped into the office. When he saw them, his face took on a grim expression.

"Good," he said. "I see you got my telegram."

"No, we didn't get any telegram. John mentioned that we should have but he didn't say what it was about. He told us to see you," Will said.

"Oh, my God, then you don't know?"

"No we don't. Just tell us what's going on?"

"Boswell and his men raided your ranch. They killed Abe and all your hands, everyone but Scooter Simpson, that is. And they took your entire herd."

"What?" Will's response was explosive. "When did

this happen?"

"Four days ago. I sent a telegram to the Bottom Stockyard in Kansas City, hoping you'd get it."

Will shook his head, sadly. "No, we didn't stay there but for a few hours, then went to our old homeplace in Missouri. So we didn't get a telegram."

"You said everyone was killed but Scooter Simpson?" Gid asked.

"Yes."

"Where is he, now?"

"He wasn't killed, but he was badly wounded. Right now, he's down at Dr. Urban's office."

"What about Moses and Maria, and Julia? Were they all killed too?"

"Moses and Maria were. Julia either ran away, or they took her. We don't know what happened to her, because we didn't find any sign of her."

"Damn," Gid said.

"Wait until you talk to Scooter. He can tell you more about what happened, just as he told me."

"Let's go," Will said as he moved toward the door.

———

Scooter was in bed, propped up by so many pillows so that he was actually sitting up. There were bandages wrapped around his middle. He was drinking a cup of coffee when Will and Gid, stepped into the his room at the doctor's office.

"Scooter, how are you doing?" Will asked.

"Well, I've had days when I felt better."

Despite the seriousness of the moment, Will smiled at the young man's response.

"What happened, Scooter?"

"We was all havin' us just a normal day, movin' some of the cattle from one range to another where there was new grass, 'n gettin' 'em all bunched up so's we could move 'em down to get 'em all on the train whenever you was ready for 'em. 'N that's when they all come up on us. They was six or seven of 'em, I ain't just real sure. 'N here's the thing of it, see. They was all armed, but 'cause all we was doin' was movin' some cows around, there warn't none of us what was wearin' a gun. All them men just commenced 'a shootin', 'n there wasn't anything we could do about it.

"I was one of the first ones to get hit, so I laid there just real still so they would think I was dead too, then I watched while they took all the cattle."

"Abe was killed?"

"Yes, sir, he was. He was out there with us, 'n he didn't have no gun on neither. Fact is, he was the first one they shot down, liken as if they already know'd that he was in charge."

"Who did it?"

"I heard one of the outlaws talkin', 'n he said he was Damon Boswell."

"Boswell," Will said. "Well, we've certainly heard about him since the day we got here, but I would never have thought he would attack our ranch and steal an entire herd. And he did it in broad daylight and while we were gone."

"How would Boswell have known that we were gone? And how would he have known that Abe was the foreman?" Gid asked.

"I don't know, but he sure as hell did know."

"The marshal said they also killed Moses and

Maria," Will said.

"Yes, sir, they kilt both of 'em, 'n then they took Mrs. Barker with 'em."

"They took Julia?" Will asked, surprised by the comment.

"Yes sir, I seen 'em ridin' out, 'n she was with 'em."

"I wonder why they killed Maria but they took Julia?" Gid asked.

"Think about it, Gid. Julia's a beautiful woman— they are a bunch of men," Will said.

"Oh Lord, that's not good at all, is it?"

Will shook his head. "No. There's no doubt but that they plan to use her. She may wind up wishing she had been killed just like Maria was. It can't be very good for her."

"Scooter, don't you worry about anything, we'll take care of you," Will said.

"Thanks," Scooter said. "And I'm real sorry we lost your herd."

"You don't need to be worrying any about that," Gid said. "We just want you to get better and we'll find Julia and get her back, too."

———

FROM THE DOCTOR'S, Will and Gid visited the undertaker. The bodies of the dead cowboys were still in the morgue as, so far, only three of them had been embalmed.

"What do you want to do with them?" Jed Nunley, the undertaker asked.

"I don't know," Will replied. "Don't they have next of kin?"

"If they do, nobody knows anything about it. Except for Abe Barker. He came down here from Illinois with General Redling, who of course has gone back to Illinois. I sent a telegram to him, telling him what happened, and he asked to have Barker's body sent to him. He'll take care of getting the body to his family."

Will nodded. "Yes, I know the two were very close, and I would expect nothing less from the general. What about the others?"

"Without any known next of kin, the county will pay for them, and they'll wind up in Potters' Field."

"My brother and I thought it might be something like that. Don't bury them in Potters' Field. We'll dig graves out on the hill next to Mrs. Redling. We'll see that they all get a decent burial."

"You're a couple of good men," the undertaker said. "I'll do as you ask."

"Thanks."

"What about the woman?"

"The woman?"

"The Mexican woman."

"Oh, yes, that's Maria, she's our, uh, that is, she was our cook and house keeper. She was from San Antonio, I believe, but she's one of us, now. She'll be buried at Brown Spur, too."

"I'm so very sorry about all this," Nunley said. "I knew a couple of your hands, and they were good boys. At least Stan Mitchell and Walt Chambers were."

"They were all good men," Gid said.

"Mr. Nunley, when you're finished here, can you get the bodies out to ranch?"

"You boys don't worry about a thing, I'll take care of it," Nunley said.

CHAPTER NINETEEN

AFTER LEAVING THE UNDERTAKER, WILL AND GID returned to the marshal's office.

"Scooter said it was Damon Boswell," Will said.

"Yeah, that's what he told me, too. I have to say, that surprises me a little. This isn't normally the kind of thing Boswell does, but Scooter is absolutely certain he heard one of the men say his name was Boswell."

"Could it be that someone is pretending to be Boswell?" Gid asked.

"Why would someone do that?" the marshal asked. "They didn't intend to leave any survivors, so who would they want to fool?"

"That's true," Will said. "What is being done about the murders and the cattle rustling?"

"Sheriff Maddox is raising a posse, and he's authorized me to appoint deputies," Coats replied. "Would you two like to be deputized?"

"Yes, on one condition," Will replied.

"What condition is that?"

"My brother and I have no wish to be part of a posse," Gid said.

"What do you mean, you don't want to be part of a posse?"

"We want the authority as deputies, but we want to work by ourselves. It's our herd that was stolen, it was our men and Maria who were killed, and the woman who was taken, lived on our ranch," Will said.

"But if there are only the two of you, you'll be badly outnumbered," Coats said.

"We've been outnumbered before," Gid said.

"I guess you have been," Coats said. "All right, raise your right hand."

When they were sworn in, the marshal gave them each a badge. "These are deputy city marshal badges," he said, "so they're only good in the county."

"We'll do just as well without a badge," Will said. "And even being deputized doesn't do that much for us, because we don't intend to halt our search at the county line. We're going to go anywhere we have to go to find these bastards."

Coats smiled. "No, I wouldn't think you would be constrained by county lines. And from what I've heard of you two boys, I've no doubt but that you will find them."

After leaving the marshal's office, Will and Gid rode out to their ranch. It was eerily similar to the time they rode out to their family farm to find their parents slain, and the house and out-buildings burned. The difference now, was that the house, barn, bunkhouse and kitchen still stood, untouched.

The house and out-buildings were all empty. There were no horses in the barn, and no cattle in the field. A breath of wind came up then, and pushed a dust-devil across the ground in front of them. In some odd way, it seemed to accentuate the desolation of the ranch.

Although there were no horses in the corral, nor cattle in the fields, there was a milk cow in the barn. There were also a few pigs in the pen, and a dozen or so chickens.

"The cow needs milked," Gid said. "I'd better take care of it."

"Yeah, we're going to have to do something about these pigs and chickens too," Will said. "They're probably starving to death. I need to feed them."

"Yeah, but what are we going to do after we feed them? We plan to get our herd back, don't we? To say nothing of rescuing Julia."

"I've got an idea," Will said.

"What is it?"

"I'm going to see if we can bring Scooter back here, and if we do, we'll need someone to take care of him. Whoever we get, can also look after the livestock."

"That sounds good," Gid said.

"Before we do anything else, let's pay a visit to Chris Dumey to let him know we're going to be gone for a while."

———

WITH THE COW MILKED, and the chickens and pigs fed, they rode over to Chris Dumey's ranch, which was adjacent to the Brown Spur.

Dumey was pumping water when they rode up.

"I thought I might be seeing you two boys," Dumey said. "What happened over at your place was as bad as anything I've seen since the war. It was a couple of my men that found ever' body."

"Yes, that's what Scooter said," Will said. "I wonder if we could visit with you for a little while, and maybe talk to Mark Worley?"

"Sure. Carol Ann just made a fresh pitcher of lemonade a while ago, why don't you boys come on in and have a glass?"

"All right, thanks, we will," Will said.

Both Chris, and Carol Ann commiserated with the Crocketts, not only for the fact that all of their hands were killed, but also because the entire herd of cattle was driven off.

"Where will all those boys be buried?" Chris asked.

"We're bringing them back to be buried at the ranch."

"Maria, too?"

"Yes. We're going to bury them out by Mrs. Redling's grave."

"The general would like that," Carol Ann said. "That's a nice thing for you to do."

"I wonder if we could talk to Mark for a few minutes?" Will asked.

"Sure, come on, we'll go find 'im."

Dumey saddled his horse, then the three of them rode out until they found Mark and two other hands working on a fence.

"Mark, the Crocketts would like to talk to you," Dumey said.

"Yes sir," Mark said, putting down his pliers and coming over to them.

"We're told you're the one who found Scooter," Will said.

"Yes, sir. How's he doin'? Is he still alive?"

"Yes, for what he went through, he doing exceptionally well. The doc thinks he should recover."

Mark smiled. "That's good. Me 'n Scooter have been friends near 'bout ever' since he came to work for the general."

"How is it that you happened to find them?" Will asked.

"Well, I was just ridin' around lookin' for any cows what might have strayed off, when I heard some shootin'. At first I thought it was just someone shootin' off maybe at a snake or somethin', then there commenced to be a lot of shootin' so I knew somethin' was goin' on. I started over toward the Brown Spur, when I saw some men moving all the cows out. They was too far away for me to tell who it was, but I was pretty sure it wasn't anybody from the Brown Spur. So, I waited 'til they were pretty much gone, then I rode on over, 'n that's when I saw ever' one lyin' dead in the field, Mr. Barker, Doodle, Walt, all of 'em. Well, it wasn't all of 'em dead, on account of I saw Scooter movin' so I rode over to check on 'im, 'n saw he was still alive yet."

"When you saw them moving the herd, which way were they going?" Will asked.

"They were goin' west."

"Thanks, you've been a big help. And thanks for getting Scooter into town to the doctor. You saved his life," Gid said.

"I didn't do nothin' anybody else wouldn't a' done. 'N like I said, me 'n Scooter's been friends for a while."

———

"WE WERE TOLD that it was Boswell and his men who did this," Gid said when he, Will and Dumey returned to the house.

"Yes, I've heard the same thing," Dumey said. "Boswell's been a real menace in these parts. Somebody needs to stop him."

"We're going to do just that," Gid said.

"That's a pretty absolute statement," Chris said.

"Absolute is the right word for it," Will said. "Because we are absolutely going to stop him."

"I do hope that you find him, and justice is done," Carol Ann said.

"We will find him, and justice will be done," Gid said. He smiled, a tight, grim smile. "Just what kind of justice, we extract from him, is yet to be decided."

"Whatever you boys do will be fine with me, 'n I expect it will be with anybody who lives in this part of Texas," Chris Dumey said.

"Is it true that they took Julia?" Carol Ann said.

"Yes, I'm afraid it is," Will replied.

"Oh, what a shame." Carol Ann shook her head. "I have to confess that Julia wasn't exactly what I would call a friend, but I can't help but feel sorry for the poor girl. I mean to have been captured by a bunch of ruffians like that, why, I wouldn't wish that on my worst enemy."

———

IT WAS an eerie feeling when they returned to the ranch. With the empty bunkhouse, empty foreman's house, empty barn, and yes, the empty kitchen of the Big House, it took on the appearance of a ghost town.

"You said something about bringing Scooter out here," Gid said.

Will nodded. "Yes, I do want to do that. I think that may help him recover."

"But he's not ready to be on his own, yet, is he?" Gid asked.

"No, he isn't, but we can hire someone to look after him," Will said.

"Who?"

"I don't know, yet," Will said.

"How about Abby?" Gid suggested.

Will smiled. "Damn, Little Brother, that's a pretty good idea."

Gid laughed. "I think Scooter might agree."

"Well, first we'll have to see if Dr. Urban will let him come out here," Will said.

————

WHEN THEY RODE INTO TOWN, they next morning, they went directly to the doctor's office.

"How's our patient doing this morning?" Will asked.

"He's doing quite well, actually," Dr. Urban said. "I got the bullet out, it didn't hit any significant organs, and there's no sign of infection, so I expect a full recovery."

"Good. Then that brings up another question. How would it be if we took him home today?"

"I think it would be good to get him into a more comfortable environment," Dr. Urban said. "That is as long as you don't leave him by himself. He'll have to have someone look after him for quite some time."

"We have someone in mind," Will said. "We'll go see

if we can make the arrangements—then we'll be back for your patient."

From the doctor's office, Will and Gid walked down to John Casey's saloon. As soon as they stepped inside, Kate greeted them warmly.

"It's good to see you two again," she said.

"Gid, entertain the lady, I'm going to speak with John," Will said.

"Entertain me? Now, there's a change. Normally it's my job to entertain you."

"Why don't we entertain one another?" Gid suggested.

Kate laughed. "Sounds like a good idea to me."

Will watched Kate and his brother find an empty table, then he stepped up to the bar and signaled John who came over to him.

"I want you to know that everybody in town is awful sorry about what happened out at the Brown Spur," John said. "Nearly ever'body know'd one or two of them boys that was kilt, most especial Art. And Scooter bein' shot like he was, ever'one's for sure hopin' he gets well."

"Scooter's who we came to talk to you about," Win said.

"Oh, no, he hasn't died, has he?"

"No, he's still alive, and Dr. Urban thinks he's going to pull through."

"Then I'd say that's good news," John said.

"But that's why we're here. I want to talk to you about him."

"What do you mean you want to talk about him? That's what we're doin' right now, isn't it?"

"Yes. But first I want to ask about Abby. We saw her

when we were in Fort Worth the other day. Is she still there or has she come back?" Will asked.

"She's back."

"Good, I'd like to ask your permission for something. We want to bring Scooter home, but we also want to chase down Boswell, and we can't leave Scooter home alone. So, if it's all right with you, we'd like to hire Abby to come out and look after him. I know it would take her away from her job here, but it would only be temporary, until Scooter's on his feet again."

"I don't have a problem with that—that is if it's all right with Abby."

"Thanks."

————

"WHAT DID JOHN SAY?" Gid asked when Will returned to the table.

"What do you mean, what did John say?" Kate asked.

"You'll see in a minute. Could you find Abby, and if she isn't busy, ask her to join us?"

"Sure, honey," Kate replied with an easy smile.

"You think she'll do it?" Gid asked after Kate left the table.

"I don't know why not. She'll be making more money than she is here, and she isn't likely to run into another man who wants to force himself on her."

"That's true," Gid said.

Less than a minute later, Kate returned with Abby in tow.

"Kate said you asked for me," Abby said with a pleased smile.

"I did indeed. Would you join us for a little conversation?"

"Sure, I'll be glad to. What kind of drink do you want?"

"A beer for me, and whatever it is that you want to drink. Oh, and Kate, you may as well get you another one, too."

"Thanks, honey, we'll be right back."

A moment later the two re-joined Will and Gid at their table.

"Abby, I have a proposition for you. Do you know the young man, Scooter Simpson?"

"Oh no," Abby said with a pained expression on his face. "I know he was shot. Did he die?"

"No, no, he didn't die. As a matter of fact, Dr. Urban said he is doing quite well. All he needs now is rest."

"Good, I'm glad to hear that. Scooter is a very nice young man."

"I'm glad you think so. Because we'd like to hire you to come out to the ranch and stay with Scooter until he recovers."

"Oh, but John..."

"I've already spoken to John, and he's all right with the idea." Will smiled. "And I'll pay you more than you're making now."

"Abby, you can't pass that up," Kate said.

A broad smile spread across Abby's face. "Yes," she said enthusiastically. "Yes, I'll do it. When do you want me to start?"

"How about today?"

"I'll pack my clothes and be ready any time you say."

"All right. I'll go talk to Dr. Urban to see if we can pick up Scooter. There's something else. If I bought a buckboard and horse, would you be able to hook it up and drive it to town whenever you would need supplies?"

"Of course, I can do that. I was raised on a farm so I know how to put a harness on and drive a buckboard."

"We've got a milk cow, a couple of pigs and some chickens. Can you take care of them, too?"

Abby smiled. "I said I was raised on a farm."

"Good. I'm going to buy a buckboard and another horse now, and we'll get started as soon as we can get Scooter comfortable."

CHAPTER TWENTY

About half an hour later, Will and Gid, now in their newly purchased buckboard, stopped in front of Dr. Urban's office.

"How's our man doing?" Will asked.

"He's doing pretty well, and he's pleased he's going to get out of here."

"We've come to do just that," Will said. "And we've hired someone to look after him."

"I think Scooter's ready to go," Dr. Urban said.

"We're ready for him," Gid said indicating the pallet they had prepared in the back of the wagon.

"Don't be in too much of a rush to get him home," Dr. Urban said. "He doesn't need to be jostled a lot—could open his wound and he'd be right back here with me."

With support, Scooter was able to walk out to the buckboard, but climbing into it was difficult for him, so Gid lifted him and put him in the back. From the doctor's office they drove back down to Casey's Saloon.

"Now this isn't fair, if you two are going in to have a beer without me," Scooter said.

Gid chuckled. "Just hold on, you'll see how fair we are."

Gid waited at the buckboard with Scooter, while Will went inside. A moment later he came back out with Abby, who was carrying a grip. There was such a stark difference in Abby's appearance that Gid had to look twice to see that it was actually her. Instead of the scanty dresses she had been wearing while at work, she was now wearing a very modest dress. Also, her face was devoid of all makeup. The effect was one of innocence and, Gid thought he had never seen her look more beautiful.

"Scooter, Abby's agreed to be your nurse for a while," Will said, as he helped her up on to the buckboardo, and then put her valise in the back.

"Abby is?" Scooter asked in surprise.

"Hello, Scooter," Abby said, shyly. "I hope you don't mind having me as your nurse."

"No, no, not at all!" Scooter said, enthusiastically. He smiled. "Damn, this was almost worth getting shot."

"Abby, you want to drive?"

Abby chuckled. "You're testing me are you, to see if I really can drive?"

"Not really, it's just if one us had to drive, we'd have to tie our horse on behind."

"No need for that."

Because Abby drove the buckboard very slowly to give Scooter a smooth ride, it took a little longer than normal for them to get to the ranch. Once there, they helped Scooter into the house.

"We thought we'd put you in what was Maria's

room, since it's here on the first floor, and this way you won't have to go up and down the stairs," Will said. "Abby there are four bedrooms upstairs, I have one and Gid has another, so that leaves you two rooms and you can choose whichever one you want."

"Oh, this is such a lovely house," Abby said, as she began walking around, examining it. She stepped into the kitchen. "Oh, my, running water?"

"Yes, you may have noticed the water tower outside. It's kept full by the windmill, and the water flows from the tower to the house. All you have to do is turn the tap," Will said as he showed her how it worked.

"I'd like to try the kitchen out. I hope you don't mind if I fix supper."

"Mind?" Gid said, with a big smile. "Heck, Abby, we're all counting on it, but I have to say, Maria was one of the best cooks I ever knew."

Half an hour later, after a meal of potatoes and eggs cooked together, thickly cut bacon, biscuits, and coffee, Gid wiped his mouth with the table napkin, and pushed his, now empty, plate away.

"Scooter, I have a proposal for you," Gid said. "How about you go with Will, and I'll stay here and let Abby cook for me?"

"Let me think about it for a moment," Scooter said. He smiled, broadly. "Uh, the answer is no. You go chasing Boswell with your brother, I'll stay here with Abby."

"I thought you might say that," Gid said with a laugh.

After supper they retired to the parlor, where Will introduced them to the music box, by playing *Moonlight Sonata* by Beethoven.

Later that night, as Abby lay in bed looking at the moon shadows cast upon the wall of her bedroom, she marveled at her good luck, and had the, perhaps irrational, wish that she would never have to go back to the saloon.

———

As ABBY SLEPT, the dream returned. It was more of a nightmare than it was a dream, and what made it particularly bad, was that the dream was true, in that it was the recalling of Abby's actual experiences. Once again, she was on a farm just outside Blytheville, Arkansas.

Abby's father had died when she was twelve. By the time she was fourteen, her mother had remarried to a man named Jed Garner. Abby had blossomed into womanhood at a young age. At first, she was too naïve to understand why she felt uncomfortable around her step-father, but as she grew older, she understood fully.

Jed Garner was always looking at her with what she came to understand were lustful glances, before she even knew the word lust. Then, when she was sixteen, it happened. Her mother was absent from the house, and she thought Garner was, too. But Garner came into her bedroom while she was dressing for school.

Abby was still half naked, and she tried to cover herself. "What...what are you doing here?" she asked in a frightened tone.

"Oh, I think you know what I have in mind," Garner said.

"Please, go away. Please, go away and leave me alone."

"No, not this time, dearie. You've teased me, and

taunted me for the last time. Now you're going to have to make good on those promises."

"I don't understand. I've made no promises."

Garner reached her in two quick steps, then jerked the camisole down, exposing her small, but well-formed breasts.

"Please, no!"

Despite her pleas, Garner took her virginity, doing so in a way that left her in pain and humiliation.

"If you tell your mother about this it will destroy her," Garner said. "Do you really want to do that? Now, get on to school before you're late."

Abby knew where Garner kept what he called his operating money, and before she left for school, she took one hundred dollars and left home. She had never been back, nor had she ever been in contact with her mother, since that day.

———

WHEN ABBY AWAKENED the next morning, it took her a moment or two to realize that she wasn't in her room over the saloon. She was in a big, beautiful home, not as a prostitute, but as a paid nurse. Smiling at her good fortune, she got dressed quickly, then went downstairs to start breakfast for the young man she would be taking care of.

Dare she hope that her life had taken a favorable turn?

———

Dido, Texas

BOSWELL, and the men with him, drove the stolen cattle from Brown Spur to what had once been a thousand-acre ranch just outside the small town of Dido. Garrison Coker, the owner of the ranch had agreed to make his land available for five hundred dollars, and ask no questions. Almost from the moment they arrived, the Boswell gang began changing the brand. The original brand was a spur, which Boswell closed to make into an oblong circle. Then the spur barb was lengthened so that a line ran all the way through the circle to protrude on the other side, creating the brand Boswell called the Circle Bar.

"Boswell, how are we going to get rid of these cattle?" Draco asked.

"I will be taking care of that," Boswell said. "There is a cattle dealer over in the next county who is willing to give us twenty dollars a head for them."

"Twenty dollars a head?" Draco challenged. "Damn, they're worth a hell of a lot more'n that, ain't they?"

"Yes, they are, and this offer will be accepted only as a last resort. I'm going to be looking around for some other options, and I'm sure we will be able to beat the offer," Boswell said.

"They would be for sure if we delivered them to the market in Kansas City," Weasel said.

"I agree. However, under the circumstances, that wouldn't be prudent. The best way to handle any stolen product is to expedite the procedure so that you keep it in your hands for as little time as possible. Even if we only get twenty dollars a head, that would be fifty thousand dollars, and you must admit, that would be a payroll of some significance."

"Yeah," Draco said. "Yeah, that would be. By the way, how's the woman doin'?"

"The status of the woman is none of your concern," Boswell said. "I will handle that."

"I just bet you will," Draco replied, the smile growing even broader.

"You would be better served, Mr. Draco, by returning to the task of branding the cattle," Boswell said, his words cold, and commanding.

"You're right. I'd better, uh, get back to the brandin'," Draco said.

Boswell watched Draco return to the pasture where the branding was taking place, then he stepped into the line shack he had set up as his headquarters. Julia Barker was sitting in a chair by the window.

"What's going to happen to me now?" she asked.

"Don't you worry about that, my dear. I have plans," Boswell replied. "You just sit tight, I'll be back in a few days."

"Yes, well, what else can I do but sit tight?" Julia asked.

Boswell chuckled. "A lady with a sense of humor. I like that."

———

Wichita Falls, Texas

WICHITA FALLS WAS A CATTLE COMMUNITY, about one hundred miles northeast of Saginaw. Because it was a center for cattle ranching, and was a good distance from Brown Spur Ranch, it seemed to Boswell, to be the ideal location for the next stage of his plan.

When he arrived in Wichita Falls, he rode through the town looking for any sign of a lawyer's office. Then, on the corner of 10th and Westlake, he saw what he was looking for. There was a small, brick building with the sign:

ROBINSON AND CRADER
Attorneys at law

Boswell checked in to a nearby hotel, then changed from the denim trousers and chambray shirt he was wearing, to a business suit, and derby hat. Checking his image in the mirror, he decided that he looked the part, so he left the hotel, walked down to the lawyers' office, then stepped inside.

"May I help you, sir?" the question came from a young man who was sitting behind a desk.

"Yes, I would like to speak with one of your attorneys who has a good base of knowledge of the cattle business."

The man smiled. "Well, sir, we are surrounded by cattle ranches, so either Mr. Robinson, or Mr. Crader would be able to help you."

"Very well then, just choosing arbitrarily here, I would like to speak with Mr. Crader."

"Who may I say is calling, sir?"

"The name is Elmer Whitley."

"Very good, sir. Just wait here for a moment and I will announce your presence to Mr. Crader."

"Thank you."

The young man left his desk for less than a minute, then he returned. "Mr. Crader will see you, sir. If you would go down this little hall, his office is the second door on the left."

Boswell followed the directions, then tapped lightly on the door to Crader's office.

"Come in, come in," he heard from inside.

When Boswell stepped into the office, Crader was already standing to receive him. Crader was about three inches under six feet tall, with dark hair that was just peppered with a touch of gray, and a well-trimmed Van Dyke beard. Boswell estimated Crader's age to be somewhere in his late forties or early fifties.

"David Crader at your service, sir. You are Mr. Whitley?"

"Yes, Elmer Whitley of Whitley, Whitley, and Dunn. We are a legal firm in Dallas."

"Hmm, I don't think I'm familiar with that firm."

"That's understandable, we only established our practice a few months ago."

"I see. So, what can I do for you today, Mr. Whitley?"

"Our firm represents Mrs. Jason Critchlow. She is a recent widow, who has come into possession of the Circle Bar Ranch. When her husband died, he left her, not only the ranch, but a little over twenty-five hundred head of cattle. She doesn't want to ranch; indeed, she doesn't even want to stay around Dallas. She has family in Philadelphia, and wishes to return there."

"And your reason for coming to see me?"

"She wants to sell her entire herd, and as her husband, while he was alive, was one of our earliest clients, we were hoping that you might be able to connect me with a potential buyer. She is prepared to sell the cattle at a price that would make the purchase of the herd quite profitable for the buyer."

Crader smiled. "You came to the right place, because

I know just the buyer for you. Have you had your lunch yet?"

"No, I just arrived."

"Come, we'll have lunch together, and discuss the details. You do intend to use me as your consulting attorney?"

"Indeed, I do," Boswell said with a smile. "After all, it is we lawyers who grease the wheels of business, is it not?"

Crader laughed out loud. "Grease the wheels of business. Yes, I like that. I like that a lot."

They discussed the business transaction over lunch and Crader agreed to find a buyer for him, for ten percent of the transaction.

"Very well, but you do understand that your ten percent will be taken from the sum that remains *after* my ten percent," Boswell said.

"Yes, yes, I do agree to that. Now, come with me, I have just the buyer for you."

———

ABOUT TEN MILES west of Wichita Falls, Crader took Boswell to meet with Burt Rowe, the owner of the Paradise Ranch. Rowe was a lean man, sun-browned, and with intense gray eyes. He looked more like a ranch hand, than a ranch owner.

"You say you're willing to offer me your cattle at a price that will give me an immediate profit. What are you asking?"

"Mrs. Critchlow has around twenty-five hundred head of Hereford cattle, and she is willing to sell them for thirty-five dollars a head."

"Thirty-five dollars a head? Why man, the last price I heard for Herefords was forty-five dollars a head," Rowe said, surprised to hear the offer.

Boswell smiled. "Yes, Mr. Rowe. That means you stand to make an immediate profit of twenty-five thousand dollars if you accept this offer."

"Who else have you made this offer to?" Rowe asked.

"Only to you, so far, Burt," Crader said. "You were the first one I thought of when Mr. Whitley came to see me."

"But why would Mrs. Critchlow agree to such a thing?"

"The ranch was her husband's dream, not hers," Boswell said. "Now that he has died, she wants nothing more to do with the cattle business. She wants to sell the entire herd, then live out the rest of her days without the stress of cattle business. And the money she will get from this transaction will allow her to do just that."

"Will I have to bring the herd here?" Rowe asked.

Boswell shook his head. "No, and that's the beauty of it. The cattle will be delivered to you."

"When?"

"There are some details that we still have to attend to, but as soon as all the legalities are seen to, the herd will be delivered to you. I only ask that you have the money ready, immediately upon transfer of the cattle to you. Mrs. Critchlow is quite anxious to return to her relatives," Boswell said.

A broad smile spread across Rowe's face, and he extended his hand. "You tell Mrs. Critchlow that she has a deal."

"Thank you," Boswell said. "She will be most

relieved. You have done a fine deed for a wonderful old lady."

"Believe me, Mr. Whitley, for twenty-five thousand dollars, it's easy enough to do a fine deed for an old lady."

Boswell laughed. "To be sure."

CHAPTER TWENTY-ONE

Brown Spur Ranch

"I THINK MARIA KEPT A PRETTY FULL KITCHEN, SO YOU shouldn't have to go into town right away," Will said. "But if you do have to buy more supplies, I've arranged for Mr. Rafferty to extend credit for anything you might need."

"Thank you," Abby said.

Will looked over at Scooter, who was sitting on the sofa. "Scooter, all we'll expect from you is to rest up, and get well."

"Yes, sir, that's just what I intend to do," Scooter said.

"You said they were taking the herd west?" Gid asked.

"Yes, sir, as much as I could see. At least that was the direction they started out in," Scooter answered.

"All right then, that's where we'll start as well," Will said.

———

HAVING GOTTEN Abby and Scooter settled in, Will and Gid started west, to track their herd, but within ten miles of their ranch they came across the trails of other herds that were being moved north. The others washed out the trail they had been following, so they had no choice but to return to Saginaw. They pulled up in front of the marshal's office, tied their horses off, then stepped inside.

"You get Scooter taken care of?" Marshal Coats asked.

"Yeah, we got Abby to go out to the ranch and stay with him."

Marshal Coats laughed. "I'll bet Scooter complained about that."

"No, at least not so as you would notice," Gid said with a wide smile.

"No, I wouldn't think so," Coats said. "So, now that you lost all your cows, what are you going to do now?"

"We're going to find our cows," Will said, resolutely.

———

Dido, Texas

"DAMN," Weasel said as he and the others were watching over the Brown Spur herd of cows. "We've had to drive these critters here, then brand ever' damn one of 'em, 'n now we're havin' to ride herd on 'em. This ain't no different from when I was cowboyin', 'n I swore when I left that I wasn't goin' to cowboy no more."

"Yeah?" Draco said. "Now, tell me again, Weasel, how much money was you makin' while you was cowboyin'?"

"Same as most other cowboys make. Twenty dollars a month, and found."

"Uh huh. Well, I've ciphered out what each of us is goin' to get from this here operation. We'll be gettin' over six thousand dollars apiece. You think you could make that much cowboyin'?"

Weasel smiled, and shook his head. "No, I don't reckon I could."

"Then this kind of cowboyin' ain't all that bad, is it?"

"No, it ain't," Weasel agreed. "Onliest thing is, when are we goin' to be a' getting' that money?"

"Soon as Boswell makes all the arrangements for the sellin' 'n such," Draco said.

"I thought he already had the cows sold. Where is he, anyway?"

"I don't know. Gettin' things all arranged, I reckon."

———

AT THAT EXACT MOMENT, Boswell was in the Pretty Girl and Happy Cowboy Saloon in Wichita Falls. He was sitting at a table with four men, who had been suggested as the kind of men he wanted, when he put the word out that he was looking for men who were particularly good with a gun. He had looked up the background of each of the men before he invited them to meet with him.

Mug Harris was thirty-seven and his body count was said to be twelve. Mug was a big man whose face was disfigured by a puffy scar on his left cheek, the result of a prison knife fight that had left him permanently scarred. That same fight had left his opponent permanently dead.

Crack Kingsley was forty-two. He was bald, and had a wandering eye so that when anyone was having a conversation with him, he wasn't sure whether he was looking at you or not. He had killed nine men, not all of them with a gun. Crack was an exceptionally large man, considerably over six feet tall, and around 240 pounds. He had a heavy brow that gave his face an ape-like appearance.

Jeter McComb was believed to be in his late twenties. He had been abandoned when he was but a toddler, and the family that took him in had no idea how old he was, so they just arbitrarily gave him an age. They let him know, quite young, that he wasn't really their child, and they treated him like an unwelcomed guest in their home, working him as if he were their personal slave. Jeter killed both of them when he was fifteen, and had been on his own since then.

The last of the four was Eddie "The Kid" Streeter. Eddie the Kid claimed to be twenty-three, but he was actually nineteen. He was exceptionally fast with a gun, and had provoked many into drawing against him. He had killed eleven men, and what set him apart from the others in the little group of men that Boswell had gathered, was that Eddie the Kid actually enjoyed killing.

Boswell looked around to make certain he wasn't overheard, then in a quieter voice, he told them what he wanted.

"Gentlemen, have any of you heard of the brothers, Will and Gid Crockett?"

"I've heard of 'em," Eddie the Kid said.

"Me, too," Crack said.

The other two didn't respond.

"What about them?" Crack asked.

"They have become well, shall we say, worrisome to me. I have a business deal underway, and I fear that the Crockett Brothers may become an impediment to the successful completion of the deal. Therefore, I think the only solution would be to eliminate them. Both of them."

"What do mean when you say you want them eliminated?" Jeter asked.

"He means he wants 'em both kilt," Mug Harris said.

Boswell nodded.

"How much are you willin' to pay to have that done?" Harris asked.

"I will give each of you two hundred and fifty dollars now. If you work together and you are successful in bringing about their demise, I will pay another fifteen hundred dollars for each of the two brothers. That would leave each of you a thousand dollars."

"If we bring about their what?" Eddie the Kid asked.

"He means if we kill 'em, you damned fool," Harris said.

"Yes, Mr. Harris is quite correct."

"Gentlemen, from this point forward, it is all in your hands."

———

Brown Spur Ranch

"I DIDN'T THINK you'd be able to track the herd," Scooter said. "It's been too long now."

"That's true, but twenty-five hundred head of cattle

won't be that easy to hide. And the cattle are no good to them, unless they can sell them," Will said.

"Scooter, while you were laying there after you were shot, did you hear anything that might be of some use to us?" Gid asked.

"No, nothing as where they would be taking the herd. But I did hear some of their names mentioned, other than Boswell's name I mean."

"That might be useful," Will said. "What are the names."

"Draco, Sloan, and Weasel. I couldn't see to tell who was who, but I did hear those names bandied about."

"Thanks, we'll keep those names in mind."

————

WILL and Gid had nothing specific upon which to base their search, so they decided that the best thing to do, would be to visit as many of the neighboring towns as they could. When they rode into Weatherford, the first place they visited was the Weatherford office of the cattlemen's association.

They were greeted by a man who could better be described as skinny, than slender. He had thinning blond hair, and a blond moustache which was so pale that one had to look twice to see it.

"Jefferson Peters is the name," he said. "What can I do for you gentlemen?" he asked.

"I'm Will Crockett, this is my brother, Gid. We're trying to trace a herd of cattle," Will said. "Have you any word of twenty-five hundred head of cattle being offered for sale?"

"I haven't heard of such a transaction. I must say you are on a rather strange quest. Why are you looking for such a specific number?"

"Twenty-five hundred head of cattle were stolen from us, and we're trying to track them down."

"Oh, my, well, I can see why you would be interested in finding them. Unfortunately, as I say, I've heard nothing about them. If by chance I did learn of such a transaction, how would I get hold of you?"

"You could get word to Marshal Percy Coats in Saginaw," Will said.

The clerk wrote the information on a piece of paper. "If I hear anything, I will certainly get word to the marshal."

"Thanks," Will said. "We will appreciate that."

"I hope you find your herd," Peters said.

"We do too," Will said.

From the office of the cattlemen's association, Will and Gid went to the Lonesome Creek Saloon. They had two reasons for doing so, one to wash down the taste of trail dust with a beer, and another to glean any information they could find with regard to someone trying to sell a herd of cattle.

Although they got no information from the saloon, they well knew that saloons were quite often a good source of information.

Two more towns and four more saloons proved no more productive, so it was necessary that they continue their quest.

"How do you know it's the Crocketts?" Mug Harris asked.

"I heard one of 'em called Crockett," Jeter said. "'N besides which, they was a' askin' 'bout anyone what was tryin' to sell a bunch of stoled cows."

"Yeah, well, then that's them, all right," Harris said.

"How we goin' to take 'em? Them boys is know'd to be just real good with guns," Jeter said.

"They's four us, 'n only two o' them," Harris replied. "I can't see as it'll actual be that big of a problem."

"How are we goin' to handle it?" Eddie the Kid asked.

Harris looked across the street toward the saloon, then he smiled. "I know exactly what we'll do."

"What? You want us to go into the saloon?" Kingsley asked, after Harris told what he had in mind.

"No, I'm the only who'll go into the saloon, and I'm goin' to call 'em out. Crack, you stay out here, with me. Kid you 'n Jeter are going to be up there, on the roof. When they come out to face us, you shoot 'em both. And make sure you start in 'ter shootin' a'fore they do. Just make sure you don't shoot me 'n Crack."

"Ha, we ain't goin' to shoot you. Why would we do that, we ain't gettin' paid nothin' to shoot you two," Jeter teased.

"Good, you just make sure you remember that," Harris said.

After laying out his instructions to the others, Harris pushed through the bat wing doors, then took a look around the saloon. He saw a couple of men standing over by a table where four men were playing cards. One of the two was a big, strong-looking man who fit the description he had heard of Gid Crockett.

"Hey, you," Harris called out. When both of the men looked over toward him, Harris spoke again.

"I hear you two men are lookin' for a herd of stoled cows."

"That's right," the smaller of the two men replied. "Do you have any information we can use?"

"Why the hell would I want to tell you where you can buy stoled cows? Someone who'd buy stoled cows is as guilty as the son of a bitch that stoled them in the first place."

"You've got it all wrong, Mister," Will said. "It was our cows that were stolen, and we're just trying to find them."

"Oh yeah? Well I say you're a lyin' son of a bitch," Harris said.

"Mister, that's awfully dangerous language to be using with someone you don't even know," Will said in a flat emotionless tone.

"Oh, I know who you are, Crockett. There ain't hardly nobody that don't know the Crocketts. I've always know'd you was a couple killers, never know'd 'till now that you was also a couple a' cow thieves."

"What's your name?" Will asked.

"The name is Harris. 'N I don't like cow thieves."

"Mister Harris, I told you that it was our herd that was stolen," Will said. "Now why don't you just go on and mind your own business? My brother and I are having a nice conversation here, and we don't have time for a belligerent bastard like you."

"I'm goin' to go outside all right, but I'm tellin' you now that when you come out, I'm goin' to be waitin' for you. We may as well settle this little argument we're havin' here, real permanent like."

Harris turned around, then pushed through the bat wing doors with such force that they swung back and forth a few times. The people in the saloon stared at the swinging doors in stunned silence.

"What the hell do you think that was all about?" Gid asked. "I never saw anyone get so mad, so fast, and for no reason."

"He wasn't mad," Will said.

"What do you mean he wasn't mad? He just said he wanted a permanent settlement with you, and to my way of thinking, that means he wants to kill you."

"Yes, but wanting to kill us has nothing to do with his argument."

"What do you mean kill us? You're the one he was arguing with."

"That wasn't a real argument, Little Brother. For some reason, we're being set up."

"Set up?"

"Whoever took our cattle is trying to take us out of the picture before we can get to them. And they have an advantage, because it's easier for them to find us, than it will be for us to find them."

Another man came into the saloon then, and seeing everyone so quiet, hesitated for a moment before stepping up to the bar.

"What's goin' on here?" he asked. "Does it have somethin' to do with them two men that's up on the roof?"

"There are two men on the roof?" Will asked.

"I'll say. They look like they're on guard or somethin' 'cause they was both holdin' guns. I almost didn't come in."

"Bartender, is there a back way out of this place?" Will asked.

"Through that door by the piano," the bartender said. "The hallway leads to a back door."

"Come on, Gid," Will said.

CHAPTER TWENTY-TWO

"I've heard of the Crocketts, but I never would 'a thought they was cowards," someone in the saloon said, after Will and Gid left.

"Hell, they ain't cowards, they're just smart," the bartender replied. "Would you want to go out there knowin' they was someone waitin' up on the roof to shoot you in your back?"

"I reckon not."

————

Will and Gid, were in the alley behind the saloon.

"What do we do now, Big Brother?" Gid asked.

"We're going up on the roof to see what those two men are doing up there."

Gid smiled. "Sounds like a plan to me."

There was a ladder attached to the back of the building and Will and Gid made use of it so that they quickly reached the flat roof. There they saw two men hiding behind the false front of the building. Both of them were holding guns, and they were looking down toward the street.

"You men looking for something?" Will asked.

Startled, the two men spun around toward Will and Gid.

"Damn, it's them! Shoot 'em, Kid, shoot 'em!" the larger of the two men shouted. Both men fired at Will and Gid, but, startled and frightened, they hurried their shots. As a result, they missed. Will and Gid returned fire, Will taking the man on the left, and Gid the one on the right. Will hit his man right in the center of his nose, and he saw a spray of blood and brain matter explode from the back of his head. Gid shot twice, both his bullets hitting his man in the middle of his chest. He went down to join the one Will had put down.

As Will and Gid approached the two ambushers, now prostate on the roof, they heard a shout from the street.

"Jeter, Kid, what's goin' on up there?" A voice called up from the street. Will recognized it as the voice of the man who had identified himself as Harris, who had challenged him in the saloon.

Will peered over the corner of the apron of the false front, and he saw two men standing in the middle of the street. He recognized Harris, but not the other man.

"I'm afraid the men you're yelling at won't be able to answer you, seeing as they're both dead. But if you two will just wait until my brother and I can get down there, we can continue our conversation about some stolen cows."

"What'll we do with these two?" Gid asked.

"Just leave them here for now."

"WHAT THE HELL, Harris? They kilt both of 'em," Kingsley said. "I'm gettin' outta here."

"No, Kingsley, wait! Don't you see? Now that them two's dead, that means we'll get their share," Harris said.

"You can't pay me enough to get myself kilt," Kinglsey said, and turning, he ran from the middle of the road.

Harris, realizing now that he was alone, left as well, so that by the time Will and Gid reached the street, both men were gone.

"I wonder what that was all about?" Will asked, as he and Gid stood in the middle of the empty street.

"Don't you figure it was just someone wantin' to make a name for themselves by shootin' us down?" Gid asked.

Will shook his head. "No, I think it was more direct than that. It's like I said, earlier. I think this may have something to do with our cows. I'm pretty sure this operation was planned by Boswell. He has to know we're coming after him and he's trying to get rid us before we can track him down."

"Now that you mention it, the man who came into the saloon was talking about stolen cattle." Gid replied. "So what do we do now?"

"We keep looking."

While Will and Gid were standing there, with their guns still drawn, they saw two men walking toward them. Neither one of them was holding a gun, so, as they represented no immediate danger, Will and Gid holstered their own pistols.

"You fellas want to tell me what this was all about?"

one of the men asked, and as the men drew closer, Will and Gid saw that both of them were wearing badges.

"We're trying to figure that out ourselves," Will said. "Apparently there were four men who wanted to kill us."

"Four?"

"Yes, two of them are up on the roof of the saloon."

"Up on the roof?"

"Yes, they're dead," Gid said.

"Did you kill them?"

"We did."

"Who are you?"

"I'm Will Crockett, this is my brother Gid."

"The Crocketts, huh? I've heard of you two. I'm Bill Ferrell, this is my deputy, Pete Conrad. How about you two fellas come down to my office, so we can talk about this?"

"All right."

"Pete, why don't you go down to the undertaker 'n tell Goff about the two men up on the roof?"

"You goin' to arrest these two men?" his deputy asked.

"No, I'm goin' to give 'em a cup of coffee. These here are the Crocketts, 'n if they kilt someone, then they more 'n likely needed killin'."

Pete smiled. "All right, I'll get the two bodies took care of."

"Now, why do you think these men were after you?" Ferrell asked. "You say there were four of 'em?"

"Yes, two up on the roof, and then two in the street. They left before we could come down from the roof," Will said.

Ferrell chuckled. "Yes, well, I can see why. If they

started out with four, and you kilt two right away, it was prob'ly smart of 'em to run. How did this thing get started, anyway?"

"They started it in the saloon, or actually, only one of them did. He invited us outside, but before we went outside, someone came in and said there were two armed men on the roof. We went up to see what they were doing, and when we spoke, they turned and fired. Then, we saw that there were two more down in the street, but like I said, by the time we got down off the roof, the two men down here were gone."

"Do you have any idea who they might have been?"

"We heard the ones in the street called Harris and Kingsley."

"Harris? A big man, with a scar on his face?"

"He was a big man, and I do believe I saw a scar on his face."

"That would be Mug Harris. I don't recognize the other name. What was it?"

"Kingsley."

"Which gets back to my question, why do you think they were comin' for you?"

"Most likely, on account of our stolen cattle," Gid said.

Marshal Ferrell snapped his fingers. "Oh, yes, I remember now, I got a message from Sheriff Maddox over in Saginaw. You had an entire herd stolen from you and all your hands were killed. You think these men had something to do with it?"

"Not all of our hands were killed. One is still alive, and he told us that it was Damon Boswell and his men who stole the cattle."

"These men you killed—were they part of Boswell's gang?"

"I don't know. Harris called up to the two men on the roof. He called one Jeter, and the other one Kid. Jeter and the Kid, might be part of the Boswell gang, but the only names we can put with him for sure, are Draco, Sloan, and somebody called Weasel."

"I've heard of those names. What makes you think they are with Boswell?"

"One of our hands was shot, but he wasn't killed, and while he was lying there, he heard the rustlers talking," Will said. "That's how we know it was Boswell. Scooter also remembers hearing the names Draco, Sloan, and Weasel."

Ferrell nodded his head. "That figures. Pete Draco, Arnie Sloan, and nobody know's what Weasel's real name is. They're wanted for murder, all of 'em. Fact is, ever' one who's runnin' with Boswell is wanted for murder, 'cause they don't often leave anyone alive after one of their jobs."

"Are you going to need us to hang around for anything?" Will asked.

"Not really, I'll talk to a few people in the saloon to see if they can add anything. But I'm sure there won't be any need to hold you."

"Then, if you don't mind, I think my brother and I are going to go on looking for Boswell," Will said. "If he set this all up, he has to be somewhere in the area."

"I hope you find 'im, and I hope you get your cows back," Ferrell said. "But, even if you don't find your cows, there's a fifteen-thousand-dollar reward for Boswell, and I think at least a thousand more for anyone that can be proven to be a part of his gang."

"That's nice to know," Will said, "but what we want is to find our herd."

"Especially when they aren't our cows to begin with," Gid said.

"What?"

"When we bought the ranch from Ben Redling, he left his cattle with us for us to sell for him."

"I see why you'd especially want to get 'em back. I suspect it'd cost you a pretty penny if you've lost somebody else's herd."

"We'll get them back," Will said with determination.

"You know what might help?" Ferrell asked.

"What?"

"If you'd stay here, at least for another day, to see if we can find out who Jeter and the feller they called the Kid are, that might give you a lead toward Boswell."

"Thanks," Gid said. "What do you say, Will? Maybe we should hang around for another day or two."

CHAPTER TWENTY-THREE

Brown Spur Ranch

BACK AT THE BROWN SPUR RANCH, ABBY AND SCOOTER were just sitting down to their noon meal of fried chicken.

"I hope you feel like eating, Abby said. "You'll need to eat, to get your strength back."

"It's not hard to eat when you can sit down to a meal like this. You make good fried chicken," Scooter said. "Why is it that anyone who cooks as good as you do would have to...uh," Scooter paused in mid-sentence, realizing that to carry his thought any further could hurt her feelings. "What I mean is you're a real good cook."

"What you mean is, you're wondering why am I a whore," Abby said.

"Abby, I'm sorry, I had no right to—"

"It's Anna."

"What?"

"My name isn't Abby. It's Anna. Anna Wilson. I grew

up in Blytheville, Arkansas, and left home when..." Anna paused for a moment, then continued, "when something unpleasant happened. But I'd rather not talk about it."

"That's all right, you don't have to say anything," Scooter said.

Anna smiled at him. "On the other hand, since I left, you're the only one I've ever told my real name."

"Damn," Scooter said with a big smile. "You tellin' me your real name, now that's somethin' ain't it? That's really somethin'. Thanks for doin' that."

"What about you? Is Scooter your real name?"

"No, my real name is Preston, but I don't like that name, so please don't tell anybody what it really is."

"All right, if you don't want to be called Preston, that'll be our little secret. I'll just call you Scooter." Anna chuckled. "Anyhow, I like the name Scooter. I think it's cute."

"Cute? H'mm, I don't know as if I ever thought of it as cute."

Anna smiled at him, and as she did so, a dimple appeared in her cheeks. It was funny, Scooter thought, he had seen her many times at Casey's Saloon, and he had thought she was pretty then. But here, sitting at the same table with him, not in a saloon but in a house and wearing a dress that was much less revealing than the way he normally saw her, he was prepared to say that she was beautiful.

It wasn't until then that he realized she was speaking to him.

"What?" he asked.

"I was just asking you, if you had always been a

cowboy?" Anna asked. "What I mean is did you grow up on a ranch?"

"No, ma'am, I grew up in Newport News, Virginia, and I went to sea when I was twelve."

"You went to sea at twelve? Isn't that a little young?"

"It wasn't too young to be a cabin boy," Scooter said.

"What did you do as a cabin boy?"

"I helped the cook in the galley and carried meals to the seamen in the mess deck and to the officers in their quarters aft. I also carried messages back and forth between officers and the rest of the crew. Sometimes I would go aloft to stow sails with the crew, but what I liked best was when the weather was good, the helmsman would often let me steer the ship.

"Like I said, I started out as a cabin boy, but by the time I was sixteen, I was what you call an able-bodied seaman."

"Able bodied?" Anna asked with a little chuckle. "That's a strange thing to say. What does that mean? Does it mean you aren't crippled or something?"

Scooter laughed. "I guess it does sound a little strange to a landlubber."

"Are you calling me a landlubber?"

"I guess I am."

"What's a landlubber? Is that something bad?"

"No, it's just what sailors call people who've never gone to sea."

"Like me," Anna said.

Scooter chuckled again. "Yeah, like you. But most landlubbers aren't," he paused in mid-sentence.

"Most landlubbers aren't what?"

"Most landlubbers aren't as pretty as you are."

Anna smiled. "Now you're making me self-conscious."

"I'm sorry."

"Don't apologize. I think it's sweet," Anna said. "Oh, you were going to tell me what an able body was."

"An able-bodied seaman is a sailor who is a member of the deck department. You don't get to be an able-bodied seaman unless you have more than two years' experience at sea and can show the ship's officers that you know what you're doing."

"What kind of things do you do as person whose body is able?"

Scooter laughed. "It doesn't have anything to do with whether or not your body is able. It's just what they call a sailor that's not an officer or anything. But, as for what an AB does..."

"AB?"

"Yeah, sometimes we were called AB instead of able bodied. And as for what we do, well, we may stand a watch, scrub the deck, row the captain's boat

or any of those things."

"Oh, my, that sounds exciting," Anna said. "Where did you go?"

"I went just about ever' where," Scooter replied. "I went to England, and France a few times. And I sailed around the horn and across the Pacific to Hawaii, Guam, the Philippines, Hong Kong and Japan."

"That sounds like such an adventure. Why would you ever give up something like that?"

Scooter thought about his friend, Ed Bivens, and how it was that he got killed, but he didn't mention that. He sensed that Anna was enjoying the conversation, and talking about Ed Bivens falling from one of the ship's masts and crashing head first into the deck would put a pall over what was a pleasant conversation.

"It sounds like more fun than it actually is. Yeah, you get to see all these places that I told you about, but most of the time you see them only from the deck, when the ship is in harbor. And no matter how big the ship is, it gets really small when it's the only thing you see for months on end. And when it's a really heavy sea, even the most experienced sailors can get sick, and believe me, there is nothing more uncomfortable than to be sea sick around a bunch of other people who are also sea sick." Scooter chuckled. "Truth to tell, I'm nearly gettin' sea sick now, just for the tellin' of it."

Anna laughed. "Oh heavens, hush. You're making me sea sick too, and I don't even know what sea sick is."

"Trust me, it's not anything you ever want to be."

"So, how did you wind up on a ranch?"

"Gerald Kelly," Scooter said.

"What? Or should I ask who? Who is Gerald Kelly?"

"Kelly was an old sailor who had been to sea for over fifty years. He was always threatening to leave the ship before the next voyage. He said he was going to go ashore with an anchor on his shoulder, and start walking inland until he got to a place where someone would ask him what that thing was he was carryin'. That way, he figured, he'd be far enough away from the sea that he would never be tempted to sign on for another voyage."

Now it was Anna's time to laugh. "So, Scooter, are you telling me you actually walked around with an anchor on your shoulder, and that's how you wound up here?"

"No, what I did was get a map of the United States,

close my eyes, then circled my finger around a few times, and put it down on the map. When I opened my eyes, it was in this part of Texas, so I came out here and got a job riding for the Brown Spur brand."

"Do you miss the sea?"

"At first I did, but as I got used to cowboyin', I found out that I liked it, and I knew I would never go back." Scooter chuckled. "Even gettin' shot has worked out all right, because I got to meet you."

"What do you mean, you got to meet me? You already knew me, silly. You met me before you were shot," Anna said.

Scooter grinned, and shook his head. "No ma'am, the person I met was Abby. I never met Anna, until after I was shot."

At those words, Anna felt a charge of emotion, unlike anything she had ever felt before. She blushed slightly, then she cleared her throat. "Yes, well, Anna is telling you to eat your dinner. You have to get your strength built up again."

"Yes, ma'am," Scooter said with what was now, a boyish smile.

Anna was glad to see that Scooter ate well, then after the meal she helped him into the bedroom off the kitchen. It was an exceptionally clean and neat room, though it was relatively small, compared to the four bedrooms upstairs. This was a perfect room for Scooter though, because he wasn't in any condition to climb the stairs.

"You get some rest," Anna said.

"Where are you going to be?"

"Well, I'm going to wash the dishes, feed the chickens, gather some eggs, a few things like that."

Scooter laughed.

"What's funny about that?" Anna asked, puzzled by his laughter.

"It's just that, here we are together in this house, just the two of us, and you're doing all these house chores. Why, it's sort of like we're married, isn't it?"

Anna laughed too, but it was sort of a reserved laugh. "Oh, I wouldn't go so far as to say that," she said. "It's more like I'm a nurse and you're my patient."

"If you say so," Scooter said. "But I think it's better the way I think about it."

"Hush, and try and get some sleep," Anna said, feeling a slight flush.

Anna closed the bedroom door, then went into the kitchen to draw some water, then heat it on the stove so she could do the dishes.

As Anna stood there, waiting for the water to start to boil, she couldn't explain how she felt, or why she felt that way. It wasn't like she was some naïve, virginal young girl dealing with something beyond her ken. She thought of how she managed to wind up here in this place, and at this time.

———

ANNA'S first job after leaving home was washing dishes in a restaurant, for which she was paid two dollars a week, plus meals. She worked there for two months, then she quit because Fred, the owner of the restaurant, told her that if she didn't have sex with him, he would fire her.

There was a woman who occasionally came to the bar named Ellie. Ellie was always dressed well, and always had money. She was always very friendly, and gradually, Anna got to know her better. Then on the day Anna was fired, she had left the restaurant in tears. Ellie happened to be in the restaurant that day, so she followed Anna outside.

"What happened?" Ellie asked.

Anna told her of Fred's ultimatum.

"If you don't mind my asking, what is Fred paying you?"

"Two dollars a week."

"Two dollars a week? How would you like to make two dollars a day?"

"Two dollars a day?" Anna asked, shocked at such a large amount of money.

"Oh, that would be a minimum. On the weekends, you could make as much as five dollars a day."

"Where would I find a job that pays that much money?"

"You could work for me. And in addition to what you'd be making, your food and a room would be furnished."

"Working for you? But, what do you do?"

"You really don't know, do you?"

"No, ma'am."

"I manage a house, where young women visit with men. You're young and pretty. If you decided to come work for me, I have a feeling you'd do quite well. You'd make considerably more than two dollars a day."

"What would I have to do?"

"Men would pay to go to bed with you."

"Go to bed?"

"Honey, are you a virgin?" Ellie asked.

Anna blushed, then looked down. "No, I...uh...that's

why I'm here. My stepfather, he...he had his way with me. After that I left, because I was afraid he might do it again."

"Are you saying you were raped?"

"Yes, ma'am."

"If you come to work for me, you'll be with men, but I only allow men who are gentlemen to visit my girls. You won't be raped, but you will be expected to have sex with the gentlemen."

"You mean I would be a prostitute?"

"We don't like to use that word, but, yes, that's what you would be expected to do."

"I...I don't know."

"I'll give you a few days to think about it. If you decide you would like to join us, come visit me at my house. I'll introduce you to the other girls. Think of it as a family. They'll be like your sisters, and they'll treat you well."

That was how Anna got started in the business, and that was where she took on the name, Abby. From Memphis, Anna went to New Orleans, then Fort Worth, and now in Saginaw.

Except that she wasn't in Saginaw now—now she was in a big house, taking care of a nice, friendly young man. And she couldn't help but wonder if anything might come from this.

No, she decided. She wouldn't allow herself to even think of such a thing. Regardless of how innocent she had been when she entered into the profession, she was now a prostitute. She was a whore.

———

LESS THAN TWELVE feet away from Ann, Scooter was having his own thoughts about Anna. She was a very pretty girl, yes, but for some strange reason, Scooter wasn't even thinking about how pretty she was.

Scooter was thinking of the tenderness of her touch as she took care of him. He was thinking of her kindness. It was as if she were tending to him, not because she was being hired to do so, but because she actually wanted to.

Was he misreading all of this? He hoped not, he sincerely hoped that she was beginning to have some feelings for him, just as he was for her. But he knew, inherently, that he should keep his own counsel, at least for now.

"Let's face it," he said, speaking aloud to himself. "No woman is ever goin' want to have anything to do with a common cowhand."

"Scooter, did you say something? Do you need something?" he heard Anna call out to him, and was embarrassed that she had heard him talking to himself.

"Uh, no, I was just trying to remember the words to a song we used to sing. It was called a sea shanty."

"Oh? Well, you'll have to sing it to me, sometime."

Scooter chuckled aloud. "Darlin', if I was to sing it to you, you'd run for the hills to get away from the caterwauling."

"Oh, you don't know. You'll have to try it someday."

"We'll see," Scooter replied, simply because he could think of nothing else to say.

CHAPTER TWENTY-FOUR

OVER THE NEXT FEW DAYS, IT WAS A MATTER OF THE Crockett brothers, and the two who had wanted to meet them in street, looking for each other. All Will and Gid had were the names Mug Harris and Kingsley though they didn't know Kingsley's first name. They did know what the two men looked like.

They were convinced that the men were with Boswell, and that he had sent the four men to kill them. So, if they could find Harris or Kingsley, they believed either one of them could lead them to Boswell.

But how were they going to find them? They knew their names and what they looked like, but nothing else. They did the only thing they could do; they continued going from town to town trying to gather any bit of information they could on Mug Harris or Kingsley.

One of the first towns they went to was Whitt, Texas. Whitt was a one – street town, lined on both sides by businesses, from mercantile to saloons. It had a newspaper, the *Whitt Moon*, a church, a stagecoach depot, and a city marshal's office. The marshal's office was their first stop.

When they went in to the office there was a man leaning back in a chair, with his feet on the desk in front of him. He was reading a newspaper so when they first stepped inside, they couldn't see his face.

The man heard them come in through, and when he lowered the paper, they could see the badge.

"You're the city marshal?" Will asked.

"I am. Thompson's the name. Who might you two be?" The marshal was a tall thin man, with a neatly trimmed moustache.

"I'm Will Crockett, and this is my brother, Gid."

"What can I do for you fellers?"

"Marshal, we're looking for two men, one named Mug Harris, the other is named Kingsley, but we don't know his first name. We believe they may be part of the Boswell gang."

"Boswell, yes, ever' body in the country's lookin' for Boswell. What makes you think these two men that you're a' lookin' for, might be part of his gang?"

"We own a ranch down in Saginaw. A few weeks ago, while we were gone, Boswell raided our ranch. He killed all our hands but one and left him half-dead, then he drove off all our cattle. We've been looking for him ever since. Then, a couple of days ago Harris, Kingsley and two other men tried to kill us. We took down two of them, but Harris and Kingsley got away."

"And you don't know Kingsley's first name?

"I'm afraid we don't. The only reason we know these two names is we heard them calling out to each other. And we know Harris's first name because the town marshal had heard of him."

Marshal Thompson shook his head. "I'm afraid I don't know Harris or Kingsley, but you might check with Mike Jensen over at the newspaper. He keeps his eyes and ears open all the time, could be that he could help you."

"Thanks, Marshal, we'll check in with him."

"I hope you find these two men you're looking for, especially if they're connected to Boswell. Boswell needs to be stopped, and more power to you, if you're the ones who can do it."

"Well, we're going to do our damnedest."

———

THE *WHIT MOON* newspaper office was a single room consisting of a Washington Hand Press, single sheet printing press, and a shelf where the type was kept. A medium height, slender man, wearing an ink-stained apron, was using a lever to operate the tympan and frisket. After the press, he removed a printed page and with a quick glance, lay it aside. Not until then did he look toward Will and Gid.

"If you are wishing to place an ad, you're too late for this issue," Jensen said. "I've already set the type."

"No, Marshal Thompson suggested that we speak to you. He said that you might be able to help us," Will said.

Jensen used a cloth to wipe some ink from his hands. "And just how is it that I may be able to help you?"

"We own a ranch, the Brown Spur, in Tarrant County, near the town of Saginaw. A little over three weeks ago Damon Boswell and his gang attacked the ranch while we were away. They killed our cook and all of our hands except for one. Then, we believe they took our foreman's wife with them."

"You don't know if he took her or not?" Jensen asked.

"We assume he took her, but our hand who was still alive can't say for sure. He didn't see her ride out with them," Gid said. "Anyhow, we've been looking for him ever since."

"A couple days ago, four men tried to set a trap for us. We believe these men might be part of Boswell's gang, and we think Boswell sent them to kill us because he knows we're after him. Unfortunately, we were put in a position where we had to kill two of the men, but the other two got away," Will said. "One of them was a big man with a very puffy scar on his face with the name of Mug Harris. The only thing we know about the other one is that his last name is Kingsley."

"That most likely would be Crack Kingsley. He and Harris sometimes run together."

"You know them? Good!" Will said.

"I know of them, yes, but I don't believe they're part of Boswell's bunch."

"Oh? And why don't you think so?"

"Mug Harris is the kind man who always wants to be in charge."

"Then I don't understand. If these weren't Boswell's men, why were they after us?"

"It could be that Boswell hired them to come after you. Harris is sort of a free-lancer."

"How is it that you know so much about Harris?" Gid asked.

"Before I came here and started my own newspaper, I worked for the *Dallas Herald*, and I covered the trial that sent Harris to prison. I also covered his release, when a smart lawyer got the verdict over-turned."

"Do you have any idea where we might start looking for him?" Will asked.

"Well, I can't tell you for sure where he'll be, but before he went to prison, he was living up in Springton."

"Thanks," Will said.

———

Cabin on the Trinity River

"THEY KILT JETER 'N THE KID," Mug Harris said.

"Was that before you killed them?" Boswell asked.

"No, they ain't dead."

"I don't understand. How is it possible that you engaged them, lost two of your men, but didn't kill the Crocketts, and yet you and Kingsley stand here before me without a scratch? Logic would suggest that in such an engagement, either you, or they, would be dead. And yet, here you are. That would lead to only one conclusion. You abandoned your cohorts."

"We didn't exactly abandon them, they was four of us, but two got kilt right away," Harris said.

"Then you ran away, did you not?"

"I told you, they done kilt two of us, shootin' 'em down like they was nothin'."

"Then the problem remains."

"Do you want 'em kilt?"

"I do believe that was our understanding. Yes, I very much want them dead."

"Then it's goin' to cost you more money, 'cause they

ain't goin' to be that easy to get rid of," Harris said to Boswell. "Ain't you never heard of the Crocketts before?"

"Indeed, I have heard of them," Boswell replied. "That's why I have put into motion an operation to eliminate them. You assured me that you, and the men you had assembled, would not fail. But now you are telling me that you did fail."

"If you'll pay me 'n Crack two thousand dollars apiece to kill the Crocketts, I can guarantee ya that we'll get the job done."

"What makes you think that the two of you can do what four of you couldn't do?"

"I'm goin' to be smart about it, this time."

"A smart Mug Harris, is indeed an oxymoron. But, if you can get the job done, then I will agree to your terms. You do understand don't you, that payment is contingent upon the successful completion of your task? Not one penny will be disbursed without verification of the Crocketts demise."

Harris was confused for a moment. "That means you won't pay us, 'til after we kill 'em, right?"

"I am glad to see that you comprehend the parameters of our understanding," Boswell said.

"You don't have to be worryin' none. Me 'n Crack will take care of it for you."

"Please put your operation into effect as soon as you can, as timing is of the utmost importance."

Harris smiled. "Consider 'em dead."

"No," Boswell replied. "I will consider them still alive, and though I have raised the reward to two thousand dollars on each of them, please understand that the money will not be paid until I have absolute proof of the death of both of the Crockett brothers. Are you fully aware of the requirements you must meet before the funds can be disbursed?"

"Uh, yeah, you're sayin' that you ain't goin' to pay nothin', lessen we kill both of 'em at the same time," Harris said.

"It isn't necessary that both be killed at the same time, however the terms of the contract stipulate that not one cent will be paid until both are dead. And by the way, I intend to let it be known that a reward exists for the Crockett brothers, and anyone who wishes can make a try to collect the money. In other words, you do not have exclusive rights to collect the reward."

"Well, they ain't gettin' kilt with us not doin' nothin' but just standin' here a' jawbonin' about it, so Crack and me need to get goin'.'"

"You do that," Boswell said. "The sooner this matter is resolved, the better it will be for all of us."

————

Springton, Texas

AFTER LEAVING THE NEWSPAPER OFFICE, Will and Gid found The Cow Palace Saloon and went inside. There were three men standing at the bar, which ran down the left side, and another half-dozen sitting at tables. There was a tired-looking barkeep at the far end of the bar replacing whiskey bottles. When Will and Gid stepped up to the bar, he came to take their order. Both ordered a beer.

"You fellas just passing through?" the bartender asked, as he set a mug in front of each them.

"Yes," Will said.

"Where you headed?"

"Oh, no place in particular. By the way, you wouldn't know if a herd of cattle passed through here recently, would you?"

The bartender shook his head. "No, not that I'm aware of. And I think I would know, because the drovers always pay me a visit."

"Thanks."

"Why are you asking about a herd of cows? Are you looking to sign on as drovers?"

"Not exactly," Will said.

"The thing is, we had a herd stolen, and we're trying to find our cows," Gid added.

The barkeep chuckled. "Sorry, I don't mean to laugh, but seems to me like it would be pretty hard to hide an entire herd."

"Well, Texas is a big state, and they could've taken the herd up into the Indian Territory or into Louisiana, or even all the way up to Kansas. But wherever they go, you're right when you say twenty-five hundred head wouldn't be that easy to hide," Will said.

"Which is why we damn sure are going to find them," Gid insisted.

"Well, I wish you fellers all the luck in the world," the bartender said.

"Thanks," Gid replied.

When none of the other customers in the saloon knew anything about the recent movement of a herd of cattle, Will and Gid left, had supper and then got a room at the Cecil Hotel. They talked, far into the night.

"Will, do you think we'll find the herd?" Gil asked.

"Of course," Will said. "It's like the bartender said. How easy is it to hide twenty-five hundred cows?"

Gid chuckled. "Well, I'd say they're doing a pretty damn good job of it so far."

"I can't argue with you there."

————

Brown Spur Ranch

A FEW MINUTES EARLIER, though Anna had protested, Scooter got out of bed and walked out onto the front porch where he took a seat in one of the two rocking chairs.

He was only there for a minute or two before Anna came out onto the porch.

"Please don't ask me to go back in. I'm tired of being cramped up in that little bedroom."

"I'm not going to ask you to go back in. I just came out here to join you," Anna said with a little smile as she held out a cup of coffee toward him.

"Thanks," Scooter said, taking the cup of coffee. He took a sip, then chuckled.

"Something wrong with the coffee?" Anna asked, concerned by Scooter's reaction.

"No, nothing wrong, I'm enjoying it. I was just thinking about all the years I did without coffee."

"They didn't have coffee on the ships you were on?"

"Oh, they had it all right, and it was what you call, 'melt your spoon' strong. I was already a little sea-sick the first time I tried it, and the coffee made it even worse. Then, the next few times I tried it, even in calm seas, I couldn't help but think of the first time, and it made me sick again. It wasn't until I came ashore that I started drinking coffee. It took me a while, but now I like it." He took another sip, then smiled over his cup at Anna. "And I especially like it when it's served by *quelqu'un d'aussi beau que le vôtre*."

"Oh, aren't you sweet, calling me beautiful."

Scooter looked at her in surprise. "You know what I said?"

"I lived in New Orleans for a while. Lots of people speak French there."

"Oh, shucks, and here I was hoping to impress you."

"Why, Scooter, you don't have to speak French to impress me," Anna said as she looked down at her hands.

Scooter felt himself blushing at her compliment.

"Why, I think you might actually be blushing," Anna said. "Isn't that sweet?"

"Blushin'? Yeah, I...I mean, damn is it showin'?"

"Like I said, I think it's sweet."

"Anna, do you think...uh, that is, would it be possible for someone like you to...uh...like someone like me?"

"Why shouldn't it be possible for someone like me to like you? And what do you mean by someone like me, anyway? Do you mean because I'm a...what I am, that I'm not capable of liking someone?"

"I mean because you're so beautiful, and I'm not exactly what you would call a handsome man."

"I'm sorry I questioned you. I'm just very sensitive now about the fact that I'm a...well, I was, but I don't intend to be a soiled dove any longer."

"Oh, that don't matter to me. Anyhow, like you said, you're not a whore anymore."

"A whore, yes. We cover it up by saying soiled dove, but a whore is a whore, no matter what you call us."

Scooter coughed, and to cover his discomfort, he changed the subject. "I wonder where the Cocketts are?"

"They're trying to find their cows," Anna replied, as anxious as Scooter was to change the subject.

"I know that, I was just wondering where they might be in their search right now, 'cause if they can't find 'em, they won't be needing any cowhands, 'n I'd be out of work."

"You don't think you could get on with another ranch?" Anna asked.

"Oh, I could, I reckon. But there's somethin' special 'bout workin' here, at this place. I really liked workin' for the General and Abe Barker, and now I like workin' for Will and Gid. So, like I say, I sure hope they can find the cows."

CHAPTER TWENTY-FIVE

WILL AND GID WERE HALF-WAY BETWEEN TOWNS WHERE they had made camp for the night. The fire they had built to cook their supper and make their coffee had burned low, but there were still, low flames putting out heat, and a dim light.

"Will, have you ever thought about what we're going to do if we don't find this herd?" Gid asked.

"What do you mean?"

"Well, think about it. This isn't our herd, these cows all belong to General Redling. We're just tending them for him. If we've lost them, well, I've done some cipherin', 'n I figure that means we would owe him seventy-five thousand dollars."

"That's a lot of money," Will said, taking a sip of coffee.

"So, what are we going to do about it?"

"Well, my solution would be to find the herd."

"Yeah, if we can," Gid said in a voice that showed his lack of conviction that they could find the herd.

Dancer whickered, then Pug followed.

"Wonder what has them spooked?" Gid asked.

"I don't know but..." Will started. "Gid, take your horse and get over there out of sight."

"Why?"

"I hear riders coming, and I think it might be a good idea to..."

"You don't have to go any further, I know what you mean," Gid said, standing up, then going over to untie Pug, he led him away.

By now the sound of the approaching riders indicated that they were close. Will pulled his pistol, then held it in his right hand, behind his leg so that anyone approaching wouldn't see it.

There were four of them, and they rode into the camp, then dismounted.

"Coffee smells good," one of the men said.

"Yeah, it was."

"Seems to me like it would only be good manners for you to offer us some."

"I'm here by myself, and I've already drunk it. I didn't make enough coffee for four more people. But, if you're of a mind to have any coffee, you're free to use my fire, and there's a sweet-water spring here, behind me."

"What do you mean, you're here alone?"

"That shouldn't be hard for you to understand. Look around, do you see anyone else?"

"You're one of the Crocketts, ain't you?" There had been only one of the four men who had spoken, and Will gathered that he was the leader of the little group of men. He was of average size, with tousled hair that hung to his shoulders, and a beard that was just as unkempt. "Where's your brother?"

"How do you know who I am?"

The questioner's smile was without humor. "I just know."

"Who's asking?"

The man smiled, showing yellowed, uneven teeth. Then slowly and deliberately he drew his gun. "The name's Titus Moore, but the only thing that name will mean to you is, I'm the one that's goin' to kill you, 'n your brother so's we can collect the reward."

"I don't know what reward you would be talking about. There's no paper out on us, we're not wanted men."

"Maybe you ain't wanted by the law, but you're wanted all right. 'N here's the funny thing, the reward ain't for dead or alive, it's only for dead. Which is why I'm about to kill you."

"You may have a hard time with that," Will said, easily.

Moore raised his gun, and pointed it at Will. Will waited until the last moment, seeing the triumphant smile on Moore's face turn to shock, then fear, as he saw Will lifting his pistol.

Moore fired, but in his shock, he fired too quickly pulling the pistol off target. Will shot back, hitting Moore in the stomach.

By now the other three men had drawn their guns, and two of them managed to get their shots off even before Will was able to return fire. One of their shots nipped Will, not burying a bullet in his flesh, but cutting a small, painful, path in his arm. Will's return shot hit the man in his chest, plunging into his heart, dropping him instantly. Will's third shot came at the same time as Gid's first shot. Without coordination, they had both shot at the same man, and he went down with two bullets to his head.

"No, no! I give up, I give up!" the fourth man shouted, dropping his unfired pistol, and putting his hands up.

"Come on out, Gid," Will called.

Gid, with his gun still in hand, made a cautious exit from his hiding place in the trees.

"What's your name?" Will asked the man, who still held his hands up.

"It's Morgan, Fred Morgan," the man replied.

"Put your hands down, Morgan."

Morgan did so, but he continued to stare at Will and Gid with a look of abject fear on his face.

"Are you goin' to kill me?" he asked.

"I don't know, yet. I might," Will said. "It depends on how willing you are to answer our questions."

"I'll answer anything you ask me."

"Where is Boswell, and our cattle."

The expression of fear deepened on Morgan's face, and he held his arms out toward Will, showing him the palms of his hands.

"Don't shoot me, please don't shoot me," he said. "I can't answer the question, because I don't know where your cows are. I don't know Boswell, I ain't never even seen 'im."

"Then how did Moore know who I was?"

"I don't know how he know'd. All I know is that we was supposed to get paid for killin' you." He looked toward Gid. "Both of you," he added.

"All right, let's say you had killed us. Where would you be going to collect your money?"

"We were supposed to go to Burleson," Morgan said.

"What is Burleson?"

"It's a town close to here."

"Who were you supposed to see there?"

"I don't know. Titus, he was the only one that know'd."

Gid walked over to look down at Moore. "He's not going to do us any good, Will. He's dead."

Will and Gid gathered the guns from the three dead men, then picked up the one that Morgan had dropped. He removed the cylinders of all four, then gave Morgan's gun back to him.

"What am I supposed to do with a gun that ain't got no cylinder?" Morgan asked.

"Why don't you stick it up your ass?" Gid said.

"What?"

"Never mind my brother," Will said. "He always gets a little upset when someone tries to kill him."

"Oh," Morgan said.

"I tell you what you do. You can take these three back to town with you," Will said, pointing to the three bodies.

"Why do I have to do it?" Morgan asked.

"Oh, I don't know. Maybe because you're still alive?"

"Oh, yeah, uh, all right. I'll take 'em back."

"We'll be nice and throw them across their horses," Will said.

"Thanks."

———

Burleson, Texas

BURLESON WAS a small town built alongside Rock Creek. It had a sawmill, a livery stable, a mercantile store, a leather goods store, two churches and three saloons lining both sides of the street. There were two cross streets both of which were fronted by houses, a total of about fifty of them.

"So, Little Brother, where should we start?" Will asked.

"What about starting in one of the saloons?" Gid replied.

Will laughed. "Now, why did I think you were going to say that?"

"I don't know. Maybe because we stopped right in front of one?"

Dismounting, the two tied their horses off at the hitching rail, then went inside. It was smaller than most of the saloons they had visited, with the bar only about half as long, and only four tables out on the floor. There was no piano, and there were no girls.

"What'll it be?" the bartender asked.

"We'll have a couple of beers," Will said, slapping a dime down onto the bar.

"I'm Will Crockett, this is my brother Gid," Will said when the beers were put before them. He said it loud enough so that everyone in the saloon could hear.

"Glad to meet you," the bartender replied. "You goin' to stay around for long?"

"As long as it takes," Will replied.

The bartender got a confused expression on his face. "As long as what takes?"

"Long enough for someone to try and kill us."

"Look here, Mister. Why would someone want to kill you?" the bartender asked.

"Apparently a man named Boswell is willing to pay to have us killed."

"What's he doin' that for?"

"Obviously, he wants us both dead."

"Why?"

"Because he stole a herd of cattle from us, and he doesn't want us to recover it, I suppose."

"Damn, I hadn't heard anything about that," the bartender said. "I've heard of Boswell of course, but I didn't know he had stoled a whole herd of cattle, or that he was willin' to pay to have someone kilt."

Will didn't mind talking about it in public, because he felt like such an open discussion might smoke out someone who could establish a connection to Boswell.

———

LOU MCGILL WAS NURSING a whiskey at one of the four tables, listening closely to the conversation. He knew that Boswell was willing to pay to have the Crocketts killed, because he had been paid one hundred dollars to connect whoever would kill the Crockett brothers.

The fact that they were here talking about it, probably meant the men had failed. And that meant that Boswell's reward was still there to be collected, so why didn't he do it?

Lewis pondered the situation for a few minutes, wondering if maybe he should recruit someone to help him, but he knew if he did, he would just have to share the money with whoever he hired. If he could collect the four thousand dollars himself, he could leave the state and go anywhere in the country.

Lewis looked at the two brothers. They were

standing at the bar with their backs toward him. He believed he could shoot one of them in the back. The first reaction of the other one would be to check on his brother, and as he did so, that would give Lewis the opening to shoot him as well.

Lewis pulled his gun from the holster.

———

WILL SAW movement in the mirror, then saw that someone was raising a gun to point toward him. He spun around quickly, drawing his pistol as he turned.

"Drop your gun!" he shouted.

Lewis lifted his gun to aim, and pulled back the hammer.

Will pulled the trigger first. He didn't want to kill the would–be shooter, because he hoped he would be able to get some information from him, so his bullet hit the man in the elbow of the arm that held the gun. Lewis groaned in pain. The shock of the impact of the bullet caused the gun to fall to the floor.

Will crossed the floor quickly, then kicking the gun away, pushed the man back into his chair.

"Who are you?" Will asked.

"I need to see a doctor."

"First, tell me who you are, and why you tried to shoot us."

"I'm goin' to bleed to death if I don't see a doctor."

"Mister, the closest doctor to us is thirty miles away," the bartender said.

One of the men who had been sitting at another table came over to look at the wound. "Bring me a couple of towels," he said. "And a bottle of whiskey."

"You a doctor?" Lewis asked.

"No, but I was in the army for a while. I've treated bullet wounds."

"Who are you?" Will asked the shooter.

"The name is Lewis."

"Why did you want to shoot us?"

"Hell, you know why. Boswell said he'd pay two thousand dollars apiece to anyone who killed you."

"Boswell?"

"Yeah, Boswell." He gasped in pain as the helpful saloon patron poured whiskey on his wound.

"Where is Boswell?"

"I don't know."

"Then how were you supposed to get the money for killing us, if you don't even know where he is?"

"I was going to meet someone."

"Who?"

"I don't know."

"Where were you supposed to meet them?"

"Here."

"When?"

"Now."

"Who?"

"I don't know. You see this here red feather in my hat. Whoever I was supposed to meet would know who I was by this red feather."

———

DRACO WAS STANDING in the little group of men who had gathered around Lewis and the Crocketts. He was here to make contact with Lewis, but not until after Moore and the others showed up here with proof of their success.

"Why are we doing it like that?" Draco asked Boswell. "Wouldn't it be easier just to have them come out here to meet with you?"

"Obviously, my good man, you are unaware of the concept of establishing false leads and protective barriers. If Moore and his men don't know where we are, then there is a very remote likelihood of them being able to give away our position. Mr. Lewis will be an additional barrier, because he not only doesn't know where we are, he won't even know who he is supposed to meet. That's why it will be up to you to establish the contact. But don't do that, until you are certain that the task has been performed."

It was now pretty obvious to Draco, that the task had not been performed. Now he had to return to Boswell with the news that the Crocketts were still alive, and still on the hunt for their cows. But before he did that, he had another task to perform.

CHAPTER TWENTY-SIX

DRACO WAITED ACROSS THE STREET UNTIL LEWIS LEFT the saloon, holding his arm that was now bandaged. Lewis mounted his horse and rode away. Draco followed him until they were about a mile out of town.

"Lewis," he called out to him.

Lewis stopped, then turned to see who had called him. "What do you want?"

"I want to talk to you about your big mouth?"

"What?"

"You told the Crocketts about Boswell."

"Who are you? Are you the man who was supposed to meet me with the money to give to Moore and the others?"

"I am."

"Well, if you was there, you know that I didn't tell 'em nothin'."

"You told 'em that Boswell was payin' the reward to have 'em kilt."

"Yes, but that was all. I didn't say nothin' 'bout where Boswell is, 'cause I don't even know. Hell, I didn't even know who was s'posed to meet me 'till you just told me."

"We won't be needin' you no more," Draco said as he drew his pistol.

"What? No, what are you about to do? Please, please, I didn't say nothin'!"

Draco raised his pistol and shot Lewis in the forehead. Lewis fell from his horse, dead before he hit the ground.

Draco holstered his pistol, then looking around to make certain there had been no witnesses, he started toward the ranch where they were holding the stolen cattle. Boswell needed to know that yet another effort to kill the Crockett brothers had failed.

———

As WILL and Gid had done in every town they had been in since beginning their search, they paid a visit to the marshal's office. Marshal Taylor had already heard about the shooting incident.

"What was that all about back there in the saloon, when you shot that feller?" Marshal Taylor asked.

"He was about to shoot us, so we shot him," Will said.

"Why was he about to shoot you?"

"A man named Damon Boswell has put out a reward for us, dead or," Will paused for a moment. "Dead."

"Oh yes, we all know Boswell. What's your connection with him?"

"We're trying to find him," Gid said.

"Isn't everyone?"

"We have a lead through a couple of men named

Mug Harris and Crack Kingsley. Are you familiar with either of them?"

"Not directly, though I have wanted posters on both of them. They're worth a thousand dollars each to whoever captures...or kills them."

"Well, it's good to have the law on our side then," Will said.

"So where do we go now?" Gid asked when they left the marshal's office.

"What do you say we go back to the ranch and check in on Scooter and Abby to see how they're doing?" Will suggested.

"Sounds good to me."

Ranch near Dido

IT WAS MUCH MORE difficult branding full grown steers, than calves, so it was taking Boswell more time than he wanted to change the brands from a Spur to a Circle Bar. So far, they had changed brands on considerably less than half of the cattle in the herd.

"Damn it, hold on to him! Keep him from running away!" Weasel shouted in frustration. Weasel was holding the branding iron while Mathis and Sloan were trying to keep the steer still enough for the brand to be changed.

"How 'bout you holdin' onto him, 'n lettin' me do the brandin'?" Sloan asked, angrily.

"Brandin' ain't your job. Gettin' them cows over here 'n holdin' 'em still is your job. Now do it right, or we'll never get all these done."

"I didn't work this hard when I was cowboyin'," Mathis said.

"Uh, huh. When we get all these cows branded 'n moved out, our share will be a little over eight thousand dollars. Does that make it easier to hold the damn steer steady?"

"Hell, I'll bite his ear if I have to, to hold the son of a bitch for you," Sloan said with a little chuckle.

Boswell had ridden out to see how the branding was proceeding and he called Cooley over to him. He had put Cooley in charge of the branding operation.

"How is it going?" Boswell asked.

"We've got near to nine hundred of 'em rebranded," Cooley said.

"Nine hundred? That's barely over a third. At this rate it'll take us at least three more weeks before we are finished."

"We can't go no faster, Boss."

"I understand, but the longer we remain here, the greater the peril of discovery. I have studied the Crocketts, and I know that they can be a formidable and resourceful adversary."

"Hell, I thought you was arrangin' to have 'em kilt," Cooley said.

"Yes, but the best laid schemes of mice and men oft gang aft a-gley."

"What? What does that mean?"

"It is from a poem by Robert Burns, and it means that no matter how carefully you plan, something can always go wrong. And as long as the Crocketts are alive, our operation is at risk. That's why we need to get the cattle rebranded as quickly as we can."

"Here come's Draco now. I'll bet he's come to tell us the Crocketts is both dead," Cooley said.

"Let us hope that is so," Boswell replied.

Boswell, who was still mounted, rode out to meet Draco.

"I hope you have come bearing good tidings," Boswell said.

"I ain't hardly doin' that," Draco said, "on account of the news ain't good. The Crocketts is both still alive."

————

Brown Spur Ranch

SCOOTER WAS SITTING on the front porch in the late afternoon when he saw two riders approaching.

"Anna," he called, "bring the shotgun."

"What?"

"A couple of riders are comin'. Bring me the shotgun, it's better to be safe than sorry."

"Oh, Scooter, you're in no shape for anything like that."

"Bring me the gun, and you go hide somewhere."

"I'll bring you the gun, but I'll be standing right beside you."

Scooter studied the riders as they drew closer, then a broad smile spread across his face.

"Never mind the shotgun," he called. "It's Will and Gid."

————

WHEN WILL and Gid pulled up in front of the house, they were greeted with two happy smiles.

"Welcome home!" Scooter called out to them.

"Well, I must say, you're looking a lot better than you did when we left you," Will said.

"Look at you, standing out here on the front porch holding a shot gun," Gid added with a little chuckle.

"Oh!" Scooter said, embarrassed. He lay the gun down quickly. "I, uh, didn't know who you were when I first saw you."

"You did the right thing, after all you've got a pretty young lady to protect," Gid said.

Scooter's embarrassment left him. "Aye, aye, sir, that's exactly what I was thinking."

"The only thing," Will started, then he stopped his sentence there.

"The only thing what?"

Will smiled. "You don't need to aye, aye, sir me. This is a ranch, not a ship."

"Sorry," Scooter said with a self-conscious smile. "Sometimes old habits die hard."

"Come in, come in," Anna said. "You're just in time, supper's almost ready."

"If you weren't expecting us, I'm not sure there'll be enough," Will said. "You don't know how Gid eats."

"I've got cornbread in the oven, and I've been cooking ham and beans most of the day, And, I made enough for a crowd." She smiled. "I'd planned to feed Scooter beans for a couple days. So you see it will work out just fine."

"Yeah, and I won't have to be eating leftovers for a week," Scooter teased. "So eat as much as you can."

"Scooter, they'll think you don't like my cooking," Anna said as she hit his arm.

"You know I'm just teasing, I love your cooking."

"You will stay, won't you?" Anna asked, addressing Will and Gid.

"Thanks, Abby, I don't need a second invitation for that," Gid said.

"Anna," Anna said.

"What?"

"My name isn't Abby. It's Anna. Anna Wilson."

"She told me that, right away," Scooter said, proudly.

"Well, then, Anna it shall be," Will said.

"Let me take care of your horses," Scooter offered.

"No, you just stay there," Gid said, holding his hand out. "I'll take care of the horses. I don't want your stitches to break."

As Gid led Dancer and Pug to the barn, Will followed Scooter and Anna on into the house.

"Would you like a cup of coffee, Mr. Will?" Anna asked.

"Yes, thank you, that would be good. And you may as well get a cup for Gid, too."

"Yes, sir, I will," Anna said.

"So, have you found the herd?" Scooter asked after Anna disappeared into the kitchen.

Will sighed. "I'm afraid not. And to make matters worse, we haven't even had the slightest lead on where they might be."

"Nothing, huh?"

"Well, I wouldn't say that, there is this to consider." Will removed a piece of folded up paper for his pocket, and handed it to Scooter.

THE LOST HERD   255

Wanted

DEAD

Will Crockett

Gid Crockett

$2,000 for each man

Scooter examined the sheet.

"I don't understand. Why are you wanted? And why does it just say 'Dead' and not 'Dead or Alive' the way most of them do?"

Will chuckled. "You'll also notice that it doesn't have who authorized it, such as a state, or a county. And that's because, this isn't a legitimate wanted poster. This is something Damon Boswell has put out on his own. He's offering to pay a reward to anyone who will kill us."

"Damn!" Scooter said.

"Yeah, damn is right. There have already been a few who have tried to collect on the bounty."

"That's awful," Scooter said.

"Not necessarily."

"What do you mean, not necessarily? If someone put out a wanted poster on me, and offered to pay money, just to see me killed, I'd be plenty worried about it," Scooter said.

"That's true, but so far the run-ins we've had with people who want to kill us are the only leads we have to Boswell."

"Have the leads actually led you anywhere?"

Will chuckled. "Uh, no."

Gid came back into the house then.

"Coffee smells good," Gid said.

"Have a seat, both of you. I'll get the coffee," Scooter offered.

When Scooter returned, he was not holding coffee cups. Instead, he said, "Anna say's supper's ready."

For the next several minutes, the four of them enjoyed their supper.

"Abby, uh, I mean Anna," Gid corrected. "Where did you learn to cook like this? This is really good."

"Why, thank you, Gid. My mama was a good cook, and I learned from her."

"You learned well, is all I can say."

Over supper they discussed the last couple of weeks during which they had been separated.

"I'm near 'bout good as new," Scooter said. "Why, yesterday I went into town with Anna, and was even able to carry the groceries out to the buckboard."

"That's true," Anna said. "He's getting along very well. It's gotten to the point to where I'm not even needed anymore."

"Ohh," Scooter said in a pained face. "No, I'm...I'm not quite *that* good. I, uh, I still hurt some."

Will laughed. "We won't send her away just yet."

"That's good. I mean, I probably could make it on my own, but I think we should keep her around, just to be safe, you know."

"Right, just to be safe," Will said with a knowing grin.

Ranch near Dido

"WE'VE GOT MORE 'n half the cows re-branded by now," Draco said. "Don't you think we ought to take some of 'em to that feller that we sold 'em to?"

"No," Boswell said. "Right now, we have him committed to buying the entire herd. I fear that if we take only what we have rebranded, he may withdraw from our agreement. It's best that we stick to our original plan."

"You're the boss," Draco said.

"Undoubtedly," Boswell replied.

Boswell walked away from Draco, and when he stepped into the little cabin, he was met by Julia.

"How long do you plan to keep me here?" she asked.

"As long as it takes to complete my business," Boswell replied.

"What if I just left?"

"Where would you go?"

"I don't know. Anywhere but here. Do you have any idea how boring it is to have to stay in this dreary cabin?"

"It's for your own protection."

"My own protection? What are you talking about? What do you mean, for my own protection?"

"Let's face it, my dear. You are a most attractive woman, and you are out here, all alone. So far, I've been able to keep any of my men from, well, let us just say, having their way with you. And as long as I can continue to exercise my authority over them, you will be safe. However, if you leave my protection, I simply cannot guarantee your continued safety."

CHAPTER TWENTY-SEVEN

BEFORE RESUMING THEIR SEARCH FOR BOSWELL AND THEIR cattle, Will and Gid decided to visit with Marshal Coates to see if there had been any additional activity from Boswell.

"No," Coats said. "It's been very quiet since Boswell's raid on your ranch."

"Humph, maybe it's because he's having to work for a change," Gid said. "He's got a herd of cattle to look after."

"That's true. And you boys haven't heard anything about him?"

"No, but he'll have to turn up eventually. He can't make twenty-five hundred head of cattle just disappear."

"I agree."

"If you hear anything, you'll let us know?" Will asked.

"And how am I going to do that? If you two are running all over the place looking for your cattle, how will I know how to get a hold of you? We tried once before, remember, and you didn't get the telegram."

"Hey, Will, why not have him let Scooter know? We'll be staying in touch with him," Gid suggested.

Will nodded his head. "That will work. If you hear anything, get the news to Scooter. We'll try to check in with him every few days or so just to let him know where we are."

"All right, I'll just do that," Coats replied.

After leaving the marshal's office, Will and Gid walked down to Casey's Saloon. Suzie met them as soon as they stepped through the door.

"Will and Gid," she said with a welcoming smile. "I take it you're back because you found your cattle."

"Actually, it's General Redling's cattle and, unfortunately, we haven't found hide nor hair of them," Gid said.

"And we're not back to stay. We just came back to check in on Scooter to see how he's doing," Will added.

"Oh, and how's Abby doing?" Suzie asked. "We've not seen her since she went out to the ranch."

"She and Scooter both seem to be doing quite well. Scooter's moving around on his own, now."

"Apparently then, Abby's nursing is helping," Suzie said.

"Apparently so," Will agreed.

"Do you think there's anything...uh...you know, with the both of them out there all alone and..."

Will chuckled. "You mean has nature taken its course?"

"Yeah, somethin' like that," Suzie said.

"I don't know, we'll just have to see, won't we?" Will replied.

"You know, a part of me hopes something is happening between them. Regardless of how Abby's been making a living, she's such a sweet girl, and it would be really nice if she found someone."

"You never can tell," Will said with a smile. "They're young, they're together, and they're alone."

Will and Gid visited with some of their friends for a while, hoping for some new piece of information they could work with, but when they learned nothing that was helpful, they bade goodbye, then rode out of Saginaw to resume their search.

———

TWO DAYS LATER, Gid felt a burning in his arm, concurrent with the sound of a rifle shot.

"Come on, we've got to get out of here!"

They turned their horses to get away from the shooter, but when they did, they encountered a shooter from the opposite direction.

"Over here!" Gid called out, as he left the road and rode into a copse of trees which gave them both concealment, and cover. Snaking their rifles from their saddle sheaths, the two dismounted, then each of them found a tree to provide cover.

There were more shots sent their way, the shooters were separated by some distance.

"You take the one on the right, I'll take the one on the left," Will said.

For the next few minutes or so, the Crockett brothers exchanged fire with their attackers, but they had no target other than the puffs of gun smoke from the opposing rifles.

"We're not doing anything but wasting bullets," Gid said.

"I've got an idea."

"What?"

"You'll see. Just be ready."

Will shouted out at their attackers.

"You've killed my brother!" He shouted. "I give up, I give up! Don't shoot anymore!"

"Throw your gun out, then come out with your hands up!" someone called back to him.

"I'll throw my gun out, but I'm wounded, I can't come out. Please, come help me."

Will tossed his rifle out.

"Toss your brother's rifle out too."

"Why, you already killed him."

"We want to make sure that you don't grab his."

"All right." Will took Gid's rifle and threw it out as well. "There."

"Now you come out."

"All right, but I'll have to crawl out. I'm wounded, and I can't stand up."

Will crawled out from behind the tree, then dropped down onto his stomach. He lay perfectly still.

"Put your hands up!" one of the attackers called.

Will neither complied, nor responded.

"Hey, Mug, you think he's dead, too?" another voice asked.

"I don't know, Crack. Maybe. Why don't you go check him out?"

"I ain't goin' out there. You go."

"All right, we'll both go."

———

"HERE THEY COME," Gid said, speaking so quietly that only Will could hear.

"Where are they?"

"About fifty yards to the left," Gid said. "Keep an eye on them, and if one of them points a gun at me, shoot him. That'll be my signal."

"You think the son of a bitch is dead?" Kingsley asked.

"Yeah, looks to me like we just made ourselves four thousand dollars," Harris said.

"Are you sure? He was just talkin' to us a few minutes ago."

"Yeah, but he said his brother was dead 'n he was hurt."

"Well, there's one way to make sure he's dead."

———

ONE OF THE men aimed his rifle at Will, and Gid shot him. The man dropped his rifle and slapped his hand over his chest.

"Son of a bitch!" Harris shouted.

Will, using the distraction brought about by Gid, raised up onto his knees with his pistol in hand. He squeezed off a quick shot, and Kingsley went down.

Now, with both men lying in the dirt, Will and Gid stood up, and approached them carefully. Both were dead.

"Well, Harris and Kingsley won't be getting their reward for killing us," Will said.

"Too bad we had to kill them. They might have been able to give us a lead to our cows," Gid said.

"We'll just have to keep looking."

Brown Spur Ranch

"I NEED to hook up the buckboard and go into town for some supplies," Anna said. "You want to come along?"

"Sure, I like it when we go into town together. Why, it's almost like we're a couple of old married folks," Scooter teased.

Anna laughed. "Oh, I don't know as I would go that far," she said. "But you're more than welcome to come with me."

"Huh, uh, I'll be driving. You'll be coming with me."

"Oh, ashamed to be driven by a woman, are you?"

"I'll drive," Scooter said without a direct response to her tease.

Scooter drove rather slowly to limit any undue pressure that would disturb his wound. When they got to town, Scooter stopped the buckboard in front of the saloon.

"I thought we were coming to town to buy groceries," Anna said.

"We are, yeah, but I always visit Casey's when I come to town. Besides, wouldn't you like to visit with Suzie and Kate?"

"I..." Anna paused for a moment, as she thought about it. Then, she smiled. "Yes, I think that would be very nice."

"Good. And a cool beer would be nice, too."

Scooter started to climb down from the buckboard, but grunted when he was hit by a little flash of pain.

"Here, let me help you," Anna offered, hurrying

around to extend her hand and steady him as he climbed down.

When the two stepped into the saloon a moment later, they were warmly greeted by Suzie, Kate, and John, as well as all the customers. After a beer and several minutes of friendly conversation, they were about to leave when Barry Patmore came into the saloon.

Barry Patmore was the Saginaw representative for the Texas Cattlemen's Association.

"I saw you coming into town a few minutes ago. The Crocketts wouldn't happen to be out at the ranch, would they?" Patmore asked.

"No, they're still out huntin' for their cattle," Scooter said. "Why?"

Patmore smiled. "We may have found them."

"What are you talking about?" Scooter asked.

"I have a pretty good lead on where their herd might be. You might tell them that, if you know how to get in touch with them."

"Where? You know where Boswell is?"

"Well, I'm not sure, but I think I do. Or at least, I think I know where he was. A man named Elmer Whitley just sold twenty-five hundred cows. That's pretty close to the number of cows in the Brown Spur herd, isn't it?"

"Whitley?"

"He said his name was Elmer Whitley, and he passed himself off as a lawyer from the firm of Whitley, Whitley, and Dunn in Dallas."

"Then that couldn't be Boswell, could it?"

Patmore smiled. "Ah, but here's the thing. There is

no law firm called Whitley, Whitley, and Dunn in Dallas."

"I'll be damn!" Scooter said. "That's him, then, isn't it? That's Boswell."

"I'd be willing to bet on it. Now, is there any way you can get word to the Crockett brothers?"

"I think so. They've been sending me a telegram every day or so, with a way to answer them if anything's happened. When they get in touch with me again, I'll pass this along. Thanks, Mr. Patmore. Thanks a lot."

"Well, I need to get back to my office," Patmore said, by way of goodbye.

"Scooter, do you think this might be Mr. Will and Mr. Gid's herd?" Anna asked after Patmore left.

"I'd bet on it," Scooter said.

"I hope so. I really hope they're able to get their herd back."

———

BEFORE RETURNING TO THE RANCH, Scooter went over to the Western Union office.

"Oh, it's good to see you," the telegrapher said. "You just got another telegram, and I was just about to send Johnny out to deliver it to you."

"Let me see the telegram," Scooter said. "Today, I will have an answer."

WE ARE IN DECATUR UNTIL TOMORROW STOP ANY NEWS

Scooter read the telegram, then smiled at the telegrapher. "Today I do have news."

———

Decatur, Texas

WILL and Gid had checked with all their usual sources but had gotten no useful information. They had just sent a telegram to Scooter, and were now having a beer in the Long Horn saloon.

"I tell you the truth, Little Brother, we need some sort of break," Will said. "We just keep running into one blind alley after another."

"It's depressing all right. And you know what bothers me most? It's Redling's cows we've lost. Do you think it's time we told him?"

"I know, but it's like Percy said. Twenty-five hundred head of cattle can't just disappear."

"What's next?"

"We haven't checked with the station master at the railroad yet. He might be able to tell us about any recent cattle shipment," Will suggested.

"I suppose," Gid said, "but it'll be like all the other depots we've checked. They've heard nothing about any cows being shipped."

"Actually, if you think about it, that's the answer we want to hear. If they've already been shipped, it might be too late for us to recover anything."

"You have a point."

After finishing their beer, the two men rode down to the depot. As there were no trains due just yet, they had no trouble speaking with the stationmaster, Elijah Gibson.

"What can I do for you gentlemen?" Gibson asked. He was of average size with a narrow face, and a well-trimmed moustache.

"Mr. Gibson, my name is Will Crockett, this is my brother Gid. We would like to inquire..."

"About an unauthorized shipment of cattle," Gibson said, interrupting Will's inquiry.

"Why, yes. You know about this? Has a shipment of cattle come through here?"

Gibson shook his head. "No, unfortunately there's been no such shipment, but I know about it because word has gone all up and down the line. Believe me, everyone on the railroad is aware of the stolen herd of cattle, and we're on the lookout for it."

"Well, that's good to know," Will said. "I mean, it's good to know that everyone's looking for our cows. Too bad we haven't been able to locate them, though."

At that moment a boy of about sixteen came up to the three men.

"Excuse me, Mr. Gibson." The boy looked toward Will and Gid. "Are either one of you a Mr. Crockett?"

"We both are," Will replied. "Why do you ask?"

"Mr. Albright said to tell you that you got a reply to the telegram you sent this morning."

"Thanks," Will said. Then, as he and Gid walked down to the Western Union office, he wondered aloud about the telegram.

"It must be something," Gid said. "We've sent Scooter four telegrams so far, and this is the first one he's answered."

"I hope you're right."

A few moments later they stepped into the Western Union office, and Albright looked up greeting them with a smile.

"Gentlemen, you've received a reply to the wire you

sent this morning." He handed over a little yellow sheet of paper.

PATMORE REPORTS SALE OF 2500 COWS IN WICHITAL FALLS

"Patmore?" Gid asked.

"Barry Patmore. He's with the Cattlemen's Association, remember?"

"Oh, yes."

"You want to send this back for us, Mr. Albright?" Will said, after scribbling a note.

THANKS FOR NEWS WILL FOLLOW UP CROCKETTS

After sending the return telegram, they returned to the railroad depot where they bought a ticket to Wichita Falls. The train would leave at seven the next morning and be in Wichita Falls by ten.

CHAPTER TWENTY-EIGHT

THE FIRST THING THEY DID AFTER LEAVING THE TRAIN IN Wichita Falls, was visit the office of the Texas Cattlemen's Association, where they spoke with Rex Daigh.

"We've been told that there was a recent transaction of the sale of twenty-five hundred head of cattle here. Is this something you can verify?" Will asked.

"Oh, indeed I can. The transaction was handled, I believe, by Mr. Crader of the law office of Robinson and Crader."

"Thank you," Will replied with a satisfied smile. "You've been very helpful."

"May I ask the purpose of your inquiry? The cattle aren't infected with any disease, are they?"

"No, but we have good reason to believe that they may be stolen cattle."

"Oh, my. If that's so, I hope you'll be able to resolve the situation."

"Thanks," Will said.

———

IT WAS but a short walk from the office of the Texas Cattlemen's Association, to the firm of Robinson and Crader. There, they asked for, and were granted an audience with David Crader.

"What can I do for you gentlemen?" Crader asked.

"Were you a recent agent on the sale of twenty-five hundred head of cattle?" Will asked.

"Yes," Crader replied. "It was a transaction between Mrs. Jason Critchlow and Mr. Burt Rowe, of Paradise Ranch."

"Mrs. Critchlow, you say?"

"Yes. She was a widow who had no wish to continue ranching, so she put her entire herd of some twenty-five hundred head of cattle on the market."

"Did you speak with Mrs. Critchlow?" Will asked.

"No, the transaction was handled by..." Crader stopped in mid-sentence. "Oh, wait a minute. As I recall now the lawyer who handled the transaction identified himself as Elmer Whitley, of Whitley, Whitley, and Dunn, which he purported to be a law firm in Dallas. But when we tried to communicate with him, later, we learned that no such legal firm exists."

"Didn't that give you cause to worry?" Will asked.

"Somewhat. But it was obvious that Mr. Whitley is a lawyer. When Mr. Robinson and I discussed it, we decided that he may have invented the legal firm to improve his position."

"Mr. Crader, have you ever heard of Damon Boswell?"

"I believe I've heard of him. He's an outlaw, isn't he?"

"Yes, but before he was an outlaw, he was a lawyer. We have a witness who knows for certain it was Damon Boswell who stole a herd of cattle from us—a herd of twenty-five hundred head. And now we think that Boswell may be the man who identified himself to you as Elmer Whitley."

"Oh! Oh my," Crader said, lifting his hand to his lips. "Are you saying that I may have played a role in an illegal transaction?"

"We're making no direct charge against you, sir, but yes, inadvertently, you very well may have."

"Is there anything I can do?"

"You could introduce us to the man Boswell sold our cattle to," Will said. "Bert Rowe, I think you said it was?"

"Yes, Bert Rowe, and of course I will introduce you to him," Crader said.

"Is Rowe an honest man? What I mean is, do you think he is someone who would willingly buy stolen cattle?"

"No, I wouldn't think so. Mr. Rowe has a very solid reputation."

"Good."

Half an hour later, Will, Gid, and David Crader met with Bert Rowe, where they told him the purpose of their visit.

"Stolen?" Rowe said. "Are you telling me that the cattle I'm buying from Mr. Whitley are stolen?"

"You said cattle that you are buying. Does that mean you haven't yet made the purchase?" Gid asked.

"No, not yet. Part of the deal is that he is to bring the cattle to me."

"If you don't mind my asking, Mr. Rowe, how much are you paying for the cattle?" Will asked.

"Thirty-five dollars a head."

"Mr. Rowe, the current market price is forty–seven dollars a head. Didn't it make you a little curious as to why he was willing to sell the cattle at such a lower price?"

"He told me it was because the widow he represented was so anxious to get rid of the cattle that she was willing to take a reduced price."

"Do you have any idea when he plans to deliver the herd to you?" Gid asked.

Rowe shook his head. "No, not exactly. He said he would let me know a few days in advance so I could be ready for him."

Gid looked at Will for a second, then he said, "Would you gentlemen excuse my brother and me for few moments so we can have a private conversation?"

"Certainly, go right ahead," Rowe said. "Mr. Crader, I have coffee inside."

"Thank you," Crader said.

"It'll be there for you two as well, when you're ready for it," Rowe said.

"Thanks, we'll take you up on it," Gid said.

"What is it, Gid?" Will asked when they were alone.

"Redling said that he would give us thirty-five dollars a head."

"Yes, he said that."

"Why don't we see if Rowe will give us forty dollars a head. That way we can pay off Redling, and still clear five dollars, without having to get the cattle to Kansas City. I know it isn't what we would make if we took the cattle to Kansas City, but we would still clear twelve thousand, five hundred dollars."

"There's only one problem with that," Will said. "What about Mr. Peabody at the Bottom Stockyard? We promised to deliver our cows to him."

"We can ask Mr. Crader to write a letter to him,

asking to break our contract," Gid said. "After all, he hasn't paid us anything yet."

Will and Gid went back into the house where they accepted a cup of coffee, then joined Crader and Rowe at the table.

"Mr. Rowe, our first intention was to take the cattle back," Will said. "But my brother and I have talked it over, and we would be willing to sell the herd to you at forty dollars a head."

"Why should I buy the herd from you for forty dollars a head, when Mr. Whitley has offered the cattle to me at thirty–five dollars a head?"

"I thought you understood," Will said. "They aren't his to sell."

"So, you're saying they are your cattle?"

"Actually, no, they don't belong to us, either."

"What?" Rowe looked at the two brothers, then at Crader. He shook his head. "No, something fishy is going on here. If they don't belong to you, how do I know that you two men aren't trying to steal the herd and then sell the cows to me?"

"It's easy enough to find out," Will said. "We can go into town to talk to Mr. Daigh at the Cattlemen's Association, then we'll talk to the sheriff. You can send telegrams back to Saginaw to Sheriff Maddox, City Marshal Coats, and Barry Patmore, who is the agent for the Texas Cattlemen's Association. They can vouch for who we are, and they can also validate that the herd was stolen. They can also validate that the herd was left in our trust by Ben Redling."

"Are you saying you can sell this herd for Redling for forty dollars a head, giving him a loss of twelve dollars a head?"

"Yes."

"Bert, it won't be very hard to check these gentlemen out," Crader said. "I know a lawyer in Fort Worth that we can also check with."

"Daniel Norton is the lawyer in Fort Worth who handled the transfer of property for us, and also the arrangement as to how we would handle the cattle. You might want to contact him as well," Will suggested.

"Yes, I've done business with Norton," Crader said. "If Norton validates their claim, we'll have no reason to doubt it."

"Forty dollars a head?" Rowe asked.

"Yes."

Rowe nodded. "That would still be a seven dollar a head profit for me. All right, gentlemen, let's go back into town so we can send telegrams to all these people you've mentioned, and if it all checks out," he stopped in mid-sentence then smiled, and extended his hand. "You've got yourself a deal."

By nightfall, return telegrams, in the names of Sherriff Maddox, the lawyer, Norton, and Barry Patmore of the cattle agency, satisfied Rowe and Daigh that Will and Gid were truly authorized to make a deal with the cattle.

"So, what do we do now?" Rowe asked.

"We wait until the cattle are delivered, then we'll take care of Boswell and his group of outlaws," Will suggested.

"Will there be shooting?" Rowe asked. "I don't want to put any of my hands at risk."

"We'll make an effort to make sure none of your hands are involved when we take them down," Will said.

"Oh, and Mr. Rowe, it might be better if you say nothing about this to anyone," Gid suggested.

"Not even my hands?"

"Especially not your hands," Gid said.

"Why not? Look here, you don't think any of my men are mixed up in this, do you?"

"No, but if they know in advance what's going to happen, they might get nervous about it. And Boswell might be an evil son of a bitch, but he's also very shrewd. I think he might pick up on anything that didn't feel right," Gid answered.

"My brother's right," Will said. "It's best that you don't say anything at all."

"All right."

"I, uh, have done my job," Crader said. "I need to get my letter off to Mr. Peabody, so if there's going to be any shooting, I'd just as soon not be around. If you don't mind, I'll just go back to town now."

"We'll go with you," Will said.

"But, aren't you going to try and stop Boswell?"

"Not until Mr. Rowe brings them to town, so he can get the money from the bank," Will said.

"Oh, but I've already withdrawn the money."

"Boswell won't know that." Will smiled. "Besides, you'll need another twelve-thousand, five-hundred to pay us."

"So that means the confrontation, if and when it would begin, wouldn't take place here."

"Yes. Oh, and Mr. Crader, it might be a good idea for you to be here with Mr. Rowe when Boswell arrives. Boswell has already met you, and if you're here, he won't question having to go into town for the money."

Crader nodded.

All right," Rowe said. "We'll go to the bank for the money when the herd arrives."

———

Brown Spur Ranch

SCOOTER LAID several pieces of kindling into the fireplace, then he put some cut wood on top, and held a match to it. The kindling caught, and Scooter watched it until the larger pieces of firewood caught as well. He saw the blaze begin to rise—blue at its origin, then orange, then yellow at the top where the little tongues of flames danced and waved while little gray and white streams of smoke rose. The smell of burning wood permeated the room.

"Scooter, don't you be doing too much now," Anna called from the kitchen. "You don't want to break open your stiches."

"Come in here and join me," Scooter yelled back to her.

"I really need to get the dishes washed and…"

"If you don't come in here with me, I'm going start to jumping up and down just so I do tear my stiches," Scooter called.

"Don't you dare!" Anna said sharply. She came quickly, into the parlor. "Why would you even say such a thing?" she asked.

Scooter chuckled. "It got you in here, didn't it?"

"You tricked me." Anna's smile told him that she wasn't really angry with him.

The flames caught a gas bubble trapped in one of

the logs, and it popped loudly, throwing up a little shower of sparks.

"Oh!" Anna said, startled by sound.

"Let's have a seat on the sofa," Scooter invited.

"This is nice, isn't it?" Scooter said, as they sat together in front of the fire.

"It's more than nice. It's beautiful!" Anna said.

"Yes, you are," Scooter said as he captured one of the curls that hung beside Anna's face. "Especially when the firelight is reflected in your hair." He began removing the pins from her top knot, and when her hair was free, he ran his fingers through it, smoothing the waves.

Anna watched him with a quizzical expression. She was no virgin; she had made her living by selling her body. But what she was feeling now was quite new to her. Scooter wasn't a paying customer, and as she looked at him, she realized that he was going to kiss her. She knew, also, that she very much wanted him to.

"Scooter, what are you...?"

"Shh, don't talk just now," Scooter said.

Scooter pulled her face to his and kissed her. And though the kiss wasn't unexpected, her reaction to it was. It was a light and tender kiss, of short duration, ending much too soon, and as she stared into his eyes, she saw a glint of doubt.

Was he having regrets? Was he thinking of her, not as a woman susceptible to his kiss, but as the prostitute?

No, she wanted to say. *You need have no doubt. I'm not a prostitute, and I will never be one again. I have returned your kiss, because I wanted to. Oh, Scooter, please know this.*

Scooter started to say something but the words caught, and he cleared his throat before he spoke.

"Anna, I...I'm sorry, I mean we are here, all alone, and I don't wish to take advantage of you. I know it makes no sense. I'm nothing but a cowhand, I don't make enough money to support you, but it's just that I, well, I've fallen in love with you."

"You're right, it makes no sense," Anna replied. Then she smiled and laid her fingers on his cheek. "But I've fallen in love with you, too."

CHAPTER TWENTY-NINE

IT HAD TAKEN BOSWELL AND HIS MEN FIVE DAYS TO DRIVE the herd from the ranch, which was just outside of Dido, to within five miles of Wichita Falls, Texas.

Just before they reached Wichita Falls, Boswell called Draco and Mathis over to him.

"Draco, you keep the herd moving, you've got about ten more miles to go before you get to Paradise Ranch. I've got some business to take care of. I'll rejoin you, just before you reach the ranch."

"What kind of business?" Draco asked.

"I fail to see that that is any of your concern," Boswell replied. "Now, before we get there, I have a question to ask you. Who am I?"

"What do you mean, who are you? Hell, you're..." He stopped in mid-sentence. "Oh, you mean who are you pretending to be, don't you?"

"And who would that be?"

"Uh, White? Whittaker? Uh..."

"Draco, what is wrong with you? I must have told

you what name I will be using a dozen times or more. Now, who am I?"

Draco frowned for a moment, then he smiled. "You're Whitley," he said.

"And, what is my first name?"

"Why hell, it's Mister."

For just a second, Boswell had an irritated expression on his face, then he relaxed and smiled.

"All right, Mister Whitley is good enough. Now, you may proceed, but don't actually go onto the ranch until I have rejoined you. I shall want you to accompany me to Mr. Rowe's house where we will conclude the deal. Then, once we have the money in hand, we'll find some place to divide it all up."

"And how much of it is we goin' to be gettin'? I mean, after you take your cut."

"Each one of you will be getting ten thousand dollars," Boswell said.

Draco smiled. "Damn, that's a lot of money. How much is it that you'll be 'a gettin'?"

"It is no concern of yours what my share will be. Just keep your wits about you, and do not say or do anything that will foul this up."

"I'll do good, Mr. Whitley. I'll do real good," Draco said with a broad smile.

"See that you do. You may continue with the drive, but remain on the environs of the ranch until I return."

"Do what?"

"Don't take the herd onto the ranch until I come back."

"All right," Draco agreed.

Boswell left the herd then, and pushing his horse into a rapid trot, he reached Wichita Falls in a little under an hour. As soon as he arrived, he tied his horse off in front of the Lone Star hotel, then, taking his panniers with him, went inside and stepped up to the front desk.

"My name is Elmer Whitley. I believe my wife may already have arrived."

"Yes, Mr. Whitley, she's here. She's in room 206, you may go on up."

"Thank you."

Boswell went up to room 206, opened the door, then stepped inside. Julia Barker smiled at him.

"Did you get the money yet?" she asked.

"Not yet. I need to get cleaned up and dress for the occasion."

"Before you dress for the occasion, suppose you get undressed for the occasion?" Julia suggested with an inviting smile.

"I swear woman, you are insatiable," Boswell said.

"I'm also brilliant," she said. "You wouldn't have a herd to sell, if it weren't for me."

"Yes, and now it is about to pay off. I will be seeing Rowe within the hour, then I'll return here, with your share of the money."

"For me, it's a double victory. I got rid of old Abe and I'll be getting enough money to start over somewhere. With you, perhaps?" she added.

"This will be the second husband I've gotten rid of for you, won't it?"

Julia made a face. "Yes, Mr. Byrd. You handled my divorce. For which you were paid twice," Julia said.

"Twice?"

"Fifteen hundred dollars from my husband, and," she smiled, "sexual favors from me."

"But, my dear, you enjoyed it fully as much as I did. I wouldn't call that payment; I would call it shared pleasure."

"And now the pleasure will continue, especially after you get the money from Mr. Rowe. You wouldn't be in this position had I not told you about the Crocketts absence from the ranch."

"You did well, my dear," Boswell said as he kissed Julia lightly.

"You have to admit that passing you off as my brother was a stroke of genius," Julia said.

"As was sending two letters in every envelope, one for you to share your 'brother's' letter with your husband, and a second letter that was personal and private meant only for you."

"How would you feel about something personal and private right now?" Julia asked, coquettishly.

Boswell smiled. "Oh, my dear, I fear you would wear me out."

"Perhaps, but wouldn't it be a fun ride?" Julia asked.

"I've no doubt but that it would. But now, I have nothing on my mind but collecting the money for selling a herd belonging to the widow Critchlow."

"You can take a little time before you leave, can't you? Let's celebrate," Julia invited with a seductive smile, as she began removing her clothes.

———

LESS THAN AN HOUR LATER, a clean, well-dressed, and satiated Damon Boswell showed up where Draco had stopped the herd, holding them until Boswell arrived.

Then, for the remaining couple of miles, Boswell

rode clear of the herd so that he wouldn't get dirty from the cloud of dust that the cattle were kicking up. As they crossed over the property line onto the Paradise Ranch, they were met by half a dozen of the Paradise ranch hands. One of them came out to meet them.

"I'm Pete Crowley, I'm the foreman here," the rider said. "Which one of you is in charge?"

"That would be me, Elmer Whitley," Boswell said.

"All right, Mr. Whitley, all these boys can go on now. We'll take 'em from here."

"Draco, you come with me to meet Mr. Rowe and get our money," Boswell said. "The rest of you gentlemen can wait right here, I'll pay you off here, then you're free to go anywhere you want to go."

All the men smiled at the prospect of becoming rich, and they gathered in a small group as the men who were riding for the Paradise brand took the herd onto ranch pastureland.

Boswell and Draco rode up to the main house where they were met by Rowe and Crader, the lawyer who had helped Boswell broker the deal.

"Well, Mr. Whitley, I see that you made it here," Crader said. "Any difficulty with bringing the herd? Any deterioration in the numbers?"

"Not at all, Mr. Crader." Boswell replied. "As a matter of fact, though our deal is for twenty-five hundred head, I'm proud to report that the final count is some twenty head beyond that. And," he added, "I am willing to include those strays as a bonus."

"Where is the herd now?" Rowe asked.

"Your hands have taken control of the herd. So, as soon as you get an accurate count, you can pay me, and our business will be concluded."

"Yes, indeed," Rowe said. "As soon as we go to the bank."

"Go to the bank? Are you telling me that you don't have the money ready for me?"

"Oh, my dear Mr. Whitley," Crader said. "Surely you didn't expect Mr. Rowe to have that much cash money in cash here at the ranch, did you? I advised him against it, as I'm sure you would have done had he been your client. But, not to worry, the bank has been apprised of the upcoming business transaction and has the cash ready to be disbursed."

"Very well. Mr. Draco, if you would gather the men and bring them into town, I will pay them as soon as I receive the funds," Boswell said.

"All right," Draco said.

"Gentlemen, I shall ride in with you," Boswell said to Rowe and Crader.

———

WHEN THEY GOT to town half–an–hour later, Boswell excused himself, saying he had to pick up something from his hotel room.

"I'll meet you at the bank," he said.

"Very well, we'll have the cash ready," Crader replied.

As Boswell started toward the hotel room, Crader and Rowe continued on toward the bank. They were met there by Will and God, who had been waiting for them. C.D. Malone, the president of the bank was there as well.

"Is everything ready?" Rowe asked Malone.

"Yes," Malone said. "I've temporarily closed the

bank so that we have no customers nor employees. I'm the only one here, and I have a bank draft of eighty-seven-thousand, five-hundred dollars made out to Benjamin Redling, and another for twelve-thousand, five-hundred made out to Will and Gid Crockett. You need only to sign the drafts to activate them."

"Good," Rowe replied. He turned to Will and Gid. "The man you say is Boswell has stopped by the hotel. He will be here shortly."

"I'm going to enjoy the look on his face when he learns that his plans have gone awry," Will said with a satisfied smile.

———

A FEW MINUTES later Boswell arrived. There were six men with him.

"I hope you don't mind that I brought my men with me. As I shall have no further use for them, I intend to pay them here, then let them be on their way," Boswell said, explaining the situation.

Boswell turned back toward the door and held it open for another to enter. "Come in, my dear," he said.

To Will and Gid's surprise, they saw that the person Boswell had just invited in, was a smiling Julia.

"Julia!" Will called out, the expression in his voice mirroring his shock at seeing her.

For just a moment, the expression on Julia's face was one of surprised horror. Then she shouted out loud.

"Damon, it's the Crocketts! Kill them! Kill them!"

Boswell, Draco and the others reached for their guns, and within seconds bullets began flying as Will and Gid traded shots with Boswell and the six men with him. Julia, Rowe, Crader, and Malone dropped to the floor, while Will and Gid remained erect, exchanged shots with Boswell and his men.

Boswell was hit in the chest, Draco in the head. The other five men hurried their shots as bullets crashed into the half wall that surrounded the teller's cages. The gun battle was over within seconds as the remaining five men were felled by the accurate shooting of Will and Gid. Gid went down with a bullet in his hip.

"Gid!" Will called out.

"I'm all right, make sure they're all dead," Gid replied in a strained voice.

Will checked the others, only Boswell was still alive, but Will had seen such wounds before, and he knew Boswell would soon die.

"I could have been the Missouri state attorney general," Boswell gasped.

"Yeah, well speaking as a Missourian, I'm glad you weren't."

"Hic est finis," he said with his last breath.

Julia, Crader, and Malone stood up then, and looked around nervously.

"Hang on to her," Will said, as he went back to check on his brother.

"It's in the hip," Gid said. "It hurts like hell, but I don't have anything down there that can kill me."

At that moment three armed men came in through the front door, and Will swung around, pointing his gun at them.

"No, Crockett!" Crader shouted. "It's Lee Hicks! He's the marshal!"

Will holstered his pistol.

"What happened here?" Hicks asked.

Crader told the marshal and his two deputies what happened, then pointed out that one of the dead was Damon Boswell.

"Damn!" he said. "So somebody finally got the son of a bitch! Excuse my language, ma'am."

"No need to excuse yourself to her," Will said. "She was one of them. She needs to be in jail."

"Will, no! You don't mean it!" Julia said.

"Tell me, Julia. When you had Art, and everyone else at Brown Spur murdered, did your husband say 'you don't mean it', to you?"

"Come on, Miss, we've got a jail cell waiting for you," Marshal Hicks said.

"I'll get Doc Kaufman for your brother," Crader offered.

CHAPTER THIRTY

WHEN WILL AND GID RETURNED TO BROWN SPUR, Scooter was fully recovered, so Will asked Anna if she would be willing to stay on a while longer, to take care of Gid's wound.

"I'd be glad to," Anna said. "I'm getting pretty good at this nursing business," she added.

"About the only caring for that I'll really need, is for you to make sure I've got something to eat when I'm hungry," Gid said.

"Oh, well, that shouldn't be all that hard," Scooter said. "Anna's a great cook."

———

ABOUT A MONTH LATER, Sheriff Maddox rode out to the ranch to have a visit.

"Hello, Sheriff," Will greeted. "What brings you here?"

"A couple of things," Maddox said. "I thought you

might be interested in knowing what happened to Julia."

"Oh, what did happen to her?"

"She was given a thirty-year sentence in the women's prison at Folsom."

"That's where she belongs," Gid said.

"I'm a little surprised," Maddox said. "I thought she'd hang, but the judge had mercy on her, I suppose. I don't know why, six men and a woman died because of her."

"Well, at least justice was done," Will said.

Maddox smiled. "But, I've also got some good news for you. The state of Texas has authorized the payment of the rewards for Boswell, and the men with him. The bank in Fort Worth is holding the money for you, twenty-one thousand dollars."

"Wow, that's a lot of money," Gid said.

"Yes, it is. So don't go spending it all in one place," Sheriff Maddox teased. He picked up his hat. "I guess I'd better get back into town to continue my fight against crime and or evil," he said with a little laugh. "I'll see you boys around."

After Sheriff Maddox left, Will looked over at Scooter and Anna, both of whom had been present during the sheriff's visit.

"Scooter, since both you and Gid are just about fully recovered, we won't be needing Anna to take care of you anymore, will we?" Will asked.

"Uh, no. But I plan on taking care of Anna, now," Scooter said.

"Oh? You say you want to be taking care of her?"

"Aye, aye, uh, I mean, yes, sir." Scooter put his arm around Anna's shoulder and drew her closer to him.

"Well now, look at that," Gid said with a big smile. "I guess you two got to know each other just real well, while Anna was out here, didn't you?"

"That's no problem for you is it?" Scooter asked. "I mean, I can continue to work here."

"That depends," Will said.

Scooter got a confused look on his face. "Uh, depends on what?"

"Will our share of money from the sale of the cattle, plus the reward we just received, be enough to build up a new herd?"

"Yes, sir, I'm sure that it would be."

"But Gid and I have talked it over, and neither one of us wants to settle down as full-time ranchers yet."

"Oh," Scooter said, his voice reflecting his concern.

"So whether or not you continue to work here, will depend upon whether you would be willing to take on the job of ranch manager."

"Ranch manager?"

"Yes. As I said, Gid and I have decided that we're just not cut out to stay in one place all the time."

"Yeah, we like to travel around," Gid said.

"But we don't want to get rid of the ranch," Will added. "That means we're going to have to find someone to manage the ranch for us, and the job is yours, if you want it."

"I've never been a ranch manager before. I've never been anything but a seaman and a cowboy. What would I have to do?"

"Well, to begin with, you're going to have to hire some new ranch hands," Will said.

"And buy a string of horses, and start a new herd."

"Where would I get the money for all that?"

"We'll establish a working account for you at the bank, plus pay you a decent wage," Will said.

"The only thing is, it would mean that you would have to move into the house here," Gid added.

"Oh, Scooter!" Anna said with excited joy. "Yes, tell them yes!"

"I don't know," Scooter said. "This is an awfully big house for me to be living in all by myself. I would have to..."

"Yes, yes, I'll marry you!" Anna said, happily.

"Well now, damn, girl, you didn't even give me a chance to ask you."

The look of joy on Anna's face was replaced by an expression of confusion and concern.

Scooter smiled. "So, I'll ask you now. Anna, will you marry me?"

"Yes, yes, yes!" Anna threw her arms around his neck, and kissed him without embarrassment or concern that she was being so demonstrative in front of Will and Gid.

———

Three weeks later

THE WEDDING TOOK place in Casey's Saloon, and Anna's bridesmaids were Suzie, Millie, Kate and Sally. John Casey was Scooter's best man.

The Reverend Snellgrove had to be convinced to conduct a wedding service in the saloon, but a five-hundred-dollar donation to the good reverend's church, persuaded him to set aside his concern.

After the wedding, Will and Gid, having set up an

operating budget with the local bank, bade their friends goodbye, then left town.

"Which way, Little Brother?" Will asked.

"That way," Gid said, pointing in the northwest direction.

"Why do you want to go that way?"

"I don't know. Why don't we go find out?"

Will chuckled. "That's as good a reason as any."

IF YOU LIKED THIS, YOU MIGHT LIKE:
THE TENDERFOOT

Master of the Western adventure, *New York Times* best selling author Robert Vaughan is back with another page turner sure to please Western fans of all ages.

When Turquoise Ranch hand Curly Stevens went into Flagstaff to meet a new employee arriving on the train, his first impression of Rob Barringer is of how big and strong the tenderfoot is. Rob's eagerness to learn and his willingness to take on the most difficult jobs wins everyone over, including ranch foreman Jake Dunford, and Melanie Duford, his beautiful daughter.

Rob is well-educated, and his demeanor and intelligence catches the attention of Melanie, causing him difficulty with ranch manager Lee Garrison, who believes he has an exclusive right to Melanie. Garrison makes life difficult for the ranch hands, and Rob in particular.

When Jake Dunford makes a public accusation that the ranch manager is stealing from the ranch, Garrison reacts by firing everyone, but it is Garrison who is in for a big surprise.

"Vaughan offers readers a chance to hit the trail and not even end up saddle sore."—*Publishers Weekly*

AVAILABLE NOW

ABOUT THE AUTHOR

Robert Vaughan sold his first book when he was 19. That was 57 years and nearly 500 books ago. He wrote the novelization for the mini series Andersonville. Vaughan wrote, produced, and appeared in the History Channel documentary Vietnam Homecoming.

His books have hit the NYT bestseller list seven times. He has won the Spur Award, the PORGIE Award (Best Paperback Original), the Western Fictioneers Lifetime Achievement Award, received the Readwest President's Award for Excellence in Western Fiction, is a member of the American Writers Hall of Fame and is a Pulitzer Prize nominee.

Vaughn is also a retired army officer, helicopter pilot with three tours in Vietnam. And received the Distinguished Flying Cross, the Purple Heart, The Bronze Star with three oak leaf clusters, the Air Medal for valor with 35 oak leaf clusters, the Army Commendation Medal, the Meritorious Service Medal, and the Vietnamese Cross of Gallantry.